PRESS YOUR LUCK

AN AGE GAP SECRET PREGNANCY OFFICE ROMANCE

AJME WILLIAMS

D1715566

ALSO BY AJME WILLIAMS

Ajme Williams writes emotional, angsty contemporary romance. All her books can be enjoyed as full length, standalone romances and are FREE to read in Kindle Unlimited .

Books do not have to be read in order.

High Stakes (this series)
Bet On It | A Friendly Wager | Triple or Nothing | Press Your Luck

Heart of Hope Series
Our Last Chance | An Irish Affair | So Wrong | Imperfect Love | Eight Long Years | Friends to Lovers | The One and Only | Best Friend's Brother | Maybe It's Fate | Gone Too Far | Christmas with Brother's Best Friend | Fighting for US | Against All Odds | Hoping to Score | Thankful for Us | The Vegas Bluff | 365 Days

Billionaire Secrets
Twin Secrets | Just A Sham | Let's Start Over | The Baby Contract | Too Complicated

The Why Choose Haremland (Reverse Harem Series)
Protecting Their Princess | Protecting Her Secret | Unwrapping their Christmas Present | Cupid Strikes... 3 Times | Their Easter Bunny

Dominant Bosses
His Rules | His Desires | His Needs | His Punishments | His Secret

Strong Brothers
Say Yes to Love | Giving In to Love | Wrong to Love You | Hate to Love You

Fake Marriage Series
Accidental Love | Accidental Baby | Accidental Affair | Accidental Meeting

Irresistible Billionaires
Admit You Miss Me | Admit You Love Me | Admit You Want Me | Admit You Need Me

Check out Ajme's full Amazon catalogue here.

Join her VIP NL here.

DESCRIPTION

Rules for dating your hot, *much* older boss:
Don't fall in love.
Don't meet his family.
Keep it light, fun and hot.
***Don't* let him get you pregnant...**

Todd Marshall is my hot boss billionaire I've been semi-successfully resisting... until I fall into his lap at a wedding.

Suddenly he's no longer the intimidating handsome playboy who pays my bills. He's a man I cannot keep my hands off of.

I break all my rules with him.

All hell breaks loose when his ex arrives in town with their grumpy teenage son... in time for me to realize I'm going to have Todd's baby, too.

Everything will be okay... I just have to keep this pregnancy a secret.

Forever.

PROLOGUE

Betts

I lifted my champagne flute to yet another toast to Naomi and Pierce's nuptials. I smiled and cheered, possibly a little bit louder than I should because this wasn't my first glass of champagne.

On the outside, I was thrilled for them. On the inside, I was happy for them as well, but I was also envious.

My three best friends had found true love and were living happily ever after, the dream I thought I'd achieved, but it had all been a lie.

Just over a year ago, I thought my life was perfect. I had a wonderful fiancé, my childhood best friend, Analyn, had moved to Las Vegas to room with me, and I had a great job with a supervisor who appreciated my work.

Today, all that was gone.

My fiancé was cheating on me, and he'd even hit on Analyn. Then I had to watch as she fell in love with her boss, Reed, and then they were married with a baby.

Through Analyn, I met Ruby and Naomi and watched as they too fell in love, got married, and both of them were expecting babies soon. As if that wasn't bad enough, a few months ago, my company was sold and I was laid off.

I had a new job, thanks to Naomi, doing marketing for the Silver Nuggets' minor-league hockey team. I couldn't complain too much because it paid better than my last job, which meant I didn't have to worry about my rent anymore.

But Naomi had made it seem like Todd Marshall, the owner of the team, was overly involved in the team's marketing. In my experience, however, he was detached from it. It was almost as if it didn't interest him anymore.

I couldn't decide whether that was a good thing because I was basically able to do whatever I wanted with little supervision, or a bad thing because perhaps Mr. Marshall's disinterest meant he was bored with the team and might sell it, which meant I could be laid off again.

I downed my drink and waved at a passing server who had a tray filled with flutes of champagne. When he stopped by, I took two glasses because it never hurt to have an extra glass in reserve.

"You sure like champagne."

I looked at the man sitting next to me. I'd practically forgotten he was there. Technically, he was my date, but as nice as he was, I just wasn't feeling it.

It was the classic "it's me, not him" situation. I tried to appreciate Ruby setting me up with Pete, who she knew because he was her daughter, Laina's, teacher, but it was difficult. Ever since my engagement went up in flames, I'd become increasingly numb to the world.

Because he was a nice guy and it wasn't his fault that I was a terrible date, I mustered a smile. "What's not to like?" I picked up one of the flutes, saluted him, and drank the bubbly liquid.

I watched as Analyn and Ruby chatted with Naomi, and I felt left out. But again, that was my own fault because I was sitting here drinking champagne like a woman dying of thirst instead of mingling about like they were.

They all turned to look at me, and I gave a slight wave. Ruby excused herself and made her way over to our table. I sat up straight and plastered on another smile so that they wouldn't know the truth of my misery.

"Are you guys having fun?" Ruby asked as she reached the table.

"Everything's been great. I was excited to hear that the event was going to be held here because on a teacher's salary, I don't think I'd ever be able to come here otherwise," Pete said.

"You just have to fall in love with a billionaire," I quipped.

Ruby's head tilted to the side, and she arched a brow.

Oh, crap, did I say that out loud? I was never motivated by money. As long as I had enough to live, I was happy. But it didn't go unnoticed by me that my three friends had all married very wealthy men who were completely devoted to them.

"You okay, Betts?" Ruby asked.

I lifted up the other champagne glass. "I'm great. I'm so glad that Naomi and Pierce finally got their issues worked out."

Ruby had an expression that suggested she wasn't buying my comment, but she smiled and glanced over at Naomi and Pierce, who were now dancing. "I'm just glad the babies decided to wait until after today to be born."

Naomi did look like she was about to pop. Those triplets were taking up a lot of space.

I glanced up at Ruby. "How's little Buck?" I really needed to try harder to be happy and engaged with my friends, which was why I asked Ruby about her new son, Buck, born a few months ago.

Ruby's smile was as bright as any I'd ever seen. It matched the ones Naomi and Analyn always sported. "He's such a sweetie pie. And Laina is such a doting big sister."

"I can't tell you how many stories she tells about him at school," Pete said. "She recently wrote an essay about wanting to teach them how to skate."

Ruby laughed. "Figure skate, right? Not hockey?"

He nodded. "Yes, figure skating." His brows drew together in question. "Would Bo be all right if Buck became a figure skater?"

"I won't deny that Bo would much prefer Buck to become a hockey player, but that's only because it was his passion. But I also know that whatever Buck decides he wants to become, Bo and I will support him one hundred percent."

I was really a terrible friend because all this happy talk was only pulling me into a darker pit. I rose abruptly, nearly knocking my chair over. Pete reached out to grab and right it. They both looked at me wide-eyed.

"I'm sorry. I just really need to go to the restroom." I grabbed my clutch bag and hurried out of the ballroom into the open area of the lodge overlooking the desert of Las Vegas. Pete was right in that it was designed for people with wealth. It had been built in the 1800s during the silver mining days by a rich mine owner.

More recently, my boss bought it and refurbished all the systems while maintaining the essence and opulence of the era in which it was built. I think he came here by himself for a time and only recently had started opening it up for corporate groups and weddings with a price tag that only the rich and famous could afford.

I made my way to the powder room, locking the door behind me. I sat on the toilet to do my business when my phone rang. I opened my purse to see who was calling. I suppose it was sort of disgusting to answer the phone while sitting on the potty, but I'd had enough champagne to not really care. Besides, the caller ID said it was likely spam, so I poked the dismiss button, popped the phone back into my clutch, and snapped it shut.

When I finished my business, I stood pulling up my panties, glad that I had decided to wear stockings instead of nylons. I was one of those women who liked to wear pretty lingerie, even though no one was ever going to see it. It made me feel pretty and sexy, although recently, knowing I had nobody in my life who was going to see it, I'd started to feel sad and pathetic.

I pushed the skirt of my dress down, but I'd accidentally closed some of it in the clasp of my purse. I jerked it loose in frustration and then went to the counter to wash my hands. I avoided looking at myself in the mirror because I didn't like seeing the pitiful person staring back.

I exited the bathroom, but as I stepped outside, something didn't feel right.

I looked down to the source and discovered a tear in the seam of my dress along the upper part of my thigh.

"Goddammit." It was a metaphor, I decided, showing how my life was unraveling.

"Is something wrong?"

I jerked my head up to find my boss, Todd, looking at me in concern. I let out a breath, leaning against the wall. Just what I needed, my boss finding me tipsy with a rip in my dress. Not a good look. "I got my dress caught on something and now it's ripped."

He looked down to where my hand clutched the seam to keep it closed, but it was long enough that my leg was still exposed.

He made a strange sound and shifted.

"And of course, I don't have a sewing kit on me. But I can't walk back in there with my dress about to rip apart."

I wondered if he'd be willing to get Ruby or Analyn to help me.

"Here, come with me."

I followed him down the hall and into a library because why not? Maybe he had a sewing kit.

We entered the library and he shut the door behind me. For a moment, I thought I was about to get sacked. It seemed like it was on par for the night.

Instead, he removed his boutonniere from his lapel and kneeled down next to me.

"What are you doing?" Perhaps I should have been concerned that my boss had just closed me into a room and was now kneeling in front of me, but honestly, I was mostly curious.

Todd was such an enigma to me.

When I'd gone for the interview, he wasn't what I'd expected based on what Naomi said. First, she said he was close to fifty, and while that might have been true, he didn't look middle-aged. Sure, he had some salt-and-pepper in his dark hair, but my first impression had been *wow, he's sexy in that distinguished gentleman sort of way*.

Naomi had also indicated that he was driven and passionate, and while his ideas could be crazy, his success suggested they worked. During my interview, he was professional and friendly, but I didn't see drive and passion. In fact, once I was hired, I hardly ever saw him.

So now, I was curious about the man who was my absentee boss who was now holding up a pin from a boutonniere while on his knees.

"I figured I'd pin the seams together until we could find a sewing kit," he replied.

Oh. Right. That made sense.

He reached out, taking the fabric of the dress. His fingers brushed over my skin, sending a little sizzle to my girly parts. I hadn't felt anything like that in a long time. Not since Paul, that lying bastard.

When the pin was in, he stood up, standing very close to me. Probably closer than was appropriate, but I didn't care because he looked at me in a way that made my breath stall in my chest for a moment.

"Are you all right now?" he asked.

Holy hell, I wanted to jump my boss. Up close like this, I felt a pull to him.

He lifted his hand, pushing my hair back from my face, the tips of his fingers brushing over my cheek.

My breath hitched at his touch and the way he looked at me. Was he feeling this moment too? The world fell away. All the betrayal and sadness. All the hurt and loss. For the first time since I learned Paul cheated on me, I felt something that wasn't soul-crushing. That had to be why I leaned into him and kissed him.

The minute our lips met, panic slid through me as I knew it was wrong and I'd likely be fired. I started to pull back and beg for him not to fire me, only I couldn't pull away. His hands gripped my hips and his mouth opened to devour mine.

Ah . . . okay. This was still wrong, but as his hands roamed over my body, making me feel seen and wanted, I gave into it. Chances were he didn't know who I was, anyway. He hadn't said my name. He ran a huge corporation with many businesses. What were the chances he remembered the lowly marketing person for the hockey team he no longer focused on?

Neither of us said a word, maybe because it would break the spell. Instead, lips fused and hands sought skin. He let out a frustrated growl and sank to his knees again as his hands pushed up my dress.

His hands slid up my thighs. "Sexy," he murmured. His fingers slid under the waistband of my panties and drew them down.

Was I going to do this? His finger slid along my folds. Yes, I was going to do this. I leaned back against the door, knowing I'd sink into a heap without the support.

He drew his tongue where his finger had just been, making an *mmm* sound.

I gasped as pleasure shot out. I was going to embarrass myself by coming quickly, but I didn't care. I wanted this. I wanted to feel good. A warning in the back of my head tried to pull me back to good sense, but I turned it off.

Instead, I let go and let this man, my boss, do wicked things with his tongue on my pussy. Then his fingers slid inside me, finding that one perfect spot as his lips wrapped around my clit and sucked.

My orgasm blasted through me like an inferno. I rocked against his mouth and fucked his fingers, wanting it to last forever, not thinking about what would happen when it ended.

1

Todd – Two Months Later.

I stood alone in the luxurious conference room in my high-rise building in Las Vegas, looking out over the desert. Some CEOs like to march in after all members of the meeting had arrived to make a statement. They wanted everyone to know that they were the most important person, and nothing started without them.

I knew I was the most important person in my company and that no meetings would ever start without me, but I always showed up early. Showing late could suggest an inferiority complex in needing to be seen, or conceit, rubbing in that the others were peons.

But for me, making a show of walking in late indicated a disregard for the business and the people who worked there. By being early, I set the example that this business and the people who worked for me were important and were expected to treat the business as important. Someday, I'd be gone, but the business would endure. The business deserved the reverence, not me.

Then again, with my teenage son showing no interest in the business or me, I couldn't be sure the company would endure, or who would run it if it did. But I still had a few years to figure that out. I was only forty-nine, which was young in businessman years.

Today, I was meeting with all the department heads for the corporate entity, as well as the company heads for each of the companies I owned and operated. I was particularly interested in seeing the report for the Silver Nugget hockey team. I had extricated myself from the day-to-day business of the team once they won their league championship. I'd achieved my goal, checked it off the list, and now was on the hunt for a new challenge.

However, I'd purchased the team on a dare from my college roommate and still good friend, Levi Wexford. I'd been complaining about boredom, and Levi, having just read about the probable demise of a ragtag minor-league hockey team down in Henderson, bet me I couldn't take it from nothing to something in a season.

I took that bet, hiring Naomi Withers, now Jackson, to coach the team to add to the challenge.

But Naomi wasn't a token pretty face with tits to bring the fans into the stands, although it didn't hurt. She had been a great hockey player in her own right until her early retirement. I knew she had the goods to take the team all the way. But winning a championship was only part of the bet. All the money invested in the team needed to be recouped and then some. Between Levi and me, the ultimate measure of success was money.

Even though I didn't have the final numbers yet, I had already moved on from the project, and boredom was sinking in again. So far, I hadn't found anything to pique my interest. Boredom was my natural state, and nothing seemed to elevate me out of it except for these occasional high-risk projects.

The only exception was at Naomi and Pierce's wedding, when my normally cool and aloof marketing director for the hockey team became a passionate, fiery woman. I had already noted that she was a woman who stirred something inside me, but at the wedding, she took me from zero to one hundred with a single kiss. I wasn't ever a womanizer, but I'd been with my share of women, and none of them had lit me up from the inside out and given me an orgasm that made me forget my name like she had.

The image of the sweetest, sexiest pussy I'd ever encountered flashed in my mind. I could still taste the juice from her orgasm. It had driven me mad. Before she could come down, I'd maneuvered her to the desk and stripped her bare, needing to see her body.

Her perfect, round tits and the way the nipples had hardened in my mouth came back to me. The memory of the way her pussy tightened around my cock when I, in a wild frenzy, plunged into her had me shifting to adjust my cock swelling in my slacks.

Jesus, I'd never had a sexual encounter like that before.

We hadn't spoken. Instead, it was as if we both gave full rein to our bodies and they knew exactly what to do. I hadn't felt that good, that alive, in a long time. If only there were a way I could make her a project, at least in my bedroom.

But of course, it couldn't happen. What we did in the library at the lodge went against everything I believed. The biggest factor was that I was her boss. But then there was also the fact that she wasn't yet thirty and I was quickly approaching fifty.

To be honest, I wasn't sure what the red-headed woman with the captivating green eyes saw in me. How she was taken by another man was a fucking mystery.

The door to the conference room opened, interrupting my reverie. But who needed a memory when the real thing walked in wearing a charcoal pencil skirt that hugged her phenomenal legs in a way that made me salivate?

She wore a crisp white shirt that tapered at the waist, teasing me with the way it accented her tits. Her gorgeous red locks were pulled back from her face but were freely hanging down her back, and my fingers itched to run through the soft, thick locks.

"Good morning, Mr. Marshall." She sat at the table and pulled out her phone.

Ah, the ice queen was back. The contradiction of ice and fire concerned me a little bit. Had she been too drunk to remember the night we'd fucked in the study? The idea of that didn't sit well with me. I wasn't a man to take advantage of a drunk woman. She hadn't seemed drunk to me. Had she been drinking?

Yes, but she'd been lucid and clear when she pressed her lips to mine and ignited an inferno. Maybe, like me, she knew what we had done could cause problems and was opting to pretend it never happened. We were back to business as usual. There was relief in that thought.

Except why was she here today? She wasn't a department or company head.

"Good morning to you, Miss Adams. Tell me, is your department head not coming today? Are you coming in his stead?"

She lifted her gaze from her phone and looked at me, those fabulous green eyes staring at me with something that looked a bit like contempt.

"The department head retired a week and half ago and you promoted me to his position. You signed the paperwork. Don't you remember?"

I didn't remember.

"I sign a lot of papers, Miss Adams." In my mind, it was a good thing that I couldn't remember, despite the fact that Betts almost looked hurt by it. But considering that I had fucked her two months ago and then not long after gave her a big promotion, that could look suspicious. So why was she annoyed with me? Did she think I gave her the job because of what we had done? Was she expecting more perks?

I shook that thought away because while I might've signed the paperwork to give her the promotion, I hadn't seen her since the wedding. In my experience, a woman who was after something was much more manipulative and involved in making it happen.

If Betts wanted something more from me, she would've been spending much more time trying to get close to me. Looking across the table, I got the feeling that she didn't want to be anywhere near me.

I sat down in my chair, noting that forgetting that I'd signed paperwork to promote her wasn't the first time I had a lapse in memory around business. It was one of the signs that I had lost interest in my company again. I needed to put more energy into finding my next project.

As the other members of the meeting strolled in, I scanned my brain for the various options I had already looked at but dismissed. Maybe there was one that I had too easily passed up. The only somewhat interesting idea was an island resort for sale. But I wasn't one for vacations, and I had no need for palm trees and coconuts.

I started the meeting, but once the heads were making their reports, I was in my own head again, trying to find something to make me feel alive. Hearing that I had indeed won the bet from Levi was nice, but it didn't do much to stir my soul.

Thinking of stirring brought me back to Betts. For so long, my dick had been dormant. It usually took work to get him revved up and going, which was why he'd had very little action in a long time.

But from the moment Betts walked into my office, it was like my dick had a fucking mind of his own, and now wasn't any different because now that I was thinking of her, I was back in that study, sinking into that sweet, tight pussy of hers. The woman was a walking, talking, breathing wet dream come to life.

When I had walked out of the library, I was adamant that it couldn't happen again. I couldn't risk potential lawsuits or bad press. For a while, I was grateful that she occasionally haunted my dreams, as fantasizing about her made jerking off more satisfying. But it wasn't the real thing, and I was growing frustrated at the idea that I wouldn't be able to touch her again.

Could I?

We got away with it once, at a wedding, no less. Perhaps with ultimate discretion, we could again. The fact that she hadn't sought me afterward, hoping to get something more from me, whether it was money or love, told me she wasn't seeking anything permanent, either. She'd needed a good, hard fuck that night too.

I wondered if she'd be open to a no-strings-attached affair. I glanced to the other end of the table at her. As if she knew I was looking at her, her head lifted, and her brow arched in an obstinate expression.

I took that to mean that the ice queen's vote would be no on the subject. But what about the fire queen I met in the library? Could I reach her and convince her to have another night of forbidden lust?

The more I thought about it, the more I wanted it. Yes, it was risky, but that was what all my projects had in common. They all had an element of recklessness which made them exciting.

As the meeting finished, I decided it was settled. Betts Adams was my new project.

2

Betts

I left the meeting and headed straight to the ladies' room. I spent a long time looking at myself in the mirror, recognizing myself, and at the same time, I knew I wasn't the person I had been just over a year ago.

Back then, I'd been on top of the world with a great job and a fiancé. Today, not only was all that gone, but it seemed like everything I did had turned to dust. The latest interaction with my boss was proof of that.

I was livid at him for not remembering me from the library at Naomi's wedding. Granted, it was a hookup, but was I so forgettable? I was angry at myself for letting control go for one night and giving in to desire. Had I not followed Todd into that library, I wouldn't be standing in the ladies' room feeling angry—and worse, insecure.

I wasn't a woman who went around thinking I was a raving beauty, but I knew I wasn't ugly. At least I hadn't been years ago when it seemed like I could attract a man easily, and they would remember me. But ever since I discovered my fiancé cheating on me, it was like

I'd become an old, shriveled up spinster. Whatever mojo I had was gone.

The only thing good to come out of the meeting this morning was knowing for sure that Todd hadn't promoted me because I'd had sex with him at Naomi's wedding. That had to mean I got the job based on merit, or maybe it was just that I was the only choice. Mr. Weathers had been the head of marketing for the Silver Nugget hockey team, and I was hired to do publicity. When he retired, I was promoted, but nobody was hired to replace me. So basically, I was doing it all.

Not that I didn't have any help. At the corporate headquarters, there was a large marketing department, and I had access to people there to help me in executing marketing and publicity for the team. As a result, I often traveled between Henderson, where the team was located, and Las Vegas, to the corporate offices, to confer with the marketing team there. I was here today for the department meeting, as well as to work on the new campaign for this upcoming season.

I splashed water on my face and pinched my cheeks to bring color back into them. I had a job to do, and I was going to do it to the best of my ability.

I headed out of the bathroom and back up to the twentieth floor where the marketing department was located. I had a corner of the office that was ideal because even though it wasn't private, I had lots of wall space to hang up various ideas as well as a Kanban board on the progress of all the marketing campaigns I had going on.

Right now, we were working on a billboard to bring excitement to the team. We were only a few weeks away from preseason training. While the team won their division last season, this year, they didn't have their two star players, Max Blake and Big Ed Sampson, as both of them moved up to the National League. Further, it wasn't going to help things that their coach, Naomi Jackson, was taking some time off.

Newly married and with triplets, she would be dividing her time between coaching and her family.

That meant the team would have two coaches. While the new

assistant coach seemed good, there was no doubt that Naomi was instrumental in getting the team to the championship and winning. Between Max and Ed's departure and Naomi's reduced schedule, repeating a championship win would be a challenge.

I completed my work for the day and then headed out, driving directly over to Naomi and her husband, Pierce's, home. Not long ago, our friend Ruby had come up with the idea of a monthly girl power hour where we would get together and drink wine and talk about everything except work, men, and children.

When I arrived, I joined the ladies with an extra full glass of wine. As I sat on the couch, I was still simmering with hurt and anger about Todd. Why couldn't I just accept what happened for what it was? A hookup.

"Are you okay, Betts?" Ruby asked.

I looked up and nodded, only then realizing I was ruminating instead of participating in engaging conversation with my friends. "Yes, just a challenging day at the office."

Naomi did a large eye roll. "Oh, God, don't tell me Todd is trying to publicize something about your love life."

I flinched. Did she know? "You know I don't have a love life."

Analyn, my best friend since we were kids, looked at me with sympathy. I loved that she cared for me, but I hated the pity.

"I didn't either at the time," Naomi said. "I just happened to be photographed talking to Max, and that was all it took for the media to make assumptions. Todd thought it was a great idea to bring in fans."

"Todd doesn't know I exist," I quipped.

Analyn arched a brow.

"For one, I'm not the face of the team," I said quickly to cover up my bitter sounding comment. "Besides, whatever interest he had in the team last year seems to be gone. Until today, I hadn't really seen him since I was hired." Okay, so that wasn't quite true. I saw him at Naomi's wedding, but I wasn't going to reveal that. "I walked into a meeting today, and he didn't remember that he'd promoted me."

Naomi frowned. "That doesn't sound like Todd. Last year, he was all about getting fans in the seats and making money."

I shrugged. "I guess he sees that goal as met. In fact, today, he got the report that indicated the team had made money. I guess now that he's achieved it, he doesn't care as much anymore. He hasn't been down to the rink since I started working there."

"That's so strange." Naomi's brow continued to furrow. It was almost as if we were talking about two different people. "I bet that's going to change. With Max and Big Ed gone, winning the league a second year in a row isn't guaranteed. My guess is when the season starts and tickets need to be sold, he'll be in your office all the time."

My heart made a strange thump in my chest that I determined was indigestion. I didn't want Todd in my office all the time. I didn't need to see him and be reminded of how I gave myself over to him in passion and he didn't remember it. The man had flattened my self-esteem, and I didn't need constant reminders of it.

"Maybe that'll give Pierce, Bo, and Reed an opportunity to win this year," Ruby said. "Bo has been planning all sorts of new strategies and workouts for the team."

"Oh, yeah, I heard that Pierce was giving more rein to Bo," Analyn said.

Everyone looked at Naomi, knowing she was likely the source of Pierce's stepping back from coaching.

"As Pierce tells it, he achieved all his career goals and now he wants to focus on the new things in his life, which include me and the babies and Porter."

Naomi absolutely glowed with love, and once again, envy struck me. I hated being the only one who didn't know what it was like to have love and devotion from a man. They were all living these happy, glamorous, fulfilled lives while I was still living alone, doing a job that I didn't hate, but it wasn't my passion either.

I wondered what I did to offend the universe to end up like this. I had thought I had a perfect life in my grasp, but it was cruelly taken away. Was I being given lesson after lesson in humility? Like I wasn't pretty enough, or smart enough, or deserving enough? Just thinking those thoughts made me feel pathetic. I certainly didn't have it as bad as some people. Maybe it was all my whining that was bringing on my misery.

"Mrs. Jackson." We all turned to look at the nanny Naomi and Pierce had hired to help them with the triplets. As far as I could tell, Naomi and Pierce were hands-on parents, but three babies were a lot, and once the hockey season started, they'd need the extra hands at home and on the road.

"The babies have woken and are ready for their feeding."

Naomi gave us an apologetic look. "I'm sorry, guys."

"Not at all," Analyn said. "Bring the babies out here. I know the girl power hour is supposed to be just us, but they're so cute and we can help you feed them."

"As long as we don't have to nurse them," I joked. I was the only one who wouldn't be able to nurse a baby. Well, Analyn wouldn't because her son was weaned, but she'd nursed at one time.

Everyone laughed, and I was glad I was able to bring levity to hide my misery.

Naomi looked at her nanny. "I'll nurse one of them, and we'll have bottles for the other two."

I considered excusing myself and going home. I know it sounded negative, and I really was happy for my friends, but being with them and their husbands or their babies only highlighted how much I was missing.

Why couldn't my fiancé have been faithful? Why couldn't Pete, Ruby's friend I met at Naomi's wedding, be someone I was attracted to? No, I had the misfortune of a momentary lapse in judgment and had sex with my boss. The real kicker was, if I had the chance to do it again, I probably would. How dumb was that?

Even as I sat in the board meeting today, angry that Todd had not remembered that he'd promoted me or had sex with me, I couldn't stop the feelings of attraction that I had toward him. I should've just seen him as a middle-aged man getting his rocks off with a younger woman, but instead I saw a sexy, distinguished, hard-working busi-nessman, too focused on business without time for anything else except an occasional hookup which he clearly forgot the minute it was done.

A few moments later, there was a baby in my lap, and I was holding a bottle as it suckled. I looked down into his sweet face, and yearning welled inside me. I wanted what my friends had, a loving husband and beautiful children.

Maybe I'd have to settle for something else. There was no rule that said I couldn't have a child. I made enough money and had good benefits, so I could probably afford to have a baby on my own.

Those thoughts stayed with me when I returned home to my apartment and finished off the half-bottle of wine I had in the fridge. As I climbed into bed, I noted that if I did want to have a child on my own, I'd have to cut back on the wine. But I was okay with that. It would be worth it to have someone to love and who'd love me back.

For a moment, I wondered how I would find a father. Maybe Pete would volunteer, not to sleep with me but to donate to the cause. I wondered how much it cost to go to a sperm bank, although it seemed impersonal to pick a baby daddy from a list of characteristics without actually knowing him. It was just my luck that an image of Todd entered my mind. Thankfully, my anger at him and disgust with myself had me vanquishing him.

If I were going to get out of this funk I was living in, I needed to stop wallowing in all the misfortunes of my past. What was done was done. It was time for me to look forward and plan my future.

3

Todd

When I left the meeting this morning, my spirits had risen. The only thing that tempered my excitement at taking on the challenge of wooing Betts was the fact that her attitude was decidedly against me.

The fiery, passionate woman I saw in the library was locked up tight behind Betts's cool demeanor. For that reason, as well as several others, it probably wasn't a good idea to turn my conquest of Betts into a challenge, but I found it difficult to let the idea go. But I also knew I couldn't force myself upon her.

In the few times I'd run into her, I had noticed her cool manner, but today, there was a little edge to it as if she were angry at me. Was it because I hadn't remembered that I had promoted her?

Maybe she thought I'd forgotten our evening in the library. When that thought had dawned on me, I had nearly gone rushing to her office to let her know that I had remembered her.

What stopped me was how inappropriate and possibly creepy that would have been. I was her boss, after all. Plus, there was a part of me that didn't want to become *that* man. The one who was decidedly older and filthy rich who had affairs with his much younger, model-beautiful employees. Even without a lawsuit, it could hurt my reputation and make me seem like a man who took advantage of women.

Even so, it was a risk I was willing to take where Betts was concerned. I would be walking a very dangerous tightrope as I found a way to pursue her without her feeling uncomfortable or pressured.

I managed to finish my day, although Betts was never far from my thoughts. When it was time to head out, I had my driver take me over to the Golden Oasis, a techno oriented club with decor from Las Vegas's golden age. It was established several years ago by two young men from a money family in New York. At first, I thought Las Vegas would chew the Clarke brothers up and spit them out, but as it turned out, the club did good business, partly because they were able to cater to Las Vegas locals as well as tourists, and also to men like me who wanted atmosphere and privacy as well.

I entered the club and made my way back to one of the private rooms. When I entered, I saw that Levi had already arrived. He stood, smiling as he came over to shake my hand and give each other a half-hug. We'd been friends since college, and whenever he was in the western U.S., he always made sure to stop in Las Vegas for a visit. As it turned out, it was a good time as I had the report from the Silver Nuggets to prove I'd won our last bet.

As we sat at the plush booth, a server entered with a $400 bottle of wine.

"I hope you don't mind that I ordered already," Levi said. He never spared any expense. We were similar in that we were both successful businessmen, but whereas I had earned all my money and tended to be a bit more frugal, Levi came from old money and was happy to spend it without a single thought.

"Not at all."

Once the wine was poured, Levi held up his glass. "Good to see you, old buddy."

I clicked my glass with his. "You too. In fact, you've picked a good day to show up." As we each took a sip of the wine, I pushed the report across the table to him. "The Silver Nuggets team is in the black. Pay up, old friend."

Levi laughed as he shook his head and looked at the report. "Midas Marshall does it again."

I smirked. "Oh, ye of little faith."

"Are you kidding? I know you. Everything you touch turns to gold. I'd envy you if I didn't like you so much."

I shrugged and sipped again. That old feeling of having accomplished something, but now it was done, swept through me again, leaving me feeling agitated and empty. It was a sure sign that my idea of pursuing Betts still concerned me.

"For someone who's just won a million bucks, you look like someone stole your favorite toy," Levi said, sitting back in the booth.

I shrugged.

Levi shook his head. "You're like that poor little rich girl. You have everything, and yet you always seem so miserable. Have you ever been happy?"

I bristled, not because I was offended but because his words hit their mark. I was very rarely happy. I was beginning to think I'd have to live my life feeling like something was missing and only having fleeting moments of fulfillment.

"You were married once. Surely, you were happy then," Levi said.

"Until I wasn't." I didn't like thinking about my ex-wife, Taylor. At the time we married, I supposed I thought I was happy, but in retrospect, I'm not sure I was. I had done everything I was supposed to do, from attending college to growing a successful business. When I met Taylor, getting married seemed like the next step in my life's progression. As it turned out, that hadn't been a good reason to get married.

"So, there wasn't a time when you and your wife were happy?"

I shrugged. "Maybe in the beginning. But then she didn't like how much I had to work, even though when I didn't work, she was frequently complaining or wanting more money. After a while, it just seemed easier to give her the money she wanted and walk away. I was happy when my son was born." That was true, but even that soured somewhere along the way. At first, I was an involved father, but then

Taylor took our son and moved to Los Angeles, and slowly over time, my son and I became estranged as well.

Levi studied me as he swirled his fancy wine in his glass. "Seriously, man, when was the last time you were happy?"

Immediately, the image of Betts in the library came to mind. It didn't really make sense. Yes, it was exciting, exhilarating even. So much so that I wanted to do it again. But was I happy?

I wasn't about to tell Levi that I had hooked up with one of my employees. Not that he would judge me for it because I was pretty sure Levi had hooked up with his employees. But there was something about Betts and my attraction to her that I wanted to keep to myself.

"I liked winning the championship and my bet," I said instead.

Levi laughed. "Well, how about this, then? If competition and challenge are the only things that give you a hard-on, how about a new bet? Double or nothing? The team did well this season, I'll give you that, but with your coach out on maternity leave and your two best players having moved on, I really question whether you can pull it off a second year in a row."

In my mind, I'd already moved on from the hockey team looking for a new challenge. But of course, I had recently decided I wanted to make Betts my new challenge, and what better way to do that than to start reinvesting my time in the hockey team and working with her on the marketing element?

I nodded. "You're on."

"That's it? No negotiating?"

I shook my head. "You're right. The team as it is now will be an even bigger challenge than it was last year. But I feel confident I can make it happen." And if I lose two million dollars, so be it. It will be money well spent if it gives me the opportunity to spend time with Betts.

Levi poured us both new glasses of wine, and we held up our glasses, clicking them together. "Double or nothing."

"Double or nothing." As I sipped my wine, my phone rang. Pulling it out, I looked at the caller ID and rolled my eyes. "Speak of the devil. Excuse me for a minute. I have to take this." I pressed the answer button. "Taylor. Is something wrong with Dean?" Taylor never called me unless there was an emergency, or of course, she wanted money.

"It's not an emergency, but I am having trouble with Dean. He needs a fatherly influence. He's a teenager now, and I am tired of having to hire new housekeepers and au pairs to keep up with his pranks and bad attitude."

"I can arrange to have new staff hired—"

"That's not why I'm calling."

"Dean is a young man who is full of himself, as all kids his age are. I'll arrange to have somebody who can help keep him in check. But I'm sorry, I need to go now." I hung up, trying not to feel guilty that I'd just brushed off my ex-wife, or more accurately, my son.

"How is your son?" Levi asked.

"You know how it is. He's sixteen."

Levi grinned. "One of the best years of my life. I got a car, and I got laid for the first time in it."

I laughed until I considered what he was saying. "I'm sure he's fine, and Taylor's probably just overreacting. Boys will be boys, right?" I felt like I was trying to talk myself into believing that. Guilt filled me that I wasn't being more involved, but after years of being pushed out, I'd finally given up.

"Do you ever miss being married?"

I shook my head vehemently. "Not to Taylor, I don't."

"So you're open to falling in love again."

Again? I couldn't say for sure I was in love with Taylor, or that I'd ever really been in love with anything but my work. "I haven't met a woman who can keep my interest very long." Strange then that two months after fucking Betts in the library at Naomi's wedding, I was still thinking about her.

"Sort of like your businesses, eh?" Levi chimed in.

I nodded. "Right."

"Are you sure you want to stick another year with the hockey team? I could come up with a new bet."

I shook my head. "No, I'm actually excited about this new bet."

Levi studied me like he didn't quite believe me. "You already proved yourself, though. It's not really a challenge."

"As you said, my aces in the hole are gone or are on leave." Of course, that wasn't where the real challenge came from. The challenge would be using this bet as an opportunity to spend time with Betts. Would the pull of attraction continue?

If it wore off like all my other interests, that would be good. She'd be out of my mind and my system. If not . . . well . . . as I'd told Levi, no woman ever held my interest for very long. Betts struck me as a woman who wasn't interested in love either, based on how cool and aloof she was, so there wasn't a risk she'd want more from me than I could give.

I hoped that Betts and I could have some enjoyable times while the chemistry lasted. And when it ended, she'd have her job and I'd move on to new projects. No harm, no foul. But first, I needed to get past her guard to find the fiery woman I met in the library.

4

Betts

I was working in the Las Vegas office today putting the final touches on the billboard I'd designed to promote the team. Last season, Max Blake and big Ed Sampson were the two stars who got most attention, except for Naomi, who was the focus of publicity.

Now that I was in charge, my goal was to move away from sensationalism and scandal and instead promote a hockey team. I wanted to spread the attention out over all the members, starting with a single team-centered billboard.

It'd been a week since the department meeting, and I hadn't seen Todd since then except for the few times he showed up in my dreams. I really hated it when he did that. It made me wonder if I needed to get out more and try to meet somebody new. It was bad enough thinking your boss was attractive, but to have actually given into it and had sex with him, sex he didn't remember, bruised my ego and made me feel pathetic. I didn't want to experience that again.

There was a muffled commotion, and when I looked up, Todd was walking across the marketing department toward my corner. Several of the other marketing team said their hellos or quickly looked busy.

As he approached, I tried to ignore how fabulous he looked in his expensive tailored suit. I wondered if he went to Italy for his fittings. Realizing I was ogling, I made sure my face didn't give my attention away.

"Good morning, Ms. Adams. I need to talk with you."

My stomach had this strange flutter which I quickly told it to knock off. I managed to put on a cordial smile. "Of course." I looked around for a chair for him to sit in.

"This won't take long." His eyes twinkled, and his expression told me that he had something up his sleeve. His gaze drifted over to my wall where the mockup of the billboard hung. When he turned his attention back to me, he said, "This is good, but unfortunately, we're going to have to scrap it."

Immediately, my hackles went up. "What do you mean? It's on the verge of being executed." Feeling peevish, I sat in my chair, letting him know I wasn't interested in his new idea.

He grinned like a Cheshire cat. "That's why I'm here. We need to talk about a new marketing campaign."

"All right," I said through gritted teeth.

He came around my desk and held out his hand, which I stared at like it had cooties. "I'm not going to tell you about it. I'm going to show it to you. Come on."

For a moment, I wondered what he'd do if I told him no. But he was my boss, and I needed the job. I refused his hand as I stood up on my own.

If he was offended that I'd treated his hand like he had the plague, he didn't show it. "Grab your purse and we'll head out."

I got my purse from the bottom drawer and followed him out of the marketing area to the elevator.

"Where are we going?" I asked as he poked the button to the ground floor.

"To the rink. There's something I want you to see there."

He could have done this yesterday or tomorrow since both of those days, I was at the rink. Was he being difficult on purpose? Nah. Men like Todd didn't think about the schedules of others, especially his subordinates. We were going because it was convenient for him. My timetable didn't matter.

I let out a sigh but didn't say anything as I remembered the line about not biting the hand that feeds you.

We reached the lobby and exited the elevator, and I followed him through the building and out to an SUV waiting at the curb. He held the door open as I got in, and then he slid in next to me. The driver pulled away from the curb and started the drive down to Henderson.

"So, what is this new marketing idea that you have?" I asked.

Todd looked at me affably as he shook his head. "Nope. Like I said, I want you to see it first."

I gave a slight nod and turned my head to look out the window. This looked to be a long ride.

"Have you read any good books lately?" he asked. I turned my head to look at him, curious about the question. Once again, there was a gleam in his eye. "I have found that the library has very scintillating reading."

Oh, my God, he was referring to Naomi's wedding. The heat on my cheeks told me I was blushing, and I was annoyed to have had that reaction.

I quickly turned my head to look back out the window and murmured, "So you finally remember?"

"Remember? I never forgot."

When I looked back at him, my brow was arched, letting him know I didn't believe him.

He studied me for a moment and then leaned closer to me. "I might forget things that happen at work, but I never forget things that happen in the library." He used his index finger to point to his temple. "It's seared into my brain."

I couldn't deny the ego boost knowing that he hadn't forgotten, but it still didn't change the fact that he was my boss, and an irritating one at that.

"Besides, we were in a meeting, and it didn't seem like the appropriate time to mention it," he finished.

I glanced at the driver and then back at Todd. "And now is?"

Todd laughed. "I think our secret is safe here." He cocked his head to the side. "You really thought that I had forgotten?"

"You forgot that you promoted me, so why wouldn't I think that you'd forgotten . . . the library too?"

He leaned even closer to me, his deep brown eyes still twinkling and precariously close to ensnaring me. "You're not a woman someone forgets."

The praise boosted my ego again.

Todd gave me a wink and straightened in his seat, and I was relieved to have the extra space to pull my wits together again.

"But right now, we need to focus on the team."

Thank goodness, I thought. "I was beginning to think you lost interest."

"I suppose I had, but it's been recently reinvigorated. So, I've made some arrangements that involve redoing our marketing plan. Hence the ride to Henderson."

When we arrived, Todd led me to the rink where a single hockey player and the assistant coach, Connor Tolson, were doing drills on the ice.

"Connor," Todd called out over the ice. "Can I talk to Mikael for a moment?"

Connor nodded to the hockey player, who skated over to us. The young man looked barely out of his teens. He had a boyish smile, and his cheeks were red from the cold of the ice. His pale blue eyes shone with excitement until he reached us, and then they did a thorough tour of my body that had me stepping back.

"Betts, I want you to meet Mikael Virtanen, the newest player of the team and the one who's going to take us to the championship again this year."

It wasn't completely unexpected that Todd would bring in new players to the team. But I wasn't quite sure how this changed our marketing plan, except that I'd have to get a picture of Mikael and Photoshop him into the existing marketing campaign.

Mikael took his glove off and thrust his hand toward me. "Hello." He had a thick accent I couldn't place.

"Hello, Mikael. Nice to meet you." I shook his hand and listened as he spoke to me in a language I didn't know, but the waggle of his brow and the sparkle in his eye made me feel like he was hitting on me. I glanced at Todd to see if he had a clue what Mikael was saying to me.

"So, I want to build a campaign around Mikael, kind of in the same way we did with Max and Big Ed."

I gaped at Todd. "You didn't have campaigns around Max and Big Ed. If I remember correctly, you built a questionable campaign around Naomi." But then I remembered part of Naomi's campaign was hyping news that she and Max were dating when in fact, they weren't. One news article had her in a love triangle with Max and Big Ed. Naomi had hated it but had gone along with it. She was way more important than I was, so maybe I needed to go along with this too.

"You can get back to work," Todd said to Mikael. Mikael put his glove back on and skated backward toward Connor, blowing me a kiss.

I rolled my eyes and turned to Todd. "We need to talk about this." He hired me to market the team, not one guy.

Todd was either clueless to my irritation or he didn't care. "That's why I brought you here. Let's go back to your office and talk."

As I followed Todd back to the offices, I played out all the different ways that his idea was a bad one. Yes, his idea seemed to have worked with Naomi since he had filled the stands and had taken a team that was on the verge of becoming extinct and took it all the way to the championships. But he had hired me for marketing, so I was going to have to stand up and be the expert and not let Todd get carried away with wild marketing ideas.

When we reached my office, he opened the door but stood aside so I could enter first. He had a friendly smile, and like what happened in the car, I found myself momentarily mesmerized by it. But as I entered my office, I gave my head a quick shake.

Don't lust after the boss, I chanted to myself.

5

Todd

I wasn't sure what to expect when I told Betts about Mikael and my intention to make him the center of our marketing campaign. What I got was a similar response to that I had gotten from Naomi last year when I talked to her about how we could bring fans to the games by letting the media hype a story about her and Max. She hadn't liked it either, but she had gone along with it, and as a result, we all got what we wanted, her recognition as a great coach and me a team that won a championship and was making money. I didn't see any reason I wouldn't be able to get Betts on board with this new plan.

In many ways, Mikael reminded me of Bo Tyler before marriage, when he'd been the bad boy of the NHL. Mikael was good-looking, which meant women would be interested in coming to see him play. He was athletic and had finesse on the ice, which would bring in the men. And yes, he had the reputation of being a ladies' man in his home country of Finland, and while I didn't want him to do anything that was offensive or disrespectful, I knew that Bo's antics had made him popular and I was hoping that Mikael would do the same for us.

I held the door open for Betts so she could enter her office, and then I stepped in, closing it behind me. Maybe it wasn't a good idea to shut us off from the rest of the world because even when she was wearing her ice princess persona, she was fascinatingly sexy.

She leaned against her desk and looked at me like I'd grown a third eye in the middle of my forehead.

I gave her an affable smile. "So, what do you think?"

"Do you really want to know what I think?"

"I wouldn't have asked you if I didn't." I braced myself for her negative commentary, feeling confident that I would be able to overcome any and all of her objections.

"I seriously wonder how you've become the bazillionaire juggernaut that you have because this is not a good idea."

I took in a breath to steady the sizzle of agitation. People questioning my business acumen was not unusual, but considering how successful I was, I figured by now, they would notice that while my ideas might be a little bit outlandish, they always worked.

"I know you spent a lot of time on the other campaign, but we really need to switch gears and focus on Mikael."

"Why? Hockey is a team sport, so you should highlight the team. And how do you think the rest of the team is going to feel when they're pushed aside for an unproven player?"

My jaw clenched because I didn't like what she was insinuating. Maybe it was unfair to the rest of the team, but this was a business, and businesses only succeeded when they brought in money. Without it, there wouldn't be a team.

"And are you really going to put everything behind this kid we've never seen skate? What if you do that and it turns out he sucks?"

I shook my head. "He doesn't suck. I've seen him play, and back home in Finland, he is extremely popular. He's the kind of player hockey fans love to watch, and he's got the charisma that's going to make people interested in him, and through him, interested in us."

"Charisma? Is that what it's called now? Because I'm pretty sure he hit on me, and while I don't know what he said, it's quite possible that it could lead to a lawsuit."

I stepped closer to her, partly because I wanted to impress upon her how important this was, but also because I loved the way her eyes fired with heat when I drew near. I wanted to get a better look at them. "That's why I brought you here. I want you to help him clean up his rough edges. We'll get him into some English classes and give him lessons in how not to be a douche. It's a big job, and I'm asking you to do it."

Her head was shaking before I even finished my sentence. "I wasn't hired to babysit or tutor players."

For the first time in a long time, I was beginning to think I wasn't going to win the battle of wills. I stepped closer to her again, loving the way her breath hitched and her eyes widened for a moment. She was irked at me, but whatever the chemistry was between us, she felt it too.

"I plan to be involved in this project as well. Do you have a problem working closely with me?"

For a moment, she looked tongue-tied, and it felt like a victory.

Finally, she said, "It's a big risk. It could blow up in your face."

I wondered if she was talking about Mikael or our working closely together. I suppose it was true for both, but that was what I liked about this situation. The risk gave it a bigger thrill.

Taking a chance, I stepped even closer, so close that it was inappropriate.

To her credit, she stood her ground. "Naomi said that you had crazy ideas and you didn't much care about the impact they have on other people."

"You say that like it's a bad thing, but look at what happened. Naomi is a trailblazer, coaching a men's minor-league hockey team. My tactics might've been infuriating to her, but in the end, she secured her place in the world of hockey, earned herself a championship, and I suspect if I asked her, she'd be willing to endure it again. And it's not like I'm asking you to do anything similar to what she was asked to do." The truth of the matter was if there were going to be any stories about Betts dating anyone on the team, it was sure as hell going to be with me.

We were supposed to be talking business. While standing this close to her, I was trying to provoke the passionate woman inside her, but my plan was working against me as I felt myself ensnared by her beautiful green eyes and the scent of her perfume. I'd felt the same at Naomi's wedding. Completely captivated.

"I can't believe you think I forgot about the library. Not only have I not forgotten, but I couldn't if I wanted to."

For a second, her eyes flashed with the passion I'd seen in the library, but she quickly tamped it down.

Undaunted, I continued, "I haven't seen the woman who was in the library since, but I'd sure like to."

"You're my boss." Her eyes worked to stay defiant, but the quaver in her voice gave her away. She was affected by me. Good. I didn't want to be alone in feeling helpless.

I nodded, holding her gaze, feeling it like a tether between us and not wanting to let it snap. "I was your boss then too."

"It shouldn't have happened."

It was a disappointment to hear her say that, but I didn't get to where I was in business by giving in easily. "But it did."

I leaned in closer, half expecting her to push me away. For a moment, her eyes looked down, and I worried that I'd lost the connection.

Still, she didn't move away. As I studied her, I could feel the tug of war going on within her.

"Life is full of disappointments and hassles, so it's nice every now and then just to give in to something that feels good, don't you think?"

She lifted her gaze back up to mine, and while she didn't answer, I felt certain she was in agreement.

"I don't know about you, Betts, but I don't often feel very good. That night in the library . . . I hadn't felt that alive in a long time."

"It's not appropriate."

"Maybe."

"If anyone found out, they'd think that was why I got my promotion."

"But it wasn't. Unless that was your plan. Did you seduce me for a promotion, Betts?" I knew the answer, but I also knew that by asking the question, she would be forced to disprove her concern.

Her green eyes flared with that wild heat I was growing addicted to. "Of course not."

"Then there's no problem." I was done hearing excuses, so I closed the distance between us, pressing my lips against hers. I didn't dive in and take, but instead, I was tentative in case she was going to push me away. When her fingers clutched my lapels, they pulled me closer, not away. Her head slanted, and she parted her lips, inviting me in.

My intention was one little taste, a morsel to get me through the rest of the day. But Betts wasn't something I could just have a little taste of. I needed the whole thing.

The kiss sent an inferno through me, and my hands went to her hips, lifting her and setting her on the desk as I pushed her skirt up so that I could step between her thighs. I ground my dick against her panty covered pussy and groaned with the need to be inside her.

She groaned as well, and it was like gasoline on fire, making me crazy with need. I was so desperate that I barely registered the click, click, click of heels outside the door, and then there was a knock. "Mr. Marshall."

"Fuck," I said under my breath as I stepped away.

Betts jumped down from the desk, pushing her skirt down and turning away, straightening her clothes but also reestablishing that cool demeanor she wore.

"Yes, Carol," I said once I adjusted my dick.

The door opened, and the rink's admin, Carol Slaughter, stepped in. "I'm sorry to bother you when you're having a meeting, but your wife is looking for you. She called up at the main office, and they let her know that you were here. She's on line two."

Mother fucker. There was a reason I left my phone in the car, and it was because I didn't want to be interrupted by anyone, but especially by my ex-wife.

I turned to the desk to pick up the phone. Betts looked at me, her eyes round with a look of horror. It took me a minute to realize what she was reacting to.

"Ex-wife. She's my ex-wife." Jesus fuck. I was many things, but a cheater wasn't one of them.

Betts's expression didn't change, and I was moving from being annoyed at Taylor to being pissed off if she ruined things for me and Betts.

"We share a son, so I need to take this call. But don't go anywhere because we still need to talk." I picked up the phone and poked the button for line two. "Taylor, I'm in a meeting."

Betts pushed around me and out the door. Dammit!

"If you would return my calls or texts, I wouldn't have to interrupt your work. Dean is—"

"I will call you to talk about Dean when I can. But right now, I can't." I had to go after Betts and make sure she understood that I wasn't married. I hadn't been in a long time. Hell, I hadn't been in a relationship in a long time.

Another part of me told me to cool my jets. For one, Betts might be attracted to me, but she clearly didn't want to be. I couldn't be sure whether her attitude was simply because I was her boss, but I'd be a dick to dismiss her concerns.

Then there was my pride. When she said she thought I'd forgotten about the night of Naomi's wedding, I could see how that would have hurt her pride. It was important that I let her know that I hadn't forgotten and in fact, it was a memory that was seared into my brain. But she was still rejecting me, and even if her reasons were solid, they didn't feel good. Maybe I needed to let Project Betts go and just focus on my bet with Levi.

6

Betts

I almost had sex with my boss in my office. If Carol hadn't shown up, it was quite possible that I would've let Todd have his way with me. My hormones were disappointed at the interruption, but my common sense told me that I had been saved from making a big mistake. What was wrong with me that whenever he got near, all my senses sizzled while my brain stopped working?

When Carol said his wife was calling, I nearly threw up. The idea that I was an indiscretion by a married man made me sick.

He insisted that it was his ex-wife, and just to be sure, when I arrived home that evening, I Googled Todd. I'd done research before, but my focus had been on business, not on his personal life. I was relieved when I found information online that indicated they had divorced years ago.

Todd hadn't been linked to a woman since then. A man who was nearing fifty years old who hadn't had any relationships for nearly a decade suggested a man who didn't want to be tied down.

I wasn't a prude. I had no problem with casual flings, but I was at a time of my life where I was looking for something serious. I wanted a husband and kids, just like my friends had. But clearly, he didn't want that, which gave me a whole other reason to squash my attraction to Todd.

Over the next two weeks, Todd spent more time at the rink, but I did my best to avoid him or to have other people around so I wasn't alone with him. The few times I was alone with him, my irritation at 'Project Mikael', as he called it, kept my hormones in check.

Mikael was handsome and strong and skated with a great deal of flair, but emotionally, he was like a teenage boy just starting puberty. More often than not, he was looking at my breasts, not my face, when I was talking to him. He frequently made inappropriate comments. The only thing that kept me from filing a complaint against him was that there was an innocence about him that suggested he really didn't understand that what he was saying could be offensive.

I couldn't be sure if the words came out wrong because of the language barrier or if he was so sheltered growing up that he had no clue how to behave around women. Maybe he was playing a role he thought he was supposed to play, a bad boy, womanizing hockey player.

He was a hard worker, I had to give him that, but progress was slow. I'd arranged for him to take English courses and asked Connor to be his special buddy, taking him out and showing him the ropes to help him settle into life in Henderson.

When Naomi came in, I made a special trip down to the ice to talk to her about Mikael. While on the one hand, she agreed with me that he was immature and needed a muzzle whenever women were around, she seemed to agree with Todd that there was something special about him that would bring fans to the games and could help offset the loss of Max and Big Ed.

The season was getting ready to begin, and Todd had arranged with the Buckaroos' owners, Reed Hampton and Pierce Jackson, to have a press conference to introduce the teams to Nevada fans. As much work as I had put into helping Mikael grow up and assimilate, I'd also put into Todd and his presentation, telling him repeatedly to follow the script.

"It's not like I haven't done press before," he said with his usual affable smirk.

I had a bad feeling that he was just patronizing me. After all, he didn't say he'd stay on script.

The event was set in a ballroom in a hotel in Las Vegas. Todd had rented a suite for all of us attending the press conference to meet in before the event. I did a last run-through with everyone, and as long as everyone played their part, I felt like Todd would achieve his goal of building interest in coming to Henderson to watch the Silver Nuggets.

I was standing at the back of the ballroom with Analyn and Ruby as Todd prepared to make his presentation. Alongside him stood Naomi and Connor, and behind him was the team.

"Don't mess this up, Todd," I said under my breath.

Next to me, Analyn nudged me. "What could go wrong? They all look great. Confident."

I wasn't sure exactly what could go wrong, only that it could if Todd went off on one of his wild tangents.

"If he goes off script, wouldn't it be more likely that he'd focus on Naomi and the fact that her husband is part owner of the rival team?" Ruby asked.

I shrugged. "He doesn't really talk about that. All his excitement is around his new Finnish player, Mikael."

Analyn and Ruby looked up at the stage, presumably to study Mikael.

"He is cute," Analyn said.

"I imagine he'll have his share of puck bunnies," Ruby added.

"As long as they don't care that he's emotionally fourteen years old and tends to view women as sexual objects."

Both ladies looked at me.

"I get the feeling that he was raised without a mother. Or without any women around. He's a nice kid, but he was terribly sheltered or something."

"Well, this should be interesting, then," Ruby said.

I shook my head. "No. We don't want this to be interesting."

I was glad to see that Todd had the index cards that I had prepared for him, and as he started to speak, he was using them, going through all the talking points I told him were important.

The team had been underdogs last year, not only because they were on the brink of ruin before Todd bought it, but also because he'd hired a woman to coach. Even though they had won their championship last season, the loss of their two main players and Naomi's part-time status as coach for a few months had made them the underdogs again.

In my mind, Naomi's being a coach could further prove that women and mothers could be successful in a man's world. I had no doubt that she would be asked questions about being a mother and a coach, whereas it was unlikely that Pierce would be asked about being a father and a coach.

"We are very proud of Max Blake and Ed Samson and their successful promotion to the NHL. It is definitely a loss that we feel, but I am very excited by the team we have this season."

I tilted my head to the side because that wasn't exactly what I had written.

"In particular, we are thrilled to have Mikael Virtanen here from Finland. He's an amazing young man with a bright future. Mikael, why didn't you come up here and say hello?"

"No, no, no, no, no," I hissed under my breath.

SEVERAL REPORTERS' hands flew up, and Todd pointed to one.

"Mikael, you were set to be a top hockey player in Finland. Why did you decide to come to America to play for a minor league team?"

Mikael gave his usual boyish smile. "Because this is America. There is so much. So much space. So much to do. So much money. So much beautiful women."

I rolled my eyes.

Todd laughed and patted him on the back. "To be young again." Todd pointed to another reporter.

"Mikael, how are you getting along with the rest of the team?"

He nodded. "I get along very good. I come to be a star and they help me."

Behind him, the team stood stoic, but I saw the subtle signs that they were not happy to be relegated to secondhand players behind Mikael.

Another reporter waved her hand and Todd called on her. "Nevada is a lot different from Finland. Are you liking it here?"

Mikael gave her a wide grin. "It's hot here. But so are the women." He waggled his brows.

"Oh, God, I've got to put a stop to this." I marched to the front of the room and then up on the platform set up for the event. Todd, Naomi, Connor, and Mikael looked at me in surprise, as did the rest of the team.

I ignored them all as I stepped in front of the mic. "We are very excited to have Mikael here playing with the Silver Nuggets, but we don't want to forget the rest of the team. Last season, Dylan Katz blocked what could've been a goal from the Buckaroos, thereby saving our win and the championship. Dylan, why don't you come up and answer some questions?"

As I looked at the team, they were surprised, and then they stood a little taller at being recognized.

Dylan stepped forward, glancing at Naomi and Todd as if he felt he needed their permission. Naomi smiled and motioned to the mic. I glanced at Todd, who was giving me a hard stare, suggesting he didn't like what I did.

I stayed on the platform, making sure Todd didn't muck things up again. Once our time was up, we exited the platform, and Pierce Jackson and Reed Hampton stepped up along with Bo Tyler and their team.

I didn't get very far away from the platform before a hand gripped my arm and stopped me in my tracks.

"What do you think you were doing?" Todd looked down at me in disapproval.

"What were you doing?" I shot back.

"I was doing exactly what I set out to do, which was to highlight Mikael and get attention on him."

"Did you hear the things he was saying up there? He's going to make you and the rest of the team look like a bunch of misogynists. And after everything that you did to Naomi last year, everybody's going to think all you care about is sex. This is a hockey team, Todd. Not Mikael's team. Not let's-have-a-scandal to make money."

His jaw tightened. "It's been my experience that all publicity is good publicity."

"Well, after tonight, I suspect you'll find out that's not true."

"Mr. Marshall?" Todd and I looked to see a photographer with their camera trained on us. Todd slid on a smile as his arm came around me. He leaned over as the photographer took a picture. "We need to talk about this, but not here. I expect to see you up in the suite once this is all over with." With that, he walked off.

I stood for a moment, holding onto my righteous indignation. I felt certain that the things Mikael said were going to be used as soundbites to make Todd and the rest of the team look bad. But Todd's reaction suggested that perhaps my job was at risk.

I had been between the proverbial rock and a hard place. My job was to market the team, but to do it in a way that was good for the team as a whole, I had to stop the interview of Mikael because he wasn't ready. But in stopping it, I'd gone against my boss. He hired me because I knew my job, but clearly, he didn't trust me.

I blew out a breath and left the ballroom, heading straight to the bar. I figured I had another fifteen or twenty minutes before Todd expected me in the suite to reprimand me or fire me.

I downed my drink wondering what I'd done to deserve such a string of bad luck, starting from my fiancé cheating, getting laid off, and now pissing my boss off for doing my job.

7

Todd

Usually, I found Betts's defiance stimulating. And this time it was no different. Seeing the fire in her eyes as she confronted me turned me on.

But I was also pissed off.

She'd marched up onto the platform and taken control of the press conference, which might've been admirable except for the fact that she'd embarrassed me. With our two best players gone and Naomi splitting coaching duties with Connor, we had a lot to do to entice fans back to the game. Making me look ineffectual wouldn't do it. I gave my employees a great deal of leeway in how they interacted with me, but there was a limit, and Betts crossed it.

I was ready to let her know just how egregious her behavior was when a photographer pointed his camera at us. I pushed my anger away and smiled with my arm around Betts, hoping he interpreted the move as saying that her little stunt didn't faze me. It was clear that now wasn't the time for me to have a serious talk with Betts about boundaries. I let her know that I planned to talk to her later and then walked off so as not to make a scene.

I made my way over to where Naomi stood at the back of the room with her friends Analyn and Ruby while their husbands were on stage, introducing their team.

Naomi glanced at me. "Well, that went well."

I looked at her, not sure whether she was being serious or snarky.

"I guess we'll find out when the media posts the story," I replied.

Naomi gave me a sheepish smile. "You did go off script. Betts was clear that we were supposed to stay on point."

Next to Naomi, her friends, Ruby and Analyn, watched, apparently more intrigued by what happened to me on stage than what was currently going on up there with their husbands.

"First, I never agreed to stay on script. This isn't my first rodeo. "

"Was it the first time you got bucked off?" Ruby asked.

Next her, Analyn snickered, and even Naomi's lips twitched up until she caught my glare.

Naomi patted my forearm. "Knowing you, Todd, you'll figure a way to spin it into something that will bring the fans in. You always do, right?"

Damn straight, I do.

When the press conference ended, all my staff and team gathered except for Betts. I wondered if she pulled another act of defiance and simply left.

"All of you did great tonight. I really appreciate all you've done, and I look forward to another successful season. You're free to leave tonight. Connor?" I called over to the assistant coach.

He stepped up to me. "Can you make sure Mikael gets home alright? It's okay with me if you want to gamble or party, but I'd appreciate it if you kept him out of any situations that might keep fans from wanting to come watch him skate."

"Sure thing, Boss."

As I started to leave, I saw Naomi with her husband Pierce and her friends with their husbands. For a moment, I watched them, noting how happy they all looked. I wondered what their secret was? I tried marriage and family, and it blew up in my face. Had I chosen the wrong woman? Had I been a terrible husband?

I pushed the thoughts aside and went over to them.

"Good acquisition, getting Mikael," Pierce said.

I studied him and determined he was being sincere. "Well, he needs a little work socially, but I have high hopes for him."

"I know what it's like to have a player who is socially a problem." Pierce glanced over at Bo.

Bo grinned and put his arm around his wife. "Thank God, the love of a good woman has turned me around."

Everyone laughed.

"I guess I need to find Mikael a good woman," I quipped. I couldn't imagine a woman ready to take him on, though.

"Betts is a good woman," Analyn said.

My gut clenched as the image of Mikael and Betts tangled together naked in bed flashed in my brain.

"I think he's more of a project than Betts can put up with," Ruby said.

Analyn nodded. "Betts has been unlucky in love, but she deserves a man who will worship the very ground she walks on."

I didn't disagree. And yet at the same time, I knew that I couldn't be that man. It wasn't because I was her boss. It was because my experience with Taylor told me I was terrible at marriage and family.

"Is that what she's looking for?" I heard myself ask.

Naomi arched a brow at me, and I worried that she could see through me to my attraction to Betts.

"To be honest, I think she's given up on finding true love. She deserves it, but it will take a special man to help her believe in love again," Analyn said.

Disappointment filled me because I knew I wasn't a special man. But at the same time, they made it sound like Betts, while deserving of a happily ever after, wasn't looking for one and didn't believe in one. Maybe that would work to my advantage.

I excused myself, telling everyone good night, and then I headed up to the suite, texting Betts to let her know I was expecting her to meet me there.

Once in the suite, I poured myself a shot of whiskey and downed it, asking it to give me the strength I needed to be her boss and not get sidelined by my attraction to her. In retrospect, I probably should've waited to have this discussion in the office. It would be safer since my thoughts might veer off track.

And then I remembered the other day in her office when I nearly fucked her on her desk. The reality was that there was no safe place for me to be alone with Betts and not want her.

I was about to pick up the phone to call her and demand her presence when there was movement at the door. I heard the latch of the lock, and she entered the room using the extra key I'd given her earlier that night.

I studied her, noting she'd put on her ice princess face. With cool, hard eyes on me, she entered the living area.

"Have a seat," I said, glad that my voice sounded authoritative.

She crossed her arms over her chest. "I'll stand, thank you."

Irritation flared, and I cocked my head to the side as I glowered at her. "If I said the sky was blue and the sun was yellow, would you contradict me?"

"Only if the sky was gray and the sun was orange that day."

I walked over to the minibar, grabbing another tiny bottle of whiskey and dumping it into my glass. "You do know that I'm your boss, don't you?" The minute I said it, I regretted it because that was the very reason she had given me to say we couldn't spend personal time together.

I hurriedly continued, "Why did you think it was appropriate for you to make a fool of me by marching onstage and pushing me aside like I was a petulant child?" That's what really galled me. I didn't grow up with money, and before I had it, the wealthy people I mingled with always treated me as insignificant. Only Levi had shown me respect. Now that I had more money than many of the people I had mingled with before, no one ever made me feel small. Not until tonight.

Her eyes narrowed. "You hired me to market the team. That's what I was doing. And as far as making you look like a fool, you can blame Mikael for that."

I downed the whiskey and took several large steps toward her, propelled by irritation. Her eyes widened at my approach, but she didn't retreat.

"This is my team, and Mikael is my project. I will do whatever the fuck I want to with both. You are welcome to disagree with me, but under no circumstances are you to belittle me or make me look small."

Her brows drew together quizzically. "Small?"

Dammit, I'd revealed more than I wanted to. "The point is, at the end of the day, I make the final decisions, and I decided that we needed to highlight Mikael. Maybe he wasn't a hundred percent ready, but he's a good kid and his faux pas are endearing. Even if they aren't, all press is good press."

"You tell that to the countless athletes and celebrities who've been canceled for being insensitive, sexist, racist, you name it."

I shook my head. "He wasn't that bad." Was he?

She leaned in closer to me, both hands on her hips. "Once they pick and choose their soundbites and manipulate the narrative, it will be bad."

I mimicked her, leaning in closer, willing my libido to stand firm against the intoxicating scent of her perfume and the wild heat in her eyes. "If it fails, it's on me, Betts."

For a moment, we glared at each other, with every passing second, the tension building and building. My gaze drifted to her lips, and the desire to taste them threatened to overwhelm everything I was trying to do.

Goddammit, I was helpless, and I started to move toward her.

She jerked back and stepped away. All the fire in her expression dissipated, replaced by the cool façade of the ice queen.

She held her hands out to her sides in surrender. "Fine. I quit."

What the fuck? I didn't want that. "You didn't strike me as somebody who gives up."

She shrugged. "I can't give up something I never had. You hired me to do marketing, but you've pretty much scrapped everything I've done for you. So why am I here?"

"Can you really afford to just walk away?" It was an asshole thing to say, but I wasn't about to apologize or beg, even though both sat on the tip of my tongue.

"It's not your concern. I have skills, and I'd rather work for somebody who appreciates them instead of doing all this work, only to have it ignored. Oh, and by the way, the rest of your players, I'm sure, feel the same."

I felt her words like a slap in the face. Maybe I wouldn't have minded them so much if they were delivered in the same passionate anger she'd had a few moments ago. This dismissive attitude was making me nuts.

I stepped closer to her, looming over her, daring the fire to reignite in her. "I don't accept your resignation."

Her eyes continued to stay cool, but I saw the quick uptake of the pulse in her neck.

"I want you, Betts."

The ice began to melt, replaced with uncertainty. She swallowed. "Are you talking about the job or something else?"

"I want the strong, passionate, fiery woman marketing for my team and in my bed." Might as well put it all out there.

Her breath hitched. "You can't have both."

For a moment, I wondered if she was saying if I let her quit her job, I could have her personally.

"I'm only available for the job."

There was something in her eyes that told me her statement wasn't true.

I reached my hand out, my thumb brushing over the soft lips I desperately wanted to taste. "We both know that's not true." I didn't wait for an answer, mostly because I couldn't. The need to consume her was more than I could fight. I covered her lips with mine, half expecting her to push me away or slap me. But she moaned, and her lips went pliant against mine.

The tether of control broke. I swept her up and carried her to the bedroom. With each step I wondered if she'd resist. But she didn't. She kissed me back.

I set her by the bed, and our hands raced to undress. It occurred to me that we were in a hotel with a bed, which meant I had all night if I could convince her to stay. I wanted to ravish her body, but that would be quick, and I wanted this to last all night.

Once I tugged her panties off, I laid her back on the bed. I still wore my boxer briefs and prayed they'd help me keep control while I took my time savoring her luscious body.

Her fingers slid to the waistband of my boxers, but I pushed them away. "Not yet." I kissed her, preventing any protest she might wage. With my lips, I lulled her to surrender to me. With a sigh, she gave in, and that's when I started to explore every inch of her, from the angle of her jaw to the curve of her neck. Her skin was soft and smooth like ivory.

Her tits were round and full, so fucking perfect. I settled in to taste them. Her nipples were pink and hard as rocks as I lapped my tongue over them and then sucked them, one and then the other, until her body writhed underneath me.

"Todd."

My name on her lips was like the most perfect sound I'd ever heard. I rewarded her by sliding my fingers through her pussy lips as I suckled her nipple. Her body arched up into me, and my dick hated that he wasn't seeped inside her. But he'd have to wait as her wet pussy called to my lips.

I cascaded kisses down her body, pushing her thighs apart as I settled between them.

"You're so wet," I murmured as I took in the wetness glittering her pussy.

She moaned, and again, her hips arched up.

"You want me to eat you, Elisabeth?"

She gasped, but I couldn't be sure if it was from the question or that I was using her real name.

I used my finger to brush over her clit. "Say my name." It was fucking crazy how much I needed to hear it again from her.

"Todd."

I slid my hands under her ass and lifted her pussy to my lips and feasted. Back in the library at Naomi's wedding, I'd gone down on her, but I hadn't been able to savor it. I'd given in to my desperation, and there was the element of concern that anyone could walk in, so it was a fast feast. But tonight, I planned to take my time. I lapped and sucked and drank in her essence until she was again writhing with need.

Her fingers gripped my head, holding me to her, her panted breaths urging me on.

Finally, I used two fingers, sliding them inside her, finding her sweet spot as I sucked her clit.

She cried out and bowed off the bed as her orgasm slammed into her. Her juices rushed out, and I lapped up the delicious nectar.

I kissed her inner thighs, giving her a moment to catch her breath, and then I did it again.

"Oh, God," she said on a long moan as I took her up to the heavens again. My dick ached like a motherfucker, but I knew the minute I gave in to my own needs, the night could come to an end, and I didn't want that. I wanted all night, and even that probably wouldn't be enough. I had this moment to convince her that this crazy chemistry between us was worth indulging. I wanted nothing from her except her admittance that she felt it too and her willingness to stop denying it.

8

Betts

I t wasn't that I didn't hear the warning bells clanging in my head
regarding Todd. The only time they had stopped sounding the
alarm was when I realized just how angry he was for my interrupting him at the press conference. Todd was a man who used his
affability and charm to get what he wanted. That and the fact that he
had money and he was the boss. But he didn't exude affability or charm
when he demanded to know why I'd marched onto the platform.

It became clear that what I had done had tapped into a past
trauma or insecurity. He said I'd made him feel small, and it made me
wonder who had done that to him in the past, and in a weird stroke of
irony, I wanted to go back and lambaste whoever it was.

I hadn't wanted to make him feel small. I had wanted to stop him
from letting Mikael make a fool of him and the team. But he clearly
wasn't seeing that. Instead, he lorded his authority over me, and it
made me feel small.

I wondered why he'd even hired me. I remembered Naomi and
how I'd gotten the job because he'd heard of me through her. Had I

been part of some negotiation where she told him to hire me? The idea of that made me feel even smaller. I hadn't been hired because of my skills but so Todd could appease his star coach, Naomi.

I was a token marketing person, but he wasn't going to use any of my ideas, so why should I stay? So I disengaged from the argument and was surprised to see disappointment in his expression when I did. That didn't stop him from baiting me, trying to get me angry again.

Then he stepped closer to me, and all the warning bells started chiming again. I did my best to heed them, but once his lips were on mine, the power to resist faded into nothing.

He carried me into the room and used his hands and lips to do the most delicious things to my body. It was like he was there for my pleasure and my pleasure only. When I tried to touch him, he'd stop me. So I gave in, letting him make me feel so good. In the back of my mind, I knew I'd regret this, but I pushed all that away. All the reasons this was wrong were gone just for this moment in time. If I hadn't given in yet, I would have when he called me Elisabeth. It was so strange, the feeling that filled my chest to hear my real name from his lips. He said it in a way that made me feel revered. Special. Cherished.

I'd come twice already, but he was relentless as his tongue slid inside me, lapping at my sensitive walls. I was a whimpering, writhing heap of nerves ready to blast off again.

"Todd." It was the only word I could seem to utter except the occasional "oh, God."

"Come again. You taste divine, Elisabeth."

"I want you inside me." I wasn't sure I'd be able to come again after this one, and I wanted to do it while he filled me.

"Fuck." He groaned like he was uncertain.

"Please."

In a shot, he moved up my body while pushing his boxers down. "Look at me, Elisabeth."

I opened my eyes to find his intense as they looked down on me.

And then he plunged. I gasped as the invasion sent shockwaves through my already sensitive pussy.

"So fucking good . . ." he murmured as he slowly moved in and out of me. "Do you feel it? How good we are?"

I nodded because he wasn't wrong. I couldn't remember feeling things this intensely with my ex. Sex was fun, but it had been like scratching an itch. This, with Todd, felt so different, deeper, more powerful. I was quickly nearing the edge again.

"Fuck . . . I can't wait . . ." he groaned. "Come on, baby . . . come . . . I want to feel you come."

Like his words had been a command, a rush of pleasure consumed me. I held on tight to him, my legs wrapped around him as my world came apart.

"Yes!" he shouted, and then he gave himself free rein, driving hard and fast, and all of a sudden, I was coming again. Or maybe it was the same orgasm, just held up at a fever pitch.

With a final thrust, he collapsed on me. For a moment, I could only lie there, catching my breath. I felt like I had run a marathon at full sprint. I sucked in huge gulps of air as the endorphins coursed through my veins.

But as the shimmer of orgasm dissipated and my heartbeat returned to normal, so did the reality of what we'd done and how wrong it was. Maybe not for him, but definitely for me. He was my boss, which, if it got out that I'd slept with him, could make my life at work miserable. The minute it was learned a woman was sleeping with her boss, all her credibility went out the window. Nobody believed she had talent.

That thought led me to the reminder that Todd didn't recognize my talent as it was. He'd scrapped the billboard idea, and he totally went off script at the press conference. That meant only one thing. He was keeping me around because he wanted to have sex.

A wave of nausea threatened to bring up the contents of my stomach.

"Jesus fuck, that was amazing." He trickled kisses along my neck, which only made the sick feeling in my stomach worse.

I pushed him off me and scrambled out of the bed, looking around for my clothes in a panic.

He sat up and watched me. "What's wrong?"

I found everything but my panties. I hurriedly slipped into my skirt and jacket. I could barely breathe at the thought of what he'd turned me into.

I looked at him, willing myself not to cry, even though the tears sat on the very edges of my eyes. "I don't like being made to feel small either."

His expression was stricken. "What do you mean? What did I do?" He got out of the bed and walked toward me, not bothering to put on his clothes or wrap the sheet around him.

I held my hand in front of me to keep him from drawing nearer. "You only hired me because Naomi made you. And the only reason you keep me around is so you can fuck me." Again, a wave of nausea threatened.

He shook his head, and it looked almost as if panic was in his eyes. "That's not true. I mean, yes, Naomi asked me to hire you, but I wouldn't have done it if you didn't have the experience and the talent."

Maybe his words should have made me feel better, but they only made me feel worse. "Experience and talent that you don't use. You dismiss it, toss it aside. The only thing I have that you seem to really want is my body. I'm worth so much more than that."

He held his hands out like he was trying to corner a skittish cat. "You're right, Betts."

Betts. Not Elisabeth.

"You are worth more. And you're right that I like having sex with you, but that's not why you work for me. I scrapped one idea, and I went off script tonight, but I haven't axed anything else that you or the marketing team have done. Think about it." He nodded his head up and down like he was trying to get me to agree with him. "All that PR around Naomi winning the championship and continuing her career as a wife and a mother of triplets."

I scoffed. "We all know that you're happy to have any story about Naomi, even if it isn't true."

He let out a desperate grunt. "The story wasn't my idea, though. It was yours. I value your work, Betts. My being attracted to you is completely separate. I understand your concerns around it, I really do. But that doesn't stop me from wanting you."

Again, his words gave me a little flutter of positivity that I quickly pushed away because this was all wrong.

"What do I have to do to make you understand that I do value your work? I meant it when I said I wouldn't accept your resignation."

"I need you to listen to me when I tell you about a good campaign and to stick to the script."

His head bobbed up and down. "Okay."

"And I can't help you with Mikael anymore. You have to find somebody else for that."

His jaw tightened, telling me he didn't like that idea. "I've agreed to your demands. So whatever you say around Mikael, we'll do."

I shook my head because the problem in working with his and Mikael's campaign wasn't about marketing. It was about being in proximity to Todd.

"I can't do this right now." It was exceedingly difficult to have a serious conversation with Todd while he was standing buck naked and my hormones were starting to take notice. "We can talk about it at the office."

Not bothering to continue to look for my panties, I found my purse and exited the suite.

When I got home, I stripped and got into the shower, washing the entire night, and especially Todd, off me. I stood with my head under the spray, wondering how I'd gotten here.

In the library, I'd had some drinks, so I blamed being tipsy for my inhibition and inability to resist Todd. Yes, I had a drink at the bar tonight before going up to the suite, but I wasn't tipsy.

By the time he kissed me, I was stone-cold sober, and yet I was powerless to stop him. The minute his mouth covered mine, it was as if I was intoxicated by him. The guy was a master with his lips and his hands. He could be both demanding and gentle, sometimes all at the same time. He made my body feel things I'd never felt while having sex before. He made me want to do things to him I had never considered doing with a man.

And when I came, it was like being shot out of a rocket and sent soaring into heaven. It was powerful, intense, hitting something deep inside my soul. And heaven help me, I wanted to do it again.

Fortunately, my pride was more important. That and the knowledge that sleeping with my boss would only lead to more trouble. I'd been through enough heartache and challenges in the last year and a half. I didn't want to do anything to bring on more of it, and sleeping with my boss would definitely bring on more.

I exited the shower and put on a pair of pajama shorts and a tank top and went to get a glass of wine. God, the man was driving me to drink.

Once I finished my glass, I decided to call it a night and went to bed. As I lay in the cool sheets in the darkness of my room, the memory of Todd's touch tried to take root, but I fought it, pushing it away.

Todd was right in that I couldn't just up and quit my job. So I was going to have to do everything I could to avoid him at work. I'd make sure I wasn't on the project with Mikael. And while I diligently fulfilled my duties, I would begin the hunt for a new job.

9

Todd

There had been times in my life when I'd behaved like an asshole. But deep down, I knew I was a good guy. That is, until Betts accused me of completely dismissing her talent as my employee solely for the purpose of fucking her.

As the door shut behind her in the hotel and I sank to the edge of the bed, I had to seriously consider that maybe I was an asshole. Not just sometimes, but deep down in my soul.

Her words horrified me because I could see that she truly believed them. I knew what it felt like to be used and abused because I had let Taylor do it to me for years. It felt like shit, and while I didn't think I was the sort of man to do that, clearly, I had. I had to consider that I wasn't just an asshole, but a selfish one. Hadn't I made seducing her a project? God. Did it get more douchey-asshole than that?

There was no doubt that I was going to have to apologize, and a part of me wanted to run after her and do it right this minute. But I had the feeling that the sight of me would only bring her more hurt. I would give her time so the emotions weren't so raw.

I got dressed and left the hotel, leaving my room keys at the desk. I headed home and climbed into bed, the entire time replaying my behavior and terrified of the man she thought I was ... of who I might be.

After a restless night of sleep, I headed into the office the following morning, trying to push away my self-loathing and the need to make things right with Betts. Instead, I turned my attention to sports news, eager to see how the press conference had gone.

With my twenty-ounce cup of coffee I bought on the way in, I powered on my laptop and began to click on all the saved news tabs in my browser.

The first item was a news article that briefly outlined the two minor-league hockey teams in Nevada and how they'd been struggling but had made gains in the last season, with us winning the league. All that seemed pretty good.

I skimmed down until I saw Mikael's name, and as I read, I felt a knot in the pit of my stomach.

WATCHING *old footage of Mikael Virtanen in his home country of Finland, it's clear to see he has talent. We might even be able to get past the fact that he's like a teenage boy discovering porn for the first time in his eagerness to meet hot women. The challenge I see for Coach Naomi Jackson is that Virtanen believes he is the sole star of the team. I don't know if we can solely blame him for that thought as it appears the owner, billionaire Todd Marshall, seems to have put him in that position. You only have to glance at the rest of the team to see that they feel unappreciated. It was a bit surprising that coach Naomi Jackson allowed it.*

FUCK. I opened the next tab which had a video with a commentator standing outside the ballroom of the hotel. She initially started talking about the Buckaroos and the coaching adjustment they'd made in which Bo was taking the lead as coach while Pierce stepped back. All her comments were positive, even the question she asked about whether the team was finally fully gelled to reach their potential.

Then, she reported on us.

It's clear the Silver Nuggets know that a repeat of last year's league victory isn't a foregone conclusion with both Max Blake and Ed Samson gone. Team owner Todd Marshall has recruited Mikael Virtanen from Finland to be his ace in the hole this season, but it's unclear whether or not Mikael can fill either of their shoes, much less both.

She referenced some of Mikael's statistics while he played hockey in Finland, which were impressive. They were the whole reason I'd brought him out here.

But neither Mr. Marshall nor Virtanen said anything that would make Silver Nuggets fans feel confident for a second league victory. Virtanen may play great hockey, but his focus seems to be only on adopting the American way of life and finding hot women. And of course, one person, a team doesn't make, and based on the rest of the team's reaction at the press conference, it's unclear whether Mikael has fully assimilated with them. It was also clear that whatever announcement was supposed to take place wasn't happening when Mr. Marshall's team marketing director, Elisabeth Adams, came up and interrupted the presentation. It's unlikely Mr. Marshall was appreciative of that, but it was good to hear from the other team members, and along with Mikael, I think Dylan Katz would be another player that Silver Nugget fans should watch.

I continued to read and watch all the other news reports. All echoed the same thing, that Mikael might be a good player, but he was immature and held questionable attitudes toward women. Mikael's attitude didn't come off as endearing and charming, as I'd expected, but instead cocky and misogynistic. Just as Betts had said.

Thinking, or more like hoping, that the fans might have a different attitude, I perused social media looking for hashtags about the team and Mikael. The fans weren't quite as scathing about him as the sports news people were, but the only positive thing the women talked about were his looks. Even so, most of them agreed it wasn't enough to make them be interested in going on a date with him or watching him play hockey. The men called him an asshole and then told me he'd better live up to the hype or they'd switch allegiance to the Buckaroos.

"Fuck!" I slammed the lid of the laptop down and ran my fingers through my hair. Betts tried to warn me, and I didn't listen. Being wrong didn't sit well with me. It wasn't that I was never wrong. I had been. But it had been a while. Usually, my wild ideas panned out. And while I still felt like Mikael was the key to the team's success this season, Betts had been right in that he wasn't ready for the media.

I needed to fix this, and the only person who could help me do it was Betts.

I could have checked to see if today was the day that Betts worked here at corporate offices or was working down at the rink. Either way, I could go to her and discuss this situation. But I couldn't get the image of the pain and self-loathing I had seen in her eyes when she accused me of using her just for sex.

She was ready to quit, and I was a bit surprised there wasn't a resignation letter already on my desk. She wanted to be treated as a professional, and so that was what I needed to do. So instead of calling her in directly or going to her office, I did what I'd do to summon any other employee.

I picked up my phone and called my admin. I asked her where Betts was working today. She informed me that Betts was here in the corporate offices, so I instructed her to contact Betts to have her come to my office.

Impersonal? Yes, but also professional. Lording my authority might not seem like the best way to show respect toward Betts and her job, but hopefully, it would show her that I understood the need for us to be professional.

When she arrived, I wanted to stand and go around my desk, but I couldn't trust myself not to touch her if I did, so I remained seated.

"Please have a seat." I motioned to the chair in front of my desk.

Her eyes were tired and wary as she made her way toward me and sat down in the chair. I needed to apologize for the other night, but I didn't think starting with that was the best way to start this meeting. I needed to focus on the job.

"Have you seen the reports from the press conference?"

She gave me a nod but didn't say anything. She didn't have to. The expression on her face was saying "I told you so."

I gave her a sheepish smile, hoping it might lighten the atmosphere slightly. "You tried to tell me, and I didn't listen."

Once again, she nodded.

"Because I didn't listen, we're in a bit of a quandary, and I need your help to get us out of it."

She tensed. "I told you that I can't work with you regarding Mikael."

I sighed because I really wanted to respect her wishes, but at the same time, she'd been promoted to deal with marketing and PR for the team. I cocked my head to the side. "Are you resigning?"

Her eyes widened for a moment. "Not today, I'm not."

I took that to mean she was actively looking for another position. *Fuck, fuck, fuck.* How was I going to salvage this?

"I know I haven't done a great job at keeping up on your work and going along with your suggestions. I hired you to do a job, and then I made it difficult for you. I won't do that anymore. You are the head of marketing for the team, and I need you to take charge of this. Tell us how we can get out of the bad press that I got us into."

"It doesn't have to be me. You can use someone else, and I'll just oversee them."

I sat back in my chair and studied her. Maybe now was the time to apologize for the other night. "The things you said to me the other night, the accusation you made, have been burning in my gut.

It's killing me to know my behavior made you feel that way. That was not my intention. I didn't hire you or promote you for the purpose of fucking you any more than your seducing me in the library at Naomi's wedding was an attempt to use me to get a promotion."

She sat up, ramrod straight, and glared at me. "You thought that?"

I shook my head. "No. I'm just making a point. The meaning you've attributed to my behavior is incorrect. I'm not sure whether this is going to put me in more hot water or not, but to be honest, I see the two things, the attraction and the job, separately." It occurred to me that it was probably not quite true, considering I'd designed Mikael's whole campaign for the sole purpose of spending time with her. Fuck, I was an asshole.

"It's not possible to separate the two. At least not for me. If it got out that you and I had slept together, you'd be given a pat on the back. Boys will be boys, after all. But my reputation would be ruined. People would wonder about the promotion or my getting the job. And then they'd look at the way you ended my campaign and didn't listen to me when I told you Mikael wasn't ready as proof that you didn't see me as a legitimate hire."

I sat forward as irritation filled me. "I don't give a fuck what people say."

She let out a derisive laugh. "Of course you don't. You have nothing to lose."

Dammit! I was fucking up again. I leaned back in my chair and held my arms out to my sides in surrender. "Right now, the important thing is getting the hockey team back on track and getting Mikael media ready. As I said, you are the head of marketing for the team, and so I need you to do this. Whatever you say goes."

Her eyes narrowed as she studied me. "Whatever I say?"

I nodded but added, "I need to focus on Mikael. People are going to love to watch him skate, but until the season actually starts, I need people to get excited about seeing him skate."

"And what about Naomi and the rest of the team? Mikael's not out on the ice by himself."

I nodded. "Whatever other ideas you have about that, we'll do them."

She studied me again for a long moment. "You'll do that?"

"Absolutely. I won't scrap or change them. That's how much I believe in you, Betts." I had the urge to call her Elisabeth. There was nothing wrong with Betts, but Elisabeth was such a lovely name. It fit her.

Her features softened, and I finally thought that maybe I said something to lessen the disdain she had for me.

Finally, she stood and said, "Okay. I'll do it."

I stood but stayed on the other side of the desk, not wanting to fuck this up worse than I already had. I extended my hand out to her.

She looked at my hand and lifted her gaze to my face. "But from now on, all our interactions are professional only."

"As you wish." I agreed because I wanted to respect her and knew this was the only way to keep her. But as she put her hand in mine to shake and the zap of electricity shot through my arm, all I wanted to do was to jump over the table and kiss her senseless.

But an agreement was an agreement, so I stayed where I was.

I watched her as she turned and left my office. I hated that I wouldn't be able to touch her again. Not unless she wanted me to. That thought had me pausing. She wouldn't have slept with me if the attraction didn't go both ways. Yes, she didn't want to be attracted to me. It complicated her life. But just like my agreeing to keep my hands to myself didn't mean I stopped wanting her, her setting limits around our interaction didn't mean she still wasn't attracted to me. Unless her thinking that I was using her killed it.

Still...

I would keep my hands to myself as promised, but maybe there were things I could do to change her mind, to make her want me as much as I wanted her. I wouldn't cross the line, but maybe she would.

10

Betts

I t probably wasn't a good idea for me to agree to continue to work on Mikael's campaign. What was the definition of insanity? Doing the same thing but expecting a different result. I had no reason to think that my efforts this time would be any more used than they had the last time, except for the fact that Todd appeared sincere. My feeling was that he really did unintentionally make me feel used and abused. It had never occurred to him that his behavior could be misinterpreted and deemed insensitive. But why would he think that?

Men with wealth and power had very little need to consider the implications of their behavior on other people. The fact that he seemed genuinely mortified at how I had interpreted his actions meant that at least he understood and cared. And so, I agreed to continue on, giving him another chance. Not a chance to sleep with me, but a chance to trust my work.

I'd barely gotten back to my desk when Todd called and asked that I contact Mikael and have him meet both of us at a men's clothing store this afternoon. I took this to mean that he was going to work on Mikael's external image, but the truth was, Mikael needed work from the inside out. I supposed that was what Todd was putting me in charge of.

I contacted Mikael, giving him the address and time to meet both me and Todd. Then I reread all the articles and social media about the press conference, using them to decide how we could improve Mikael's reputation and likability.

When I arrived at the clothing shop, I waited outside until Mikael arrived.

"What's this?" he asked as I opened the door for us to enter.

"You'll have to ask Mr. Marshall when he gets here."

However, when we walked in, a woman who worked in the store came up behind us and locked the door. Todd had beaten us, and he stood from where he'd been sitting looking at his phone.

He walked over to us. "I've reserved the shop for us for the next couple of hours." He put his hand on Max's shoulder. "Son, it's time to clean up your image."

Mikael looked quizzically between us but then shrugged and smiled. "You make me sexier, right?"

I rolled my eyes. Todd smiled along with a quick shake of his head. "Come see what I've picked out for you."

We followed Todd to where a suit hung on a rack outside the fitting room. Todd held up the coat. "What do you think?"

Mikael studied it and nodded.

"With this shirt and tie, you will look as clean-cut as they come." Todd held up a crisp, folded white shirt and a silver tie, presumably meant to represent the Silver Nuggets.

"Why don't you put these on?" Todd handed him the clothes and nodded toward the fitting room.

Mikael took the items and disappeared behind the door.

I glanced over at Todd. "Making him look nice on the outside isn't going to fix what's on the inside."

"Probably not, but there's a reason lawyers have their clients dress a certain way in court when they are accused of heinous things.

Appearances count for something. I'm counting on you to help fix what's on the inside."

I suspected that only age and experience would help Mikael grow up, but I nodded. After all, I'd spent much of the morning coming up with ideas on how to make him more endearing.

The door opened and Mikael exited. I bit my lower lip to keep from snickering. The suit fit him all right, but it didn't match the man he was. It was like coating a bitter pill with chocolate. It just didn't fix what was underneath. Plus, there was the fact that he tugged on the collar, which suggested he wasn't used to wearing a suit. Then there was the fact that the tie wasn't tied right and was askew.

I looked at Todd, who had his chin in his hand as he studied his new protégé.

With an eye roll, I stepped up to Mikael to fix his tie.

Mikael inched closer to me and waggled his brows. "You like what you see?"

Not particularly. "We can't make a good assessment until you've got the suit on correctly." I undid the tie and then re-tied it, pulling the knot up to his neck, perhaps a little too tightly.

"Ack, you choke me. Some people like that in passion, don't they?"

My hands stilled as I gaped at Mikael. Did he see everything through the filter of sex? I released the tie and stepped back.

"You believe in love at first sight, or should I leave and come back again?" Mikael grinned. That line was so bad it had to be something he'd heard in a bar or on TV.

"Mikael, you need to stop talking to and about women like that." It was about time Todd stepped in.

Mikael looked genuinely perplexed. "But in America, women like bold, arrogant men, do they not?"

The truth was, some women did, but Mikael's execution of boldness and arrogance came off as icky.

"In America, writers have an expression that says show, don't tell. If you have to boast about yourself or be extremely obvious, it has the opposite effect. It makes it seem like you are nothing special. "

Mikael frowned. "But I am special. In America everyone is special."

"What Betts is saying, Mikael, is that you need to exude your specialness. Competent people don't have to try so hard. The very thing you're doing to attract women is going to scare them off. You're better off not doing it."

"Is this how you acted in Finland?" I asked him. I began to wonder if Todd got a deal on him because Finland didn't want him anymore.

He shook his head. "No. But there, women know me. They love me." He grinned.

"Well, if not acting like a cocky jerk worked at home, it will work here too. You don't need to try so hard." Todd patted him on the shoulder again.

"How do you feel in this?" I asked Mikael about the suit.

"I look like Mr. Marshall."

I laughed.

"What's so funny about that? I look good." Todd was not at all offended at my laughter as he looked at himself in the mirror, turning from side to side, sucking in his cheeks like he was a male model on the runway. And good golly, he was hot. He wore a suit like no man's business. But Mikael wasn't Todd.

"I'm not sure you pay him enough to dress like you. Are those solid gold cufflinks? I bet your shoes cost more than my rent."

Todd shrugged, telling me I was right. "I was wrong about the press conference thing, so maybe I'm wrong about this too. How do you think we should dress him?"

I studied Mikael for a minute. "Well, he's a young, athletic hockey player, so I think he should dress more according to his age and his lifestyle."

Mikael had arrived wearing faded blue jeans and a white T-shirt under a denim jacket. I decided we could stay with the style but with a few upgrades. I perused the store, grabbing a pair of dark jeans and a white shirt that buttoned at the cuffs instead of having holes for cufflinks.

Then I picked up a plain black leather coat. I returned to the men, handing the items to Mikael. "Try these."

Todd arched a brow but didn't contradict me. Mikael disappeared into the fitting room.

Todd was quiet for a minute. Then he said, "Do you think I could pull that outfit off?"

I glanced up at him, curious whether my comment about Mikael dressing his age made him feel old.

I considered teasing him and telling him no, but we had to be professional. "I'm sure you could."

He looked at me in surprise. "You think so? I'm not too old?"

"I know what we're doing here is trying to dress up something that is messy on the inside. But when you're not messy on the inside, you carry yourself in a way that allows you to wear whatever you want."

His face split in a wide grin almost as if I'd given him a gift. He turned to look at the fitting room door as we waited for Mikael to emerge. "You could pull off that outfit as well."

My girly parts flared to life, even though the words themselves were quite benign. I thought about him imagining me in tight jeans and a leather coat. I scolded myself for this thought because I was the one who'd demanded professionalism.

"You're not messy inside, Betts," he finished.

Those words made my insides go gooey because they were sweet. It told me he didn't think I was hysterical or overly sensitive when I got upset the other night.

The door opened and Mikael stepped out.

"Oh, my," I said as I took in the young athlete.

"I agree. You look like a fucking rock star, Mikael," Todd said.

Mikael turned to look in the mirror. "I look good, yes?" Then his expression fell, and his gaze went to mine through the mirror. "But I'm not to say that, right? I need to show, not tell."

I had to hand it to him. At least he was trying.

"You can take pride in yourself, Mikael. You just can't say it like you're God's gift to women.

"But I am—"

Todd shook his head. "You're going to attract more women by being chill, Mikael." Todd looked at me. "You're not worried that this plays into a bad boy persona, are you?"

"Not if he doesn't act like a bad boy. This is the type of thing the rest of the team wears. Plus, he's comfortable in it."

Todd nodded. "Then it's sold." Todd turned to me. "Pick out a couple of other pairs of pants and shirts, and maybe a few ties, and I'll go pay. This is the start of the new media-ready Mikael. We'll begin working on that next."

Mikael and I watched as Todd sauntered off to find the cashier.

"Thank you for not dressing me like Mr. Marshall. I like him very much, but he doesn't attract women," Mikael said as he continued to study himself in the mirror.

I looked at Mikael, prepared to tell him that there was more to life than chasing women, but he was just barely twenty years old, and I suppose for a young man at that age, chasing women was the highlight of life.

But that didn't mean I couldn't say anything that might persuade Mikael to tone his woman attracting efforts down. "Mr. Marshall doesn't attract women because he doesn't do anything but work. But if he were to go out to the clubs with you, he'd attract all the women. You'd have a tough time of it."

Mikael looked over at Todd, studying him like he was trying to figure out what he was missing.

"Todd exudes confidence and money, but he doesn't brag. He's also kind and generous."

Mikael's brows furrowed, and I was glad that it appeared he was considering my words.

"Go change, and I'll grab a few more items."

I was curious what Todd had set up for media training, but whatever it was, I was mostly glad that he now understood how important it was to prepare Mikael. I began to believe that Todd really would listen to me and my ideas. As long as everything stayed professional, I felt really good about my job.

Todd looked up toward me from the counter where he was

talking with the young woman ringing up the clothes. He smiled and mouthed *thank you*. For reasons that made no sense, watching his lips move reminded me of the other night and all the delicious things he did to me with those lips.

My cheeks heated, and I turned away. Dammit. Todd might be doing the right thing, but I sort of wished he wouldn't.

11

Todd

I'll admit I had some concerns about dressing Mikael to look like a modern-day James Dean, but I told Betts that I would trust her, so I went along with her advice. Maybe she was right since he looked incredibly uncomfortable in the suit but quite at home in the jeans and leather jacket. I just had to hope the kick-ass outfit didn't make him even more misogynistic.

Truth be told, the hardest part of this outing was in resisting reaching out to touch Betts. Not even in a sexual way. I wanted to push the strands of her gorgeous red hair away from her face. I wanted to reach out and touch her as easily as I'd patted Mikael on the shoulder. And if I was being totally honest, I wanted to wrap my arm around her and tug her next to me so that Mikael would know she was taken. But of course, she wasn't taken. At least not by me.

I was going to do my damnedest to respect her wishes and keep everything between us professional while I hoped beyond hope that perhaps she'd give in to the attraction I knew she had toward me. There was a brief second when I was paying for the clothes that I swore I saw heat flush her cheeks. Was it a sign that if I stayed the course, eventually, she'd give in? I could only hope and pray.

After I paid for the clothes, we took our individual cars back to corporate headquarters and into a conference room. I had arranged for several members of the marketing team to act as reporters with Mikael sitting at a table for a mock press conference.

They started by asking many of the same questions that had gotten him into trouble the other night, and because Mikael was still messy inside, his answers, while different, still skewed toward horny teenager. Even a question about the puck led him to inquire about the term "puck bunny". Jesus Christ, we had our work cut out for us.

Afterward, I pulled Mikael aside. "There's still some work to do, Son. But I can see that you really want to do well here. I know that you're going to listen to Betts as she tutors you on things like etiquette or how not to view every question that is asked as some sort of sexual innuendo."

Mikael arched a brow. "Innuendo? I don't know this word."

"Well, hopefully, you will know it soon."

Over the next couple of days, I gave Betts full reign over tutoring Mikael and working with the PR team on cleaning up his image. They wisely put out into the media that Mikael's English wasn't very good and that was why he came off sounding like such a douche. Whether the media was buying it or not, I wasn't sure. I supposed we'd find out soon. Our first game was going to be against the Buckaroos, and it was quickly coming up on us.

The next week, I met with Betts and Mikael more frequently, and each time, I left frustrated, although not because of Mikael's progress. The truth was, while I couldn't be sure he was going to be media-ready when I needed him, the kid was making an effort. No, my frustration came from spending time with Betts. She was amazingly patient with Mikael and very good at guiding him to understand what it was we were trying to elicit from him.

We not only needed Mikael to perform well in front of the press, but also out in the world, so one night, we took him out to dinner and tonight, we were taking him to a club. Maybe it wasn't wise to throw him into so much temptation, but what better way to learn to swim than to dive into the deep end, right?

I arrived early, mostly because I needed a drink before I had to guard myself against the never-ending pull I felt toward Betts. I selected the Golden Oasis club because I knew it was a place where Buckaroo fans hung out, so Mikael would be less likely to be swamped by women, or if he happened to offend them, he would be offending the other team's fans, not our own.

I stood at the bar and ordered a drink.

"Haven't seen you here for a while," Sam Clarke, one of the co-owners of the club, said.

"Just working hard."

Sam smiled. "You know what they say, all work and no play makes Todd Marshall a dull boy."

I shrugged. "How's business?"

"Awesome."

"And the family?"

Sam's smile was brighter. "Perfection."

The rumor was that over half of marriages in the world ended in divorce, so it was shocking to me to find so many people, including Sam, who were not only still married, but were extraordinarily happy about it.

A strong whiff of an exotic perfume permeated my space. I turned to see a woman probably in her early thirties, with fake blonde hair and fake tits, lean against the bar next to me.

She smiled, showing off pearly whites she'd probably had a sugar daddy pay for. "Hi." Her greeting wasn't just a hello. It was an invitation.

I gave a nod of acknowledgment but turned my gaze to the glass of whiskey I'd ordered. "Hi."

"I don't see you here very often."

I wondered if she read from the same pickup line book that Mikael had been reading. At least she was more subtle.

I shrugged. "The wife doesn't let me out much."

The woman tensed and then stepped away. I liked using the wife line when women picked up on me because it was a way to let them down without actually rejecting them.

The woman hadn't been gone for two seconds before another one, equally as fake, took her place. This one was as a redhead, though, and all I could think about was how much her red locks paled in comparison to Betts's.

I delivered the wife line, and sure enough, she left.

I'd just finished my whisky when a third woman, who appeared much younger and petite, sidled up next to me. She was dressed like a doll, and it felt perverted that she was trying to attract a man while looking like a child. What was worse was that it probably worked.

I delivered the wife line, to which she said, "The fact that she's let you out at all suggests she wouldn't mind if you were to find a friend."

Oh, for fuck's sake. My eyes scanned the room toward the door of the club, wondering where Betts and Mikael were. I caught them coming across the room, Betts with a smirk on her face, while Mikael's eyes were round.

Thank God. "Well, since she's on her way over, you can ask her."

The kewpie doll turned to see Betts heading toward me. She gave me a look and walked away.

Betts stepped up to the bar with Mikael. "I told you, didn't I, Mikael?"

Mikael stared at me like I was some sort of fucking god.

"You told him what?" I asked, feeling unsettled that Betts and Mikael were talking about me.

"Men who exude confidence and money and are not messy inside attract women by the hordes. We counted three. How many more came up to you before we got here?"

I ground my teeth, annoyed, although I wasn't sure why. Maybe it was because Betts didn't look jealous that women were trying to pick up on me. Or maybe it was that they'd been watching me this whole time. Probably both.

"And you sent them all away?" Mikael asked, his voice shocked.

I looked at him and nodded. "There's a time and place for that, and right now isn't it."

The rest of the night, we sat in a booth having a few drinks and talking to Mikael about how he could have fun, but how not to overdo it. At one point, he and Betts went to the dance floor. The man in me appreciated how she moved. I might have traded places with Mikael, but she probably would have seen it as being unprofessional.

There was a moment when she leaned closer to him, putting her hand on his shoulder as if to say something to him, and he responded by putting his hand on her hip. A red haze bloomed inside me, and it nearly had me out of my chair and onto the dance floor. She finally pulled away, and they left the dance floor, returning to the table.

Before Mikael could sit, a woman approached asking if he wanted to dance. He looked at me and Betts as if he needed permission.

Betts waved them off. "Go have fun. But behave."

As he followed the woman to the dance floor, Mikael turned back and grinned, giving a thumbs up.

Next to me, Betts groaned. "I hope that the thumbs up is saying he's going to behave and not thumbs up that he's picked up a woman."

I finished off my whiskey. "Or maybe it's a thumbs up that a woman picked him."

She shrugged. "It's like sending your child out into the world and hoping all the good work you put into him sticks."

I laughed because she wasn't wrong. In some respects, the way we were tag teaming Mikael felt like parents. But thinking of that made me think of Dean and what a fuck-up of a father I'd been.

At the end of the evening, I walked Betts out to her car. She was the one woman I would allow to pick me up, but even though I occasionally saw signs of attraction toward me in her eyes, she was hell-bent on ignoring it.

"He did pretty good," she said about Mikael, who was safely in a ride-share heading back to his place alone.

"He did." This time, I didn't stop myself. I reached out to push a red curl out of her face.

She tensed and looked down, but I saw pink on her cheeks. If I pushed it, would she give in?

No. I couldn't push. I promised her that I'd behave. I stepped back, and for a moment I thought I saw disappointment in her eyes. But that was probably wishful thinking.

"Good night, Betts."

"Good night, Todd."

WE WERE a day before the big game with the Buckaroos, and while Michael had made progress, it remained to be seen if it was enough for the upcoming press conference. I, Betts, and the marketing team did all we could to get him ready. There was only one more task to put him through, a mock interview with Johanna Price, a Las Vegas TV journalist.

I arranged for a car to pick Michael up and bring him up to Las Vegas. I instructed Naomi and Connor to make sure that he was showered and dressed after practice and to remind him to treat this as a real interview.

By luck, Betts was working here in the corporate office today, so I invited her to ride with me over to the station.

"What do you think?" I asked once in the SUV. "Do you think he's ready now?"

"He's had plenty of practice, and I think he understands proper behavior. As long as he isn't overly excited and forgets himself, I think he'll be okay."

I was glad to hear what she said because if she told me to pull the plug at this point, I'd have a difficult time doing it.

We arrived at the news station and were escorted back to an area just off the main news set.

Johanna's expression lit up when she saw me. She gracefully slipped out of her director's chair and sauntered toward me.

"My God, it's been a long time, Todd." She leaned in and kissed me on the cheek, and I did the same in return.

"It's good to see you, Johanna. This is the team's marketing director, Betts Adams."

Betts's expression was quizzical as she looked from me to Johanna and back. I knew women were observant and insightful, so I wondered if she caught on to the fact that Johanna and I had, on occasion, been more than friends. Not that we had been in a relationship, because we hadn't. We were two people focused on our careers, but when we felt the itch for physical companionship, we'd reach out to each other, knowing there would be no strings. Our get-togethers had been fairly regular for a while but over the last year or so had dropped off.

I couldn't quite remember the last time we had been together. I recalled that she had called me a few days before Naomi's wedding, and I'd considered taking her as my plus one but ultimately decided against it. One, I didn't want people to get any ideas that I was dating anyone. And two, I just wasn't feeling the itch anymore with Johanna. Hell, I hadn't been feeling it with anybody until Betts kissed me in the library at Naomi's wedding.

Johanna smiled and held out her hand. "It's good to meet you. Todd has told me how much you've been working with Michael, and I'm sure after today, we will have him completely media ready."

Betts accepted the extended hand and shook. She even smiled, but I could see suspicion in her eyes, and weirdly enough, it thrilled me. Was Betts jealous?

12

Betts

I knew the look that Johanna gave Todd. I was sure there were many times I'd had that same expression on my face when I looked at him, despite the fact that I didn't want it. It was the look of longing and lust. I had noticed it on the women at the bar, but it hadn't bothered me because I could tell that Todd had absolutely no interest in them.

But Johanna was a different story.

There was a familiarity between them that suggested they had heated up the sheets in the past. Maybe they were still heating up the sheets, in which case I should be glad that he had moved on or moved back. But I wasn't glad. No, that feeling rising in my gut was envy. It angered me to feel that. It was like I'd had my chance and blown it, except I hadn't. There was no scenario in which my sleeping with Todd ended in anything but embarrassment, or worse, heartache.

I studied him, wondering if I could decipher how he felt about her. His smile was genuine and his eyes were warm, but I didn't necessarily see desire. That little green monster in me liked that.

"Thank you for taking the time to help him," I said in response to her.

And then speaking of the devil, Mikael came in with his usual swagger and wide-eyed enthusiasm, like a kid who just walked into Wonka's factory.

"This is for TV, yes?" he asked as he stepped up to us.

"That's right, this is a news station, but you won't be broadcasting today. Instead, Johanna here has agreed to do a mock interview with you. Your final rehearsal before the real thing tomorrow."

Johanna and Mikael shook hands. Then she leaned toward Todd. "Can I talk with you, just for a minute?"

"Sure thing." Todd looked at me and Mikael. "I'll be right back."

I watched as they stepped aside, and Johanna put her hand on Todd's forearm as if she had every right to do so. I had a terrible urge to rip out her long blonde extensions. The woman was gorgeous on TV, but in real life, she was beyond stunning. Seeing her and Todd standing together, they looked like the perfect couple.

"When we're done, we should go for a drink," Mikael said to me.

I shook my head. "I don't think so."

"I am not being telling. I am trying to be showing. Showing my thank you for helping me."

When he said things like that, I felt much better about his being interviewed. Mikael was eager to do well and to please me and Todd.

Johanna and Todd both laughed at something, and her hand that had been on his arm moved to his chest. That was my limit.

I marched over to them. "I'm sorry, but we really should get started."

Still laughing, Johanna and Todd stepped away from each other.

"Absolutely. Mikael, why don't you come with me?" Johanna led Mikael over to the desk off the main news area.

"Here goes nothing, right?" Todd said as he came to stand next to me, and we watched Mikael and Johanna sit down for their mock interview.

"It appears as if he's in good hands." Did I sound bitter? I hoped not. It was bad enough to admit to myself that I was jealous. I didn't need Todd to know it.

Todd slanted a look at me, making me wonder if I'd failed to hide my true feelings. "He is."

I kept my gaze on Mikael and Johanna as I asked, "You and Johanna seem to have a history." The minute the words were out of my mouth, I regretted it. Even if I wasn't jealous, there was no way to ask that question and not seem jealous.

"Johanna and I went out a few times a while back. We've remained friends."

Friends my ass. I would bet anything that they were friends with benefits. The idea that he was taking benefits from me and her at the same time burned in my gut. The feelings of hurt and betrayal really annoyed me because I knew we'd only hooked up. It didn't mean anything, so I shouldn't care that he was screwing other women.

Except for the fact that he didn't use a condom. Dammit. Now I needed to ask him about his health and sexual history, which would take things out of the professional zone I was trying so hard to keep us in. That led me to my other annoyance, which was how easy it had been for Todd to revert to the professional zone. I'd spent the last few weeks fighting with my libido, while he'd been calm and cool. He'd found another fuck-buddy, apparently. One who was svelte and gorgeous.

Anger and jealousy swirled deep in my gut. I watched Johanna and Mikael but was unable to take in a single thing they were saying. Instead, my mind was filled with images of Todd doing all the delicious things he'd done to me to her. Inwardly, I let out a frustrated growl.

"Are you all right? I think he's doing really well."

Oh, God. Did I growl out loud? "I was just thinking about other things at work. He seems to be doing fine." Although I didn't know because my head was spinning with images of Todd and Johanna.

When the interview finished, Todd and I moved toward Mikael and Johanna.

"I think you did brilliant, Mikael," Johanna told him. Mikael grinned, and he looked to me and Todd for validation.

Todd nodded. "You looked good to me too, kid. What do you think, Betts?"

I nodded, feeling a little guilty that I didn't know for sure. But it wouldn't matter. If Johanna thought he did all right, I'd defer to her expertise and would support Mikael's being part of the press conference tomorrow.

"Thank you for this. I owe you," Todd said to Johanna.

"Of course. It was good to see you. We should get a drink." Johanna's eyes perused Todd's body. "We could catch up."

My hands fisted, either to keep from scratching her eyes out or ready to punch her.

He gave her a noncommittal nod. "Sure. I can't now, but give me a call."

"I will."

"We need to go." I tugged on Mikael's arm to escort him out so I didn't lunge at the woman trying to take the man I wanted but couldn't have.

"We have a drink now?" Mikael asked me.

"Not right now, but maybe another time." I glanced at Todd, wondering what he'd think of my having a drink with Mikael. He arched a brow, but he didn't seem concerned or jealous.

We exited the station.

"You take it easy tonight, Mikael. You've got a big game tomorrow," Todd said.

Mikael saluted him and then went to get into the car that Todd had arranged to bring him here to Las Vegas and now back to Henderson.

Todd opened the door to the car he'd arranged for us, and I slid into the backseat.

"If you want to have a drink with her, I can make other arrangements." See, I could act like I didn't care whether he went with Johanna.

He shrugged. "Not tonight."

Ugh. I looked out the window as our driver pulled away from the curb. I desperately wanted him to tell me that he wasn't into her. I hated him for making me feel like this, even though the circumstances were of my own making.

We drove, and I was practically biting my tongue to keep from asking questions about Joanna.

"She's a beautiful, intelligent woman. I'm surprised you let her get away." Dammit.

Todd looked at me, and I swore there was amusement in his eyes. He shrugged. "Maybe."

God. What was wrong with me that I was still hoping for an answer that indicated he wasn't interested in her? I wanted him to say something like she was a raving lunatic or vapid or boring.

"Well, it doesn't look like you've missed your chance. She seems interested." *What the hell is wrong with me? Shut up, Betts.*

He leaned over, and his expression confirmed that he was amused by me. "If I didn't know any better, Betts, I'd think you were jealous."

"Jealous? Me? Why would I be jealous?"

He winced and straightened. "Ouch."

I looked at him with confusion. "Why would that hurt you when you have someone like Johanna eager to see you?"

His dark eyes were intense, as if he was trying to look through to my soul. "I guess I should be grateful that at least she remembers how good it was."

Ouch.

"You easily pushed our time together away, Miss Professionalism. No one would ever have a hint about the time we spent together. Hell, I'm beginning to wonder if it really happened."

What the hell is he talking about? "You don't think I remember that?"

He shrugged. "It doesn't seem like it. But that's what you wanted, right?"

"You're the one to talk. You've been nothing but professional."

He laughed. "That's because you said you would quit if I didn't." He threw up his hands in frustration. "What do you want from me, Betts?"

I turned my head to the window to avoid telling him what I really wanted, another night with him. More than one, even. But I couldn't go there.

I shrugged like it was no big deal. "It doesn't matter. I mean, it looks as if whatever need you have will be taken care of by Johanna."

He shook his head and turned to look out the window. Finally, he turned back to me and all the humor I'd seen before was gone. Instead, there was just intense frustration. "You accused me of only keeping you around to fuck you. Now you seem upset that I agreed to your terms, which was to keep everything professional between us. It wasn't what I wanted. I did it because you wanted it. And as far as Johanna goes, it's been over a year since I fucked her and more than that since I wanted to. You're the only woman who has turned me on in a long time. And the fucked up thing is that you still turn me on. But you told me—"

I couldn't take it anymore. He didn't want Johanna. He wanted me. How could I resist that?

I launched myself into his lap and crushed my lips against his. It was stupid and wrong, but I couldn't help it. Everything about him pulled me toward him, from his honesty to his respect for me. And yes, it did my ego good to hear that the beautiful Johanna did nothing for him. I did.

13

Todd

Did I want Betts to be jealous and change her mind about our professional-only relationship? Yes, absolutely. Did I think making her jealous would work in making her change her mind? Not at all. Especially after I accused her of being jealous and she very calmly indicated there was nothing to be jealous of. I wasn't joking when I said "ouch." That hurt. Sure, I was a lot older than her, and maybe I'd been a little rusty at sex, but I didn't think I was so unremarkable that it would be no big deal for her to brush me off. And yet, that was exactly the impression she'd given me.

And then somehow, the conversation came around to where I realized that we were both misinterpreting each other's behavior. She'd thought my ability to respect her no-touch rule was a sign that she was unremarkable. I'll admit, it was frustrating to have her tell me we had to be professional and then for her to be upset when I respected that rule. She thought it had been easy for me when it hadn't. Not at all. Certainly not as easy as she'd made it seem on her end.

But as it turned out, being professional hadn't been so easy for her, either. And now she was in my lap, her skirt pulled up to her hips as her wet panty-covered pussy rubbed against my dick. Fuck, that was good. He was so hard that I was certain his tip was poking out of my waistband. I wanted to tear away her panties, shove my pants down, and thrust inside her right here, right now. I could probably do it. My driver was discreet.

But I didn't want a quick fuck in the backseat of my SUV. I wanted what I thought I was going to have the other night before everything fell apart—hours and hours of endless pleasure.

I slid my fingers under her panties and rubbed her clit. She gasped, and I took the moment to glance out the window to figure out where we were. We were just off the Vegas strip. Hotel central.

"Pull up to the hotel on this corner," I demanded of my driver. Then I dragged her lips back to mine and massaged her entrance, not wanting her to think too much lest she change her mind. I wanted her to stay in this haze of lust until I could get her to a place where I could fully dive into her body.

My driver pulled over, and I opened the door, tugging Betts out with me. I pushed her skirt down, then grabbed her hand and pulled her through the front door. The lobby, like all Vegas lobbies, buzzed and rang from slot machines.

"Are we getting a drink?" she asked as I led her to the front desk. Thank fuck, there was no line.

"We can have a drink later." I couldn't imagine the hotel didn't have room service or a bar, though I couldn't be sure it had mini-bars in the rooms. I didn't care about the amenities as long as the bed was large and the sheets were clean.

I booked us a suite, and with the keycard in hand, I guided Betts to the elevator, and when the elevator door shut, my mouth was on hers again. I'd made it this far without her questioning what we were doing or the wisdom of doing it, but I wasn't taking any chances. My mouth consumed her lips. My hand wrapped around her, tugging her close as I ground my cock against her so she knew just how desperate it was to have her. Her fingers gripped the lapels of my coat, and she moaned.

When we reached our floor, I half carried her up the hall to the room. My mouth was still on hers as I finagled the keycard over the handle. I heard the lock switch, and I opened the door, tugging her inside. I pushed the door closed and pressed her against it, dropping the key card so I could focus all my attention on her.

"Do you feel what you do to me?" I murmured against her neck as I took her hand and brought it to my dick. "That's you, Elisabeth. Not anyone else."

Her fingers wrapped as much around my dick as they could considering I still had my slacks on. I hissed out a breath as she squeezed and stroked. My eyes nearly rolled back in my head.

I dropped to my knees, pushing her skirt up and yanking her panties down. "What do I do to you?" Her glistening pussy told me what I did to her. Her arousal did my ego good, especially after thinking she'd so easily walked away from me.

This was my chance to bind her more fully to me, to keep her from walking away after this.

For a moment, I hesitated as I realized what I'd just thought. Bind her to me? What was I thinking? There was no doubt that there was something more than just sex pulling me to her, but I wasn't able to name what that was.

I gave my head a quick shake. I didn't have to define it now. I just wanted to make sure I could continue to be around Betts, spend time with her, touch her for as long as this attraction existed.

"Todd." Her voice was desperate, and again, my ego soared knowing it was me she was desperate for. I rewarded her by dragging my tongue through her folds, holding her up by her hips as her legs trembled.

"Oh, God." Her fingers threaded through my hair, gripping my head as I sucked and licked her pussy. Fuck, she tasted divine. I slid one, then two fingers inside her, making sure I rubbed against her sweet spot inside. I flicked my tongue over her clit, slowly driving her closer and closer to madness. Her hips rocked in rhythm, and she let out soft mewls that filled my chest with something I couldn't name.

"Oh . . . I'm coming." Her entire body went taut, and her juices flowed around my fingers. I lapped them up, consuming them like they were the elixir of life.

I brought her down from the high and then rose, kissing her hard so she could taste how delicious she was. Her hands went to my clothes, and I helped her get them off me. I was about to fuck her, but she lowered down in front of me.

Fucking hell. I wouldn't last if she sucked me. "Elisabeth—"

"I want a turn."

I pressed a hand on the wall to keep upright and hopefully in control as her tongue snaked out over my tip. I let out a moan as a zap of electricity shot through my dick.

"I won't last . . ." My words were lost as her lips wrapped around my dick and sucked it in deep and hard. "Jesus fuck!" Pleasure consumed me, swallowed me whole, taking me near the brink. I wanted to give in to it, to let go and watch my cum fill her mouth. But more than that, I wanted to be inside her sweet pussy.

"Elisabeth." It took all the strength I had to pull away from her fantastic mouth.

She looked up at me in question.

I tugged her up and kissed her hard. "I want to be inside you."

"Technically, you were—" Her words were cut off when I turned her around, pushing her against the door.

"Open your legs, baby."

She didn't argue. She widened her stance and tilted her sweet ass back. I rubbed one buttock cheek, admiring how sexy and smooth it was. Then I took my dick and rubbed it between her legs, searching for her entrance.

She moaned and pushed back against me.

"Did you miss this?" I asked her, my lips nipping along her neck.

"Yes."

"Good, because I missed it too." I filled her in one hard, deep stroke. This was my happy spot, where I found excitement and challenge. Betts had brought something into my life that had been miss-ing, something I'd spent many years chasing but could never quite grasp. The truth of that was startling and terrifying. This woman could hurt me. And I didn't mean hurt me like Taylor did, which was more of a disappointment and annoyance. No. Betts could hurt me emotionally. But what could I do?

14

Betts

My entire body was humming, vibrating with that torturous mixture of pleasure and desperate need. Sex had never involved every neuron in my body, but somehow, Todd was able to arouse every bit of my body. My fingers pressed against the door as he drove in and out of me from behind. Each time he thrust in, I thought I would go flying into nothing. Instead, he just ratcheted up the tension tighter until I could barely breathe.

"You feel so fucking good, Elisabeth."

He was calling me by my full name again. The fact that he did so when we were having sex somehow made it feel like more than just a physical act. I couldn't say why. It was probably wishful thinking. It was me, once again, wanting something and seeing things that weren't there. Even if it meant nothing, it was sweet.

His fingers found my nipple and started tweaking it. I felt it straight to my core, so when he thrust again, this time, he launched me to the stratosphere. I cried out as pleasure washed through me, making my entire body shudder.

"Yes!" he growled and began driving harder, faster, until he thrust hard and warmth filled my womb. Weirdly, the sensation reminded me that I'd wanted to ask him about his sexual history since we hadn't been using a condom. But then I remembered he said he hadn't had sex in a year. Was that just with Johanna or anyone?

My thoughts were interrupted when he collapsed against me. "If this door weren't here, I'd be a gelatinous heap on the floor," he said between harsh breaths.

"You're keeping me from melting to the floor."

He gave my shoulder a light bite, and then finding strength, he scooped me up and carried me to the bed. He collapsed on it, tugging me into his hard, warm body. Instinctively, I curved into him. A part of me needed to meld into him.

My opinion on this matter hadn't changed. Engaging in an affair with my boss was still wrong. I was risking all sorts of problems. But right at this moment, I couldn't bring myself to care enough to extricate myself. There was something about Todd that drew me to him, like a metal to a magnet.

But it was even more than that because when I allowed myself to be with him, there was a joy and satisfaction that went beyond the physical. I suppose it was like puzzle pieces. When locked in place, it was like this was where I was supposed to be.

I nestled against Todd, resting my head on his shoulder and my hand over his chest where I could feel his heartbeat. I knew he was attracted to me. Not just because we had sex, but because he had admitted as much. But did it extend to his heart? There was danger in my pondering that, so I quickly pushed it out of my head.

"Remind me to make you jealous more often," he murmured against my temple, followed by a kiss.

I tilted my head to look up at him. "Was that what this mock interview with Johanna was all about?"

For a moment, his expression turned concerned. "Not at all."

"I'm still not sure what you don't see in her."

"Who?"

I grinned at him.

"I meant it when I said I thought you were able to push me into the professional zone without a thought," he said. "I will admit that if I had considered you might get jealous, I might've arranged the meeting sooner."

I pursed my lips at him. "You're the one who was acting like it was easy."

He let out a laugh. "It was total and complete agony to act professional when all I wanted to do was touch you and hold you and kiss you."

I walked my fingers over his chest. "It wasn't very easy for me, either."

"What was that?" He put his hand behind his ear as if he was trying to hear better. "What did you just say?"

"You heard me." I gave his nipple a pinch.

He winced, taking my hand and bringing it to his lips in a sweet gesture. "Do you suppose now we could redefine what professional means between us?"

I moved until I was sitting up and straddling his thighs, running my hands up his strong chest. "What do you have in mind?"

His hands went to my thighs, rubbing them while his dick, a minute ago lying soft on his belly, began to swell and harden. "I'm kind of liking this."

"This?" I used my thumbs and forefingers to pinch his nipples, loving the way his dick jumped as I did so. "Or this?" I rubbed my pussy along his shaft.

His hips rose, pressing his dick tighter between our bodies. "Do I have to choose just one?"

"No." I took his dick in my hand and stroked. "Why do you call me Elisabeth when we're having sex?"

For a moment, he stared at me. It made me wonder if he realized he did it.

Finally, he said, "I don't know. I suppose because your name is beautiful. Maybe it's to differentiate Betts, my employee, from Elisabeth, the woman who lights me up."

I knew my smile was goofy, but hearing him say I lit him up

boosted my ego and made me feel warm and gooey inside. He deserved a reward for that, so I rose over him and then took him inside my body. After that, the only words were erotic and naughty until pleasure consumed us again.

As I lay sprawled over him, catching my breath, I had to admit, even if it was just to myself, that I was already in deeper than I should be with Todd. My heart was becoming entangled with his. If I were smart, I would leave now and not look back. I didn't mean just leave this room and make a vow to stay away. I meant quit my job and go work somewhere else so that I could avoid him completely. Even just seeing him across a room was enough to make my chest hurt with longing. I was in very dangerous territory here.

There'd been a time not so long ago when I had sworn off men, instead spending all the time with my friends. Over time, I'd come to want what they had, men who were devoted to them and children born from their love. But I couldn't have that with Todd. He'd been married and had a child, but clearly, it hadn't gone well. The fact that he hadn't been serious with any woman since then suggested he had no interest in trying again.

Finding a life mate and getting married took time, and I couldn't waste that time having a relationship, or whatever this was, with Todd. In fact, it was just a few hookups between people who were physically attracted to each other, right? Telling myself that made it easier to stay right where I was, my body wrapped around his, my head lying on his chest, listening to his heartbeat.

"I THINK I promised you something to drink. Maybe we could get something to eat too. I need the sustenance." Todd waggled his brows suggestively. It had its intended effect when everything inside me went sizzling hot.

"I could eat something."

He grinned and got out of bed, not bothering to cover up as he sauntered to the desk in the room to look through the menu by the phone. "I'm feeling like a burger. What about you?"

I'd had dinner with Todd when we took Mikael out, but I'd been so busy helping Mikael learn manners and etiquette, I'd hardly eaten. In other words, I hadn't really ever had a meal with Todd. Funny how with sex, I could talk myself into calling it simply a physical action, but having a meal with him after sex somehow made it seem like more. The warnings again sounded, but I again silenced them.

"Is there one with bacon and cheese?"

He grinned at me for reasons I couldn't understand.

"What? Did you think I was a vegetarian or something?"

He shook his head. "I don't think I've ever been with a woman who ate anything other than salad. I like that about you."

I arched a brow. "That I'm happy to eat like a pig?"

His eyes perused my body. "No. That if you want a burger, you eat a burger without thinking whether it will make you look like you're eating like a pig, which it doesn't."

"I don't suppose you worry about such things." I didn't hide my appreciation of his body or his willingness to show it off to me.

He grinned. "You like what you see?"

"I'll admit it's not a bad view."

"I might like what I see too, if you'd lower that sheet."

I wasn't a prude, but I'd never been an exhibitionist either. Still, I liked the way Todd's eyes heated at the sight of my body, so I got out of bed, gave him a full view, and then headed to the bathroom. While in there, I could hear Todd ordering room service.

I was washing my hands when his cell phone rang.

He let out a frustrated growl. "It's not a good time, Taylor."

I froze, wondering why his ex-wife was calling him.

"We will. But not right now. I'll call you tomorrow, I promise."

I heard the rattle of what sounded like a phone being tossed onto the table.

I looked for my clothes and began to put them on.

"Are you okay, Betts?"

It was silly, but it didn't help that he was back to calling me Betts. I didn't look at him. "Sure. Fine. I'm just thinking of all the work we need to do." I could only imagine what his driver was thinking by dropping us off in the afternoon at a hotel after our making out in the back seat of the SUV.

Todd's hand came around me and stopped me from slipping my skirt on. He turned me in his arms. "What's going on?"

Todd was surprisingly honest with me, and maybe it was time I needed to be with him too. "It's just the mood is over."

His head cocked to the side. "Why?" Then he did a big eye roll. "Not because of the call from my ex-wife, is it?"

I shrugged. The outside world had intruded, burst my bubble. For some reason, I couldn't silence all the reasons our being together was wrong.

His hand cradled my cheek. "Don't let her ruin this."

"I don't want to, but even without her call, nothing has changed. All the reasons we shouldn't be doing this still exist."

He sucked in a breath and took a moment. Finally, he said, "We don't need to figure everything out right now. Let's give ourselves this time and not think about anything else. I'll turn off my phone. You can turn off yours."

I gave him a wan smile because it sounded nice. "I think the time has passed. Like I said, the mood is gone."

One hand slid over my ass. "Let's get the mood back."

I couldn't respond with words because his lips were on mine in a searing kiss that I felt from my lips down to my toes. Every neuron in my body tingled to life. I moaned into his mouth.

What the hell. I'd give in this one time. For this one brief moment in time, I'd take what I wanted from him.

15

Todd

I was on top of the world. And it wasn't because Mikael was skating like he had wings on his feet and a laser at the end of his hockey stick at tonight's game against the Buckaroos. The kid was fucking killing it.

While watching Mikael kick ass on the ice felt good, my euphoria was from the woman standing at the other side of the owner's box watching the game and prepping comments with her assistant for the press conference afterward. The woman I wasn't supposed to be watching lest I give away the fact that I spent all of last night seeped inside her body.

The last time I ever remember feeling this energized was when my son, Dean, was born. By then, I knew my marriage was going to be a struggle, but as I held my newborn son in my arms, I remember being filled with awe. I had a newfound reverence for life and all the potential it held. I remembered thinking how perfect things could be with hard work and enthusiasm.

Back then, the feeling was fleeting. Not long after, Taylor decided we needed a mansion and nanny and things that did not come cheaply. While I'd been successful by then, in order to maintain the lifestyle she wanted, I had to work hard and often, and our already strained relationship eventually broke.

Because I knew those moments of bliss were fleeting, I understood that what Betts and I had wasn't necessarily everlasting. But I also knew that I wasn't done seeking out the pleasure that she and I could bring each other when it was just the two of us and we let the world fall away. She was like a drug. In fewer than twelve hours after my last hit, I was craving more.

But I understood the situation she was in, and I promised her I wouldn't do anything that would hurt her reputation, which meant right now, in the owner's box, watching the first hockey game of the season, I had to act like I hadn't spent last night with her having more orgasms in those few hours than I had in the entirety of my marriage. It wasn't easy, but I knew if she wanted to give me another night, I'd have to follow the rules, so I did my damnedest to keep my eyes focused on the game.

"What are you feeding that kid?" Reed, the Buckaroo's owner, asked. He sat with his wife and the wives of the coaches, Analyn and Ruby.

I grinned and shrugged. "It must've been that wholesome Finnish fresh air."

When the game finished and we'd come out with a three to one win, I knew that despite all my false steps with Mikael, I'd made the right decision in bringing him onto the team.

"Great game, Todd." Reed extended his hand, and we shook.

"Thank you. Now I just have to hope he gets through the press conference." I didn't think anyone knew how hard Betts and I had been working to get Mikael media ready. But Reed and the rest of them were good people, and I don't believe they hoped that Mikael would embarrass the team.

I turned toward Betts, who stood waiting for me. "We should go catch Mikael and get him settled for the press conference," she said to me. "I've already sent David down."

I nodded and went over to the door, holding it open and

motioning for her to exit in front of me. As we made our way out of the room and took the elevator down to the locker room level, I wanted more than anything to grab her and hold her and kiss her. Fuck the press conference. I wanted to take her back to the hotel and drown myself in her again.

I shoved my hands in my pockets and played sports stats in my head to keep myself in check. As the elevator neared the end of its journey, I asked her, "When this is all said and done tonight, would you like to go get a drink?"

I chanced a glance at her, hoping I wasn't stepping over the boundary. After all, we were in private, and it wasn't like I was asking her back to the hotel to get naked. I'd do that later.

"Maybe." But her sly smile told me that she was interested. My heart did a dance in my chest. She wasn't fighting this thing between us anymore.

The doors opened and we exited, heading toward the locker room. When we arrived, Betts went into full marketing management mode, checking in with Naomi and Connor, as well as Dylan and Mikael. Last year, most of the media interviews seemed to involve a reporter catching a player or coach coming out of the locker room. This year, I made sure the media was corralled into a specific room that we set up for interviews and press conferences.

I stood at the back of the room while Naomi, Connor, Dylan, and Mikael sat at the table at the front of the room. Over at the side door, Betts stood at the ready, prepared to intervene if anything went off kilter. I was grateful that this time, I wouldn't be the one she'd interrupt if things went off the rails. I was also grateful when the first questions asked were directed at Naomi and her coaching. It was probably sexist that they asked about motherhood and coaching as if the two shouldn't go together, but Naomi took on the questions like the true trailblazer she was. She let the world know that all things were possible for a woman. She also gave props to her husband Pierce, who was an equal parent and her biggest supporter as a coach.

The next questions were geared toward Mikael, and I held my breath as I waited for something obnoxious to come out of his mouth.

My next breath came ten minutes later when the press conference ended and Mikael hadn't said anything offensive. I waited until the press conference broke up and everyone was leaving before I went on the hunt for Betts. I found her in her office with her assistant, David. When she finished talking to him, he exited her office, and I stepped in.

"Mikael did good tonight," I said.

Betts nodded. "He did."

Betts looked at me, and I noticed the wariness in her eyes. Was she changing her mind? Or maybe she was just making sure I behaved and kept our little affair a secret. I shoved my hands in my pockets to keep from rushing toward her and tugging her into my arms like I desperately wanted to do. My desire wasn't sexual, or at least not solely sexual. I'd had a really great night, and there was nobody else I wanted to celebrate it with than with Betts. I was determined that we would celebrate, but not here.

I was trying to decide whether I wanted to invite her out for just a drink or dinner. I considered dinner and dancing, but to be honest, all I wanted to do was go someplace where it would just be the two of us like it was last night.

"Todd." The voice behind me sent a cold chill down my spine.

I turned my attention toward the doorway. Taylor. Jesus fuck, what was she doing here?

I cast a quick last glance at Betts, who stared at Taylor in confusion.

I stepped toward Taylor, blocking her from Betts. "What are you doing here?"

"I've brought Dean. He needs to come live with you for a while."

I looked over her shoulder where my son was leaning against the wall, his attention directed to his phone.

"What are you talking about? You can't just show up here—"

Taylor got up into my face. "You won't talk to me over the phone, so I've come in person. He's been kicked out of school again, and I can't handle him. You abandoned him for long enough. Now it's your turn."

What the hell? "I didn't abandon him. You're the one who took him away."

"You could come and visit."

"Not if you want all the financial support I send you." Okay, so maybe that wasn't totally true. I was very wealthy now. I didn't need to work like I had when I was married. The truth was, the last few times I had visited Dean, he'd had no interest in me. It appeared he believed all the things his mother had told him about me. Maybe I should've tried harder, but it seemed easier at the time to just do what they wanted me to do and go away.

"I have to go if I'm going to catch my flight back." She dropped a duffel bag I hadn't realized she was carrying next to my feet. "You're the one who wanted to be a father. So now you can do it." She turned on her heel and strode down the hallway.

I started to go after her, but I looked at Dean, who was still staring at his phone. I couldn't imagine he hadn't heard everything that was just said. Taylor was right. Having a child had been my idea. She'd fought it at first. How must he feel knowing that about her, plus over-hearing us argue, not about who would get to keep him, but who would be free of him? Jesus fuck, I was a terrible father.

"Dean."

"What?" He didn't bother looking up.

I picked up the duffel bag and handed it to him. "Take your bag. We're heading home."

With his gaze still on his phone, he took the strap and put it over his shoulder and then resumed typing.

I looked into Betts's office, wondering how I was going to explain this to her. "I was hoping we could go celebrate, but . . ."

She waved my comment away as she sat down at her desk. "You have more important things to worry about now."

I desperately wanted to go over to her, especially since for some reason, this felt like an ending, not just an interruption. I was torn between her and Dean, and the guilt of that was unsettling. I should be choosing my son, no question. Apparently, he was having a difficult time, and I knew he didn't care much for me, but that wasn't his fault. That was mine and Taylor's fault. I needed to do better by him.

"Thanks for all your hard work on Mikael, Betts."

She nodded and gave me a wan smile. Did she feel it too? That whatever started last night was now over?

I couldn't continue to stand there and stare at her with yearning in my chest, so I turned to Dean. "Come on, Son, let's go home."

I started up the hall, and a few steps in, I turned to make sure that Dean was following me. The kid must have eyes on the top of his head because he didn't look up from his phone as he followed me up the hall.

It was clear that in an instant, my life had changed. The fucked up part was that I wasn't sure I'd be able to manage it.

16

Betts

If Todd had invited me somewhere private to celebrate the team's victory and Mikael's success at the press conference, I would have gone. After last night, there was no denying how much I wanted to spend time with him. That didn't mean I wasn't concerned about my job or my reputation.

But Todd said he understood and would abide by my terms, which were when we were in public, particularly at work, we had to act professional. Only when I was sure that no one would see us could we give in to the desires we had for each other.

And then his ex showed up.

Todd's expression at seeing her suggested he was completely caught off guard. Anger and resentment burned in his eyes toward Taylor. Whenever he glanced at his son, there seemed to be a helplessness in him. The teenage boy didn't acknowledge either of them, and I wondered how it had to have been for him to listen as his parents argued about who was going to be stuck with him.

The knowledge of that was like a bucket of cold water poured over me. Todd clearly wasn't cut out to be a family man. When I was with him, my hopes of someday being loved and having a family like my friends took a backseat. I too easily forgot that a relationship with him wouldn't go anywhere.

I suppose I should thank Taylor for reminding me of that.

Over the next few days, I worked from my office at the rink instead of going to the corporate offices. It was my attempt to put distance between me and Todd, and hopefully, distance would make my heart grow less fond of him. I'd heard through the grapevine that he hadn't come to work the last few days. News of his son's arrival had gotten out, and apparently, he was spending time getting his son settled in and enrolled in school.

The following weekend, the team was playing in Colorado, and I made the decision to tag along to keep watch on Mikael. He had done well at the last press conference and was confident that he was ready for us to completely cut the tether on him. Each day after practice, I would meet with him, and while he did what he was asked, I could see he was getting frustrated.

"I don't need you on me like a mother hen," he finally said the day before we were supposed to travel to Colorado.

I nodded. "You're doing very well, Mikael. But in today's world, one off-color remark can derail not just you but your entire team."

He scraped his hands over his face. "How much longer will we have to do this?"

I smiled at him. "I don't think much longer. Just keep up the good work."

He stood. "I will do good, you'll see."

I had no doubt that he wanted to do well, but I was still going to be in Colorado just in case.

That evening, as I packed for my trip the next day to Colorado, I thought about how I hadn't heard from Todd all week. Of course, he had his hands full with his son, but that didn't stop me from feeling disappointed, even as I knew it was silly if my goal was to distance myself from him. I wondered if maybe I should call him to check in. Was I being a bad friend by not doing so?

I pushed that all away as I finished packing my bag and headed to bed. I hadn't had good luck with men, but clearly, it was because I allowed myself to get attached to men who wouldn't be able to give me what I was looking for in a relationship and didn't want from me what I wanted to give them. I believed Todd was a better person than my ex-fiancé, but that didn't mean there was a future for us, and I needed to remember that.

THE GAME in Colorado was much like the opener back home in Nevada. Mikael skated brilliantly, and when the media surrounded him, he was able, for the most part, to keep his comments from turning into a media nightmare.

I waited with the team as they showered and cleaned up and then rode back with them to the hotel. I planned to go to my room, but Mikael draped his arm over my shoulder as we entered the lobby of the hotel. "You still owe me a drink."

"Tonight is for you to celebrate."

"And you will join us. Come on. There is nothing fun to do in your hotel room." He was right. I figured I'd have one drink and toast to the team.

The hotel bar was filled with hockey players, several fans, and I even picked out a few sports media people.

I sat at the bar with Mikael, ordering a glass of wine while he ordered beer.

Dylan came up and patted Mikael on the back. "Dude, you're a demon on the ice."

Mikael grinned. "That pass in the third period you sent to me was amazing."

I smiled, happy to see all the members of the team getting along. I was also glad that while Mikael could still be cocky, he recognized that he wouldn't be as good as he was without his teammates.

Once again, Mikael draped his arm over my shoulder. "Betts is my good luck charm."

Dylan looked between us, a brow arched. I shook my head to let him know that if he was thinking there was something between us, there wasn't.

"I only keep you from embarrassing yourself in front of the media," I said.

Mikael let out a laugh. He leaned over and gave me a kiss on the cheek. "It's a very hard job. Is it not?"

I grinned at him. "You have no idea."

The evening wore on, and it was nice to see the team celebrating together. While the season had only just begun, there had been real concerns that they would struggle after losing their two best players from last season. But it appeared now that they felt as strong as ever.

I was just finishing my wine when one of the sports media people stepped up to Mikael. "Amazing game tonight, Mikael."

Mikael grinned. "We came to win and we did."

"Are you fully settled into the American way of life?"

Mikael nodded. "Yes. I love it here."

"And it seems you have a new friend." The man nodded toward me.

Mikael, for the third time that night, put his arm around me. "Yes, this is my girlfriend, Betts."

My brain screeched to a halt. I leaned toward the reporter on the other side of Mikael to correct him, but the reporter's phone rang and he pulled it out of his pocket. With a quick excuse, he left Mikael's side.

"Why did you tell him I was your girlfriend?" I asked.

Mikael's brow furrowed. "You're a girl and you're my friend. Girl friend."

I let out a groan. "In America, a girlfriend is someone who is more than just a friend."

He stared at me like I was speaking Greek. There was little I could do about it now, and hopefully, it wasn't something the media was interested in. I wasn't a celebrity. In fact, once I left the bar, chances were Mikael would take up with one of the several women who'd been eying him from across the bar.

I finished my wine and then patted him on the back. "I had my drink. You have a good time with the rest of the team."

"You should stay. Look over there. Dancing. We could dance."

"Why don't you go ask those women over there to dance? They seem very interested in you." I nodded toward the women at the end of the bar.

Mikael looked toward the women. He laughed and gave me a hug. "You're a good girl friend." He left his stool and headed over to meet the women.

I left the bar and headed up to my room. It was difficult to be in a hotel room and not think back to the night a week ago that I had spent with Todd. It was amazing, and in many ways, surreal. It was the type of night every woman should have at least once in her life, a man ravishing her body, giving her pleasure beyond any she could imagine. But it was one night. One night that was now gone.

As I settled into bed, it occurred to me again that it had been a week since I'd heard from or seen Todd. Time away was what was needed to end this crazy attraction I had for him. But even after seven days of no contact, I had no doubt that if he showed up at my hotel room door right now, I would let him in and give myself over to him. Time hadn't changed anything.

17

Todd

I knew I was to blame for the challenges I was having with Dean. I felt pushed out by him and Taylor, so I abdicated my role as father. It made sense that he would be resentful of me now.

But I'd spent the next week bending over backward to connect with him, to get to know him and the young man he was becoming. It fixed up a room and worked to get him settled. I enrolled him in school. But the boy barely ever took his eyes off his phone, and when he did, he looked at me with disdain. If I became stricter, he'd resent me more. But offering the olive branch and doing what I could to learn about him and be his friend wasn't working either.

I had taken off from work, something I hadn't done since the day he was born. I didn't travel with the team to Colorado this week to watch the game so that I could dedicate my time to Dean. But the kid didn't seem to give a fuck.

By Monday morning, I knew I needed to change things up, but I wasn't sure what that was to be. At breakfast, like every other break-fast since Dean arrived, he sat at the table looking at his phone and wearing his headphones. I knew that giving up on being a father was what got me into the situation, but at this moment, I was too damn tired of trying. So I let him do whatever he was doing on his phone and as I drank my coffee, I opened the sports news app on my phone.

I knew the team had won this weekend, but I wanted to check out the news sites to see what was being said about the team. I was scrolling through the feed but came to a screeching halt when I saw a picture of Mikael and Betts sitting at a bar. At first, my heart thundered in my chest. It'd been a week since I'd seen her, at least in person. She continued to make frequent visits in my dreams.

It was odd for her to be photographed in a story, so I pressed the link to open it.

FINNISH HOCKEY SENSATION *Mikael Virtanen has found himself an American girlfriend who just happens to work for the team.*

WHAT THE FUCK? I studied the picture of Betts and Mikael. They were leaning in close, and Mikael was kissing her on the cheek. The logical part of me told me that this was nothing. But even if it was something, Betts and I had no official connection. We'd hooked up a couple of times, and while I wanted that to continue, our relationship had never been spelled out.

The man in me, however, was seeing red. Mikael, of all men, should have known to stay away from Betts.

"Dean. Get your stuff together and I'll drop you off at school."

He didn't look up from his phone. I slammed my hand down on the table, and while Dean startled, his expression remained disdainful.

"Get your stuff. Time to go to school." I rose from the table to get my things.

I suppose I should be grateful that he did what he was told. A few minutes later, we were in the car, riding in silence toward his high school. Dean was still on his phone, but I was too distracted by the image of Mikael and Betts seared into my brain to try and talk to him.

Surely, the paper was wrong. But even if it was, Betts wasn't mine. Hadn't I felt it was over once Taylor dropped Dean off? So maybe she moved on. But with Mikael? The kid was immature like a horny teenager. What could she possibly see in him?

At the same time, I had to concede that he wasn't the same young man as when he arrived. He was more respectful and better behaved.

I dropped Dean off at school, and he exited the car without a backward glance. It occurred to me that Dean needed to be my focus. I couldn't worry about what Betts was doing and with whom. But fuck, the idea of her with somebody else burned in my gut. She wasn't mine in reality, but inside, I felt like she was.

When I arrived at my building, I entered and headed up to my floor. As I made my way to my office, I asked my secretary, "Is Betts Adams here today?"

"Mondays are generally the days that she comes in to corporate. I can call and find out."

"Find wherever she is and ask her to come into my office."

My secretary arched a brow. "Even if she's down in Henderson?"

I nodded. "Even if she's in Henderson."

She nodded and picked up her phone, but her expression told me that she was wondering what was going on.

I entered my office, shutting the door and tossing my briefcase on my desk. Then I went over to the window looking out over the desert. I couldn't get my mind to focus on anything else but Betts.

Ten minutes later, there was a knock on my door.

"Come in." I stayed standing by the window but turned and watched as Betts entered my office. I was prepared to confront her about the article. What I wasn't prepared for was the longing that welled in my chest the first time seeing her in a week. I had the urge to rush over to her and wrap her up in my arms. I wanted to run my fingers through her thick red hair and consume her luscious pink lips.

She moved to the middle of the room, watching me, studying me, clearly uncertain as to why I had summoned her here.

"Are you wanting a report on how Mikael did in Colorado?" she asked.

I shoved my hands in my pockets and irritation flamed in my gut. "I think I have a pretty good idea of how Mikael did in Colorado. It's plastered all over the fucking media. Mikael has a new girlfriend. I guess you were able to get over all his sexist comments. I mean, he's a good-looking, athletic guy."

Her eyes rounded as if in shock. And then they narrowed like laser beams. "What are you insinuating?"

I let out a derisive laugh. "I'm not insinuating anything. It's plastered all over the news. My star player is dating the team's head of marketing." I tilted my head toward her, mimicking the intensity of her eyes as I stared down at her. "Tell me, Betts, does he know that you've been fucking the boss too?"

18

Betts

The only other time I had wanted to strike a man was when I discovered my fiancé was cheating on me. I felt the betrayal and the anger deep in my bones. That was the way I felt now at Todd's accusation that I was sleeping with Mikael. With his words, Todd turned what I had with him into something sordid.

But maybe that was what it was. We'd hooked up. Although the situation was complicated, I had no doubt that I had wanted more than just a sexual affair even if it was inconceivable. The way Todd said that I'd been fucking the boss told me that it was nothing more than that.

But if that was the case, why did he care what I was doing with Mikael?

I considered leaving and not giving him a response. I'd gather my things and leave. Maybe I'd quit. At the very least, I would resume my job hunt. I couldn't continue to work like this.

But a little voice told me that perhaps Todd was jealous. Either way, I would tell him the truth, and then I'd leave.

I glared at him, not wanting him to see how his words had hurt me. "That article is not correct. The reporter got it all wrong. Mikael only meant to say that I was a friend who happened to be a girl. But it came out as girlfriend because he doesn't realize what that means. Before I could correct the reporter, he got a call and left. That's it." I set my hands on my hips and leaned forward. "I'm not sure why it's got your boxers all in a bunch. Aren't you the one who always encourages scandalous stories whether they're true or not? Are you going to tell me now not to deny it just like you told Naomi not to deny reports of her having a relationship with Max?"

Todd's jaw tightened. "That wasn't the same."

She arched a brow. "Oh, really? Let's invite Naomi here and you can tell her why this is any different than what you made her go through. Lucky for you, no one is going to care about this story. I'm a nobody."

"That's not true." He didn't elaborate, so I wasn't sure what he meant. Was he saying I wasn't a nobody? Was he saying that to make me feel better or because he felt like it would continue to be in the news?

"The point is, it's going to blow over. If that's all that you want, I have work to do."

He continued to stare at me with an expression I couldn't read. When he didn't respond, I turned to leave.

I just reached the door when he called out, "Betts, wait."

I took a breath and then turned toward him. He ran his fingers through his hair as he turned to look out the window. I waited until finally, he turned to me with a sheepish smile. "You handled it a whole lot better when you were jealous of Johanna."

I arched a brow, not liking being reminded of my jealousy. Especially after the way he was being such a jerk. "Is that what this is? Jealousy?"

He shrugged. "Maybe. Yeah, I think so. The red mist that blinded me when I saw the picture and article of you and Mikael gave it away." He was trying to bring levity, but I wasn't quite ready to let go of my hurt and anger.

He blew out a breath. "Look, I know that whatever it is between us has not been defined. And I know that it's because of all the complications, of my being your boss, but . . ."

I leaned forward, wondering what he was stopping himself from saying. "But what?"

"I wanted to say that I don't like to share. But like I said, this thing between us has never been defined. And now my life has gotten even more complicated."

I could hold up against his anger, but the look of confusion, like he was lost, adrift, that was my undoing.

My hurt and anger dissipated. "How are things with your son?"

He let out a humorless laugh. "I don't think it's going too well, but it's hard to tell since he won't talk to me."

"Isn't that how teenagers are, though? They like to keep themselves in. They don't like spending time with their parents."

He walked over to his desk, sitting back against it as he let out a long sigh. He looked down, shaking his head. "I don't know. Maybe." He lifted his gaze to mine. "I recognize that I have a part to play in all this. I'm doing my damnedest to reach him, and he looks at me like I'm lower than pond scum."

I wanted to reach out and hug him, to comfort him and give him strength to keep trying with his son. But like he said, things between us were unclear. He'd been jealous to hear about me and Mikael, but that didn't mean that he and I were a thing.

Instead of going to him, I clasped my hands in front of me. "Maybe you should spend time doing things that he enjoys."

"As far as I can tell, the only thing he enjoys is whatever he does on his phone."

"Then you need to try and find out what it is that he likes."

"How do I do that? He doesn't talk to me."

"We're in Las Vegas, right? There are all sorts of interesting things to do around here that a teenage boy might enjoy. Ruby told me once about this really interesting haunted house."

"It's a little bit early for Halloween. Plus, he's a little bit old."

"It runs all the time, not just for Halloween. Bo took Ruby there on a date. And don't teenage boys like horror movies and scary stuff?"

I realized maybe I was pushing it too much. "Or maybe not. I don't know."

Todd was quiet for a moment as if he was thinking. Then he turned his attention back to me. "That could be fun, but we need a buffer. Would you be willing to come with us?"

I shook my head and held my hands up to stop him. "This is about the two of you bonding. You don't need me there for that. I'll just get in the way." I realized that my growing attachment to Todd was something I needed to finally break away from, and this was the best time to do it. We'd spent a week apart, and now his focus was on his son.

"Please come with us. Chances are he's going to spend all his time on the phone anyway. Or maybe you'll be able to connect with him in a way I can't. I'm his dad, so I think, by definition, he's supposed to despise me. Maybe with you there, he won't feel so hard-core the need to keep himself closed off."

I should stand my ground. Todd and Dean needed to find their connection and build the relationship between the two of them. These two were not my problem, and getting involved would only complicate things more than they already were, at least for me. So, I needed to say no.

"Okay."

19

Todd

There was a moment when I thought I'd be going to the haunted house with only Betts. Truth be told, I would've been all right with that. Dean was a difficult kid to be around. That was my fault, so having thoughts of wishing I could leave him behind led to guilt that I was such a shitty father.

I ended up begging and cajoling, and finally, Dean, who was probably sick of listening to me, said he was willing to go if I bought him a car. Since he didn't yet have a driver's license, that wasn't going to happen.

But I did agree to pay for private driving instruction, and finally, we negotiated an outing together. Having to bribe my son to spend time with me was another reminder of how bad I was at being a dad.

In all honesty, I wondered if it was too late for the two of us. But I didn't want to be a bad father, and the universe had thrown us together, so I was going to do my damnedest to make this work, even if the best I could hope for was coming out of this with him not hating me so much.

Instead of having someone drive us, I decided I would take us in my Audi. I pulled the car from the garage, and when he didn't think I was looking, Dean's eyes lit up at seeing the car.

"You like it?" I asked.

The moment he realized I was watching him, he turned sullen and indifferent again. He shrugged in response. I sighed and got into the car and then drove us over to Betts's apartment.

"Is this your girlfriend?" There was a sneer in his tone that grated on me. I wondered if bringing Betts along was a good idea after all. I needed her there for moral support, but I didn't want a situation in which Dean would be disrespectful to her.

I pulled into a parking spot and turned off the car and then looked at him. "Betts is a friend, and she also happens to work for me. I get that you don't like me, and I know I deserve your disdain, but you won't be rude to her. Do you understand?"

He rolled his eyes and looked out the window.

I took the keys with me as I went up to get Betts. Dean didn't have a driver's license, but that didn't mean he wouldn't try to take my car.

When Betts opened the door to my knock, I was once again poleaxed by the sight of her. Her gorgeous thick red hair was pulled back into a ponytail, but soft tendrils of curls fell around her face. She wore a green blouse that highlighted the matching color in her eyes. She also wore a pair of white jeans and silver sandals from which I could see pink colored toenails that made me think of bubblegum. I never had a toe or foot fetish, but all of a sudden, I had the urge to develop one.

I cleared my throat. "Ready?"

She looked behind me. "Where's Dean?"

"He's sulking in the car."

Her smile dropped, and I worried about what had taken the happiness away. "He doesn't want me to go with you, does he?"

"He doesn't want to go with me." Unable to help myself, I reached out and pushed one of the pretty red wisps out of her face. "But I want you to come. I need you to come."

Her expression was uncertain, but she got her purse and walked back to the car with me. As we approached it, I realized Dean was still in the front seat. Jesus, I hoped he wouldn't make me drag him out of there so that Betts could sit there.

As we drew close, his door opened and without a look, he moved to the back seat. It made me think that this was not the first time he'd been brought along on a date. Of all the manners and etiquette he lacked, it was strange that he understood he needed to change seats. Or maybe he saw it as an opportunity to get away from me.

I helped Betts into the car. She turned to look over the shoulder of the seat. "Hello. I'm Betts. You must be Dean."

Dean looked at his phone but managed a hello to her. I shut her door and made my way around to the driver's side. I opened the door and got behind the wheel.

"Are you playing a game or doing something on social media?" Betts was asking Dean.

"Just some stuff on TikTok."

"Whenever I'm feeling down, TikTok always has something to make me laugh."

I arched a brow as I looked over at Betts and started the car. "You watch TikTok?"

"Usually, it's for work. But sometimes, I watch it for fun too."

I frowned. "I have a TikTok account?"

She rolled her eyes. "The team does."

I glanced at Dean through the rearview mirror, catching him rolling his eyes as well. It occurred to me that Dean was closer in age to Betts than I was. This TikTok discussion was highlighting that I was an old man.

"That one with the team doing the Cupid Shuffle on the ice was pretty good," Dean said from the back seat.

What the fuck?

Betts smiled as she turned to look over her seat again. "You saw that one? Oh my God, how they groaned about doing that. But I thought it came out pretty good."

Once again, I watched Dean through the rearview mirror. He shrugged, but there was something about it that wasn't as disdainful as it normally was toward me.

I had bought tickets to the haunted house in advance, but there was a line for us to wait until our turn for entry. As we stood waiting, Dean continued to look at his phone.

"Oh, that was funny. I'll admit, I like the ones that are lip-synching. Especially if it's dogs lip-synching," Betts said to Dean.

Dean didn't say anything, but he adjusted his stance and moved his phone so that Betts could have a better look. There was a sense of relief that he was willing to accept her and at the same time, I felt jealousy. Not the rage I'd felt when I thought she was sleeping with Mikael.

No, this was an envy that she was connecting with my son who despised me. I reminded myself that our relationship was what it was because of me. Dean wasn't going to make it easy for me to fix, and I suppose, considering what a shitty father I'd been, it shouldn't be easy. I needed to earn his respect and his love.

The sound of a chainsaw blasted through the area, and Betts startled, practically launching herself into my arms. It now made total sense to me why young men would bring their girlfriends to scary movies, to hold their woman close.

The rule with Betts after our night in the hotel was that out in public, we had to be professional, or maybe friendly, but nothing that would give away the lust that burned between us. But her body was pressed against mine, her face buried in my chest, and so I had no choice but to put my arm around her and keep her safe.

Dean looked up at me, and if I wasn't mistaken, there was a slight arch of his brow as if he was wondering what the deal was with me and Betts.

"We're not even inside yet and you're terrified," Dean said. I think it was the most I heard him say since his mother had dropped him off with me.

Betts straightened and inhaled a breath. "I was just startled for a minute. I didn't realize the scary stuff would start before we actually got inside."

Dean shook his head and turned his attention back to his phone, but I caught the slight upward twitch of his lips. It hurt that he was responding to her and at the same time, I was grateful.

The line we were in moved forward a few feet until we turned around a corner. All of a sudden, a clown jumped out in front of Betts. She screamed and once again buried her face in my shoulder.

Dean laughed. My son laughed. It was awesome to see it and at the same time sad to realize I couldn't remember the last time I'd seen him laugh.

"It's a clown," Dean said. "You can't seriously be afraid of a clown."

Once again, Betts straightened. "Have you ever actually really looked at a clown? All that makeup hides some really evil stuff."

This time, I laughed as well, long and hard until I felt I had tears in my eyes. It was strange because what she said wasn't necessarily funny, and yet there was something about it. It released the tension. I had no illusion that my son and I were now going to bond and be best friends, but for a second, the disdain wasn't in the air between us. There was just shared amusement at Betts.

Finally, the doors opened, and it was time for our group to enter. The place was dark and cool. I noted Dean shoving his phone into the pocket of his hoodie, and again, I was relieved. He was at least going to allow himself to experience this.

As we made our way through the dark corridors, a warm hand slipped into mine. I looked down to see Betts's green eyes staring up at me. I squeezed her hand, feeling so ridiculously glad that she was holding my hand.

I leaned over toward her. "I'll keep you safe from the bogeyman."

Her cheeks tinged with red and she looked embarrassed, but she said, "Thank you."

As we continued on, I didn't see the creepy crawlies or ghouls wandering about. All that existed was Betts's hand in mine and a fullness in my chest. It occurred to me that this is how it should have been with me and Taylor. She and I should've been taking Dean to things like this. But Taylor's self-care and shopping and outings with her friends took up most of her time. My work had taken up mine.

Dean had been left with nannies until a few years ago when Taylor enrolled him in boarding school.

I remembered at the time feeling that it wasn't the right decision. I'd known back then that we had both failed him by abandoning him. At the same time, I remember thinking that maybe it would be better for him. He'd be in a place that would nurture him academically and socially in a way that his mother and I couldn't. I'd been an idiot to think that because there was no way a parent should abdicate their responsibility to a school.

He lasted about six months before being kicked out, and his days at subsequent schools were smaller and smaller each time he was expelled. So far, he seemed to be doing okay at his new school. Maybe it was because he wasn't having to live there that he was doing better.

Although it was difficult, I made sure I was home every evening to make him dinner even if he wasn't going to talk to me while he ate. I vowed that this time, I was going to do right by him, but I couldn't help but think how much easier it would be to have a partner to help me. A partner like Betts.

20

Betts

When did I become such a scaredy-cat? Maybe I always was. I wasn't someone who went to haunted houses growing up. And I didn't go to scary movies. The fact that people paid to have their hearts stopped by fear made no sense to me.

I'd taken Todd's hand out of instinct, but as he squeezed it reassuringly, it felt right, like that was exactly where it should be. As we moved through the place, I found myself inching closer and closer to him, screaming and gripping him. Even when I had a sense that something was going to jump out, it still scared the crap out of me.

Behind me, I could hear Dean laughing, and while it was a little embarrassing, every time he did, Todd had a look in his face like the sun had just come out. It was as if he hadn't heard his son laugh. It was an indicator of just how far apart these two were, and it broke my heart for the both of them, although I knew that it was most likely Todd and Taylor's fault that Dean had grown into such a sullen and withdrawn kid. It looked like Todd was trying to connect with his son, and I hoped at some point, Dean would forgive his father and give him a chance.

I wasn't going to lie. I was glad when we came to the end of the scary stuff and exited into the dry desert air. I scanned the area, wanting to make sure that the tour was really done and nothing was going to jump out at me.

I felt a hand on my lower back. "Boo," a husky voice murmured next to my ear. It sent a chill through me, but not the scary kind. The gesture was intimate, and I looked over at Dean to see if he noticed, but he'd already pulled his phone out and was immersed in whatever was on the screen.

"How about we go to Lucky Buckets?" Todd turned his attention to Dean. "All you can play arcades on me."

Dean looked up and shrugged.

"I think that means yes," Todd said to me.

We got back into the car, and he drove us to the restaurant which to me seemed like a slightly more grown-up Chucky Cheese. They didn't have pizza but instead burgers and chicken.

As we sat at the booth, Dean said, "Can I go play?"

"Sure thing." Todd pulled out several twenty-dollar bills from his wallet and handed them to Dean. It seemed like an awful lot of money to me, but Todd was filthy rich, so it was probably barely a drop in a bucket. It was a reminder about how different our worlds were. It was also a reminder of the amount of work he had to do to build and maintain his empire.

Todd hadn't married again because he was married to his business. I wondered if I could change that but immediately pushed the thought away.

My friends might've gotten their happily ever after, but it was so clear to me how perfect they were for each other. While Todd and I were compatible in bed, there were so many issues, including his being a workaholic and my boss, that got in the way. In fact, it was likely that his workaholism was why his marriage ended and he was estranged from his son.

Still, as Dean wandered off and Todd scooted closer to me, taking my hand under the table, my heart yearned to have something just like we had in this moment. Almost like a family.

"Dean likes you."

I looked at Todd to see if that bothered him. "How can you tell?"

"He looks at you when you talk to him, and he actually expressed something in a full sentence. Thank you for that, by the way, because I was beginning to wonder if I was going to have to take him to a speech therapist or something."

He was being humorous, but I could still see sadness in his eyes. His gaze turned to the restaurant, tracking Dean through the arcade. "I'm really worried that I fucked my kid up."

I squeezed Todd's hand. "There's no doubt that he has issues. He's probably angry, but I don't think he's beyond your reach."

He looked at me with hope in his eyes. It was like I'd tossed him a lifeline and he was eagerly grabbing onto it. "You think so?"

"I think so. But it's not going to be easy. More than anything, he's going to need time, which means you're going to need a lot of patience with him. You can't undo in a day or week, maybe not even a year, what took several years to create."

He nodded. "You probably think I'm the worst father in the world."

"Not the worst, no. I think you made some mistakes, but what parent doesn't, right?"

"I'm not quite sure how to undo them."

I squeezed his hand again. "You just keep doing what you're doing, knowing that it's going to take time for him to believe that you are really here for him."

Todd gave me a sheepish grin. "You know, if this marketing thing doesn't work out for you, you have a career in parent counseling."

I arched a brow. "Are you saying my career in marketing is in jeopardy?"

"Hell no. I plan to keep you forever."

In my chest, my heart started bouncing around like a ball in a pinball machine. It heard something entirely different from what he meant. He meant he wanted to keep me in the job, not me personally. But oh, how I wished it could be different.

Dean joined us when it was time to eat and then ran off again to play more games.

When the night was over, they drove me back to my apartment, and Todd walked me up to my door. I really wished he would kiss me goodnight, but with Dean in the car, I understood why he couldn't or wouldn't. Hell, maybe he didn't want to kiss me at all.

"I'll see you Monday at work?" he asked, his gaze drifting down to my lips, telling me he did want to kiss me.

I considered tossing all caution to the wind and launching myself into his arms, but I stepped through my open doorway. "I'll be there. I'll be working on the next TikTok campaign."

He laughed and shook his head. "Now you're making me feel old."

"It's time for you to go home, Gramps."

He let out a laugh and gave me a wave as he turned and headed back to the car.

It wasn't too late, so I decided to end the evening with a glass of wine and soak in a hot bath. I loaded the hot water up with scented bubbles and lit a few candles, turning out the light as I sank into the water.

There had been a moment in the hotel with Todd when I wondered what it would be like to be in the tub with him. I imagined soapy water sluicing over his skin. Just the thought of it made my pussy come to life with arousal.

Whatever the chemistry was between us, it continued on. But Todd's focus was Dean, and so I was certain that our little affair was over. All I was going to have were memories and fantasies.

But what good fantasies they were. The best. For as reckless and foolish as I'd been to sleep with Todd, I couldn't regret it. Every woman should have a man make her feel the way he'd made me feel when he touched me at least once in her life.

I drew my hand down over my nipple as the memory of his lips sucking and tugging on them filled my brain. I pinched my nipple, sending sweet sensations down my body. With my eyes closed and my mind filled with Todd, I took myself back to the hotel and the wildly erotic things he did to my body.

His lips trailed down my body, over my belly and lower. My fingers flicked over my clit, imagining it was Todd's tongue. My hips rocked as need filled me. His hands pushed my thighs apart, his mouth sucking on the soft, sensitive skin on my inner thighs. It drove me wild with need.

"Todd."

"Yes." His lips slowly moved along my thigh, closer to my pussy.

"Don't tease me."

"Does it feel like I'm teasing?"

"Yes." I moaned in agony as my body cried out for attention.

"I'm savoring, Elisabeth."

The words were sweet, but my need was too much. "Please."

"Alright. What do you need? This?" His breath gently brushed over my nether lips.

I moaned and lifted my hips, seeking his attention. "More."

"How about this?" His tongue ever so softly flicked over my clit.

"Yes ... more ..."

"Or this?" He used his fingers to open me, and his tongue slid inside, lapping at my inner walls.

"Yes ... yes ..."

Todd did amazing things with his tongue, driving me up and up until I was a whimpering, writhing ball of nerves.

"Come for me, Elisabeth. Let me taste your sweet juices." With that, his finger rubbed my clit as his tongue thrust inside me. The proverbial fireworks blasted, starting at my pussy and radiating out to the rest of my body.

I rubbed my clit, drawing out the fantasy as long as I could. Then I lay quiet for a moment in the now tepid water. Bittersweet feelings washed through me. I was grateful for the time I'd spent with Todd, even as I knew it needed to end. But self-pleasure didn't come close to the real thing.

21

Todd

I woke up with my dick tenting my sheet. I was having a luscious dream about Betts. Again.

We had a lovely night last night at the haunted house and dinner. At least I thought we did. The way Betts screamed through the haunted house, and then my taking her to a burger joint with an arcade with my son in tow probably wasn't on her list of ideal dates. I really wanted to continue to see her, especially since I knew Dean would respond to her, but it wasn't fair to her.

She had her own life, her own interests, and that didn't include helping me bond with my son. Was I selfish enough to ask her to help me again? Probably. Then again, maybe there were some gains made last night with Dean. Not that I believed everything would be one hundred percent hunky-dory today, but maybe some progress had been made.

But first things first, I had to deal with this hard-on the dream of Betts had given me. I rose and went into my bathroom, turning on the shower as I dropped my lounge pants and then stepped into the hot spray. I lathered up the soap, rubbing over my body, imagining my hands were Betts's. She had great hands, small but soft, and she used them well to explore my body, finding hidden delights I didn't know had existed.

We'd filled the night in the hotel with as much sex as we could, but there was still so much I hadn't been able to experience, such as taking a shower with her. I closed my eyes, imagining it. Fantasizing her here, hot water rolling down her soft skin. Her long, red hair wet. Her green eyes knowing as she ran her hands over me, down my body until they wrapped around my cock.

I stroked my dick, letting out a groan as electricity shot through me. "Fuck, yeah."

I tugged her in, kissing her until I couldn't breathe. God, I loved kissing her.

When she pulled away, her eyes held a wicked gleam. She slowly moved down until she was on her knees. My dick thickened, standing straight up in anticipation. She held my dick, flicking her tongue around the tip.

"Yes . . ." I stroked again, focusing on the sensitive rim of my cock.

She licked and then sucked my dick into her mouth, deep.

I slapped my hand on the wall of the shower as a wave of lust punched through me. I stroked my cock faster, tighter, wishing I could slow this down but powerless to do so as the image of her on her knees, giving me the blowjob of my life, permeated my mind.

Pressure built until I bucked and shot my cum over the shower wall. I continued to stroke my dick until I'd released every last drop.

There was nothing like a hard orgasm in the shower to start the day. Of course, it would have been even better if Betts had been with me. The idea that we might never have the opportunity disappointed me.

I exited the shower, drying off and getting ready for the day. When I came out of my bedroom, I found Dean in the kitchen eating a bowl of cereal as he watched something on his phone.

"I was thinking maybe we could go out for pancakes or something," I said. After all, it was the weekend. Not that there wasn't work I could do, because there was always work. But I really wanted to do better by Dean. "Maybe after that, we could go to the movies or something."

Dean tossed the spoon in the bowl and rose from his chair. "There's a livestream I want to watch." He took his bowl, setting it in the sink, and then walked out of the kitchen to his room. He hadn't looked at me, but at least he said something to me in a slightly less dismissive tone. The kid was a lesson in contrasts. He showed me very little respect and yet would put his bowl in the sink. Then again, it would be better if he put his bowl in the dishwasher.

It didn't seem like a good idea to try and force my kid to have fun with me, so I let him go watch whatever it was he wanted to watch while I pulled out the ingredients to make an omelet. I had just finished chopping up some vegetables when there was a knock on my door.

I couldn't imagine who would be here this early in the morning, but my mind went to Betts. She had no reason to come over here, and yet a part of me wished that she felt the connection between all of us like I had last night.

I went to the door, pulling it open. Not Betts. Levi.

He stood in a rumpled tuxedo, his hair spiking all around and in his face, looking like he hadn't gone to sleep yet.

He gave me an affable grin. "A few of us flew into Vegas last night, and I figured I couldn't go home without stopping by to see you."

I shook my head as I opened the door to let him in. "You look like you've been on a bender."

He laughed. "Close enough."

"Have you eaten? I was just getting ready to make an omelet. I'd be happy to make you one as well."

Levi patted me on the shoulder. "I would love an omelet."

He followed me to the kitchen. "I tried to call you when I got in yesterday, but you didn't pick up."

I frowned as I pulled out my phone, not recalling any calls or messages.

"I left a message, thinking maybe you were busy."

I saw his number in the missed calls. "I took Dean to a haunted house yesterday, and I turned off my ringer. I must have forgotten to turn it back on."

Levi made himself at home as he brewed himself a cup of coffee. "Dean? He's visiting you?"

"More than that. Taylor dropped him off and left town. Right now, he's living with me." I heated butter in the pan and sautéed the vegetables thinking I'd make a scramble instead.

"No shit. You're a full-time dad."

I shrugged. "I don't feel like a dad. Or more accurately, I feel like a dad who fucked up and my kid doesn't want me to go a minute without knowing it."

Levi leaned against the counter and studied me. "You didn't fuck up."

I cracked the eggs into the pan "I did fuck up. Taylor didn't want me around, and I guess I just thought it would be easier to give in to her. And before long, he didn't want me around either. And again, I told myself that if that's what they wanted, that's what I'd give them. But I can see now that it was the wrong response."

"And now you have the opportunity to make it right."

I pulled out two plates and divided the scramble between them. Grabbing a couple of forks out of the drawer, I put them on the plates and then handed a plate to Levi, who sat at the table.

I took the other one and sat across from him. "The kid doesn't want to give me the time of day. He was much more responsive to Betts. They bonded over TikTok or something."

Levi's fork stopped halfway to his mouth. "Who's Betts?"

I didn't want to get into too much detail about my relationship with Betts, such as it was. "She's just a friend."

Levi finished taking the bite of his eggs, but his eyes studied me as he chewed his food. Once he swallowed, he said, "Is she the flavor of the month?"

My gut clenched in annoyance that he would refer to her like that. "Not at all." But I wasn't sure I was ready to let him know my convoluted feelings for her. "She works for me."

His brows rose as he took a sip of his coffee. "You're dating someone who works for you?"

"I don't think I'd call it dating."

His brow furrowed as he watched me. "You're not making a lot of sense. Is sex involved?"

I shifted uncomfortably. I didn't like the way Levi was talking about her, but it was partly my problem because I wasn't being clear with him. Levi was my best friend, so if I was going to talk to anybody about the craziness in my life, it would be him. "There has been some sex, yes, but it's not meaningless. It's not sordid."

He sat back in his chair, using his napkin to wipe his mouth. "I'm not sure whether I'm happy for you at finding somebody you want to spend time with or worried that it happens to be someone who works for you who can cause you all sorts of legal hassles. Did she sign an NDA?"

I hadn't even considered asking her to sign an NDA. Every time we were together, it had been a spur of the moment thing. After the night in the hotel, I began to think that perhaps we could have something steady and regular, but then Dean came to live with me. But even between those two points, I hadn't considered asking her to sign an NDA.

I shook my head.

"She must be something if you're willing to risk all that. Especially after the whole thing with Taylor."

He wasn't wrong, and yet I couldn't imagine Betts being as shallow and greedy as Taylor.

"It's all sort of moot at this point. I need to focus on Dean."

Levi shook his head in disappointment. "That's bullshit and you know it. First of all, the kid is a teenager, so it's not like he needs you hovering over him every minute of every day. Second of all, if you and Taylor were married, you'd still be going out and fucking and doing all the things couples do, right? You don't have to give up your life for this kid."

"I have a lot to make up for."

"That may be true, but that doesn't mean you have to sacrifice your own happiness. If this Betts woman makes you happy, then you should pursue that. And if she and Dean get along, that's all the better."

My heart wanted to feel hope at the words he was saying. It was likely I was just talking myself into something that I wanted. But my life wasn't just about me anymore.

Then there was the fact that Betts was still a young woman. Even if she wanted to be saddled with someone who was nearly old enough to be her father, she wasn't likely going to be interested in becoming a stepmother to a teenage boy.

"Betts is not some cheap affair, but neither is she someone I can plan a future with."

"Why the hell not?"

I sighed. "First of all, there is a pretty significant age gap. She's at a different place in her life. She's focused on her career, not settling down, and certainly not settling down with an older man who has a sullen and broody, rude, teenage boy."

Levi rolled his eyes. "Where's my violin so I can play you a sad song? Seriously, dude. It's not for you to decide what everybody in the world wants in relation to you. If you want her, you go after her. And if she thinks you're too old or doesn't want to be a stepmom to Dean, she can tell you that."

What he was saying made sense, but I told myself that it shouldn't. In reality, Betts and I had a few spectacular hookups and some enjoyable conversations, but it wasn't more than that.

As I tried to dismiss our interactions as nothing more than enjoyable sex, my heart ached. It wouldn't let me deny that what I was feeling for Betts was more than just lust or camaraderie. For the first time since my marriage imploded, I felt like I had met a woman I could make a life with.

22

Betts

I woke up the next morning feeling exhausted. I had a lovely soak in the tub last night, and I slept like the dead, so it was strange to wake up tired. I decided it must've been all the terror screaming from the haunted house yesterday.

Instead of indulging in the fatigue, I forced myself out of bed. The moment I was upright. My stomach rolled, and I hurried to the bathroom as nausea overtook me. Okay, so not fatigue, some sort of bug.

When I was finished emptying what little there was in my stomach, I brushed my teeth and then rummaged through my medicine cabinet looking for a thermometer to take my temperature and something to help with my nausea. A bottle of pain reliever and my birth control toppled out and into the sink. I set the pain reliever aside and put my birth control away because I was on the inert cycle at the moment.

As I closed the medicine cabinet, I had an unsettling feeling that something was off. I opened it and took the birth control pill packet out. Yes, I was in the middle of the week for the inert pills. It then became apparent why something was off. I wasn't menstruating.

A few days late didn't mean anything, right? Except . . . as I thought back to the last time I had my period, I didn't have one last month, either. How did I not notice that?

I pressed my hands on the side of the sink base and looked at myself in the mirror. Was it possible that I was over a month late?

That could only mean one thing, and yet, at the same time, it was impossible. I was on the pill, so there was no way I could be pregnant, right?

Were there times when I might have forgotten to take it at the same time every day? Yes.

But I usually took it within twelve hours. If I forgot to take it in the morning, I had it in the evening when I went to bed. It had never been a problem before. So maybe I wasn't pregnant. Perhaps it was just stress. Or maybe what I needed to do was take a trip to urgent care to see if there was something seriously wrong with me. With that said, it seemed likely that the first thing they would test for would be pregnancy, so maybe I needed to start there.

Telling myself I was overreacting, I got dressed and then grabbed my purse to head out to the closest pharmacy. I bought a pregnancy test from two different brands and brought them home and set about taking them. Both Naomi and Ruby had had accidental pregnancies. Ruby had had two. I remembered at the time thinking how could that be possible? And now here I was, thinking I was so responsible, and I was taking a pregnancy test. Two of them, actually.

I followed the instructions and then set the sticks out on the boxes that they came in to wait.

"There's no way I'm pregnant." I nearly threw both the tests away because it was inconceivable.

"You're being ridiculous, Betts." I reached out to swipe the tests into the wastepaper basket but stopped short when I saw one of the tests had two lines. *Oh, God.*

I checked the other stick. It didn't have lines. It had a single word. *Pregnant*

I sank down on the toilet seat lid. I felt completely numb. My brain was void of any thoughts. This was so inconceivable that my brain couldn't wrap around the reality of it.

What was I going to do?

I finally roused myself out of my catatonic state and went to find my phone. At times like this, I needed my very best and oldest friend in all the world. I dialed Analyn's number, hoping that she wasn't too busy with Reed or the baby.

"Hey, girl. I was just thinking about you."

"Do you have plans for today?"

"What's wrong?" Leave it to Analyn to notice something wrong in my voice.

"Could you come over?"

"Of course. Now?"

"If it's not too much to ask."

I could hear her moving. "I'm on my way. What's going on?"

"I'll tell you what I can when you get here."

Twenty minutes later, I let Analyn through my door. By then I was overwrought, shaking at the thought that from this day forward, my life was completely changed. I was pregnant with my boss's baby. A boss who had no interest in marriage and family. The guy could barely handle the son he had. Granted, he seemed to be trying now, but he'd been an absent father for so long. I knew for sure that this was not what he wanted.

Analyn wrapped her arms around me and gave me a hug, comforting me even though she didn't yet know what was happening. She led me over to my couch and we sat down.

She took my hands in hers. "What's going on, Betts?"

For a moment, I just stared at her, not being able to articulate the words out loud. Maybe if I didn't say them, they wouldn't be true.

Of course, that was ridiculous. "I'm pregnant."

Analyn's brows shot up to her hairline in shock. But she quickly schooled her expression back into compassion. "I didn't realize you were seeing anyone. Your shaking hands tell me that he's not excited by the news."

"I'm not really seeing anyone. Not officially, anyway." Even if

Taylor hadn't dropped Dean off with Todd, I couldn't be sure that Todd and I would have developed a relationship beyond occasional sex.

"I just took the test today, so I haven't had time to tell him."

Analyn squeezed my hands in support. "Are you worried how he'll respond?"

"I don't know if worry is the right word. I mean, I know he's not going to be thrilled about it. He's a confirmed bachelor who is estranged from his teenage son."

Analyn's jaw dropped. "You're talking about Todd Marshall?"

This time, I gaped. How did she figure that out?

"We heard through the grapevine that his ex-wife dropped his son off on his doorstep. And you work for him, so I just put two and two together."

"Yes, it's him." I noted that in her guessing that Todd was the father, nowhere was the idea that he cared for me. I'd remembered the few times I would see Naomi with Pierce, and while they acted like nemeses, it was easy to tell that they had feelings for each other. That wasn't the case with Todd. He enjoyed my company and the sex, but sex wasn't love.

"So, you don't think he'll be a good father?"

I hesitated for a moment. Not because I didn't think Todd could be a good father. I just wasn't sure that it was something he wanted.

"Todd's a good person, but he's basically married to his work. I believe he'll do the so-called right thing, but he did that with his son, and they don't really know each other."

Analyn arched a brow. "What is your definition of the right thing?"

"He supports his ex-wife and son, but apparently, once Taylor moved to California, he didn't see his son very much. I just don't want that for my baby."

Analyn gave me a small smile. "It sounds like you're planning to keep the baby."

I knew I had many different options, but I hadn't really considered them. I didn't need to think about it. I wanted to be a mother, and now I was going to be. At one time, I'd thought about doing it on my own. Now I could.

"I think it's great that you're having a baby. There's no doubt in my mind that you're going to be a wonderful mother and that, if necessary, you can do it on your own, which of course you wouldn't because you have me and Ruby, and even Naomi, once the triplets are a little bit bigger."

"Why do I feel like there's a but coming?"

"But you need to tell Todd. Maybe he won't react well to it. Maybe all he'll be willing to do is financially help you, which is no small thing. Babies are expensive. But he needs to know because it needs to be his decision, his response, not your projecting your thoughts and feelings onto him."

I knew she was right, but I was barely comprehending what was going on just with myself. I needed a little bit more time to get myself sorted before I told him.

"I will tell him. But until I do, can you promise me not to say anything to anyone? I'm not ready for Ruby and Naomi to know, and I suspect if they know, their husbands would find out, and then it wouldn't be long before Todd found out, and as you said, I need to be the one to tell him."

She nodded. "I promise I won't say anything. But you have to promise me that you will tell him. Give him the chance to do more than just the right thing." She cocked her head to the side as her eyes narrowed. "Why is your relationship with him such a secret?"

I sighed as I sank back onto the couch. "I wouldn't say it was a relationship. I'm not even sure that it would've been possible, but now with Dean, it's not possible."

"Who's Dean?"

"He's Todd's son."

"Oh, right. And why would a relationship not be possible if Dean is around, which also doesn't seem like a dealbreaker? Many people remarry and expand their family."

"Well, first of all, he's my boss. And you can't tell me that's not an issue because it is. I remember you went through the same thing with Reed."

She nodded. "The thing is, Betts, the challenge isn't really that he's your boss if you both care about each other. The challenge is worrying about what other people are going to think. It's a rotten fact of life that when a woman sleeps with a man who happens to be her boss, all of a sudden, her talents and skills are out the window and she only got the job because she was sleeping with the boss."

"Exactly." I was glad that she understood. "And maybe in your case, it didn't matter because you and Reed were in love, but that's not me and Todd."

"Are you sure about that? Naomi made a comment at one point about how much time Todd was spending down at the ice rink after he'd been nearly MIA most the summer."

"The summer is the off-season. And while yeah, it did seem for a while like he'd lost interest in the team, now that he brought in Mikael, Todd is excited about it. He's asked me to help him get Mikael media ready."

She arched a brow in one of those knowing looks. "So he isn't just spending time at the rink with Mikael, but he's spending time at the rink with you?"

I waved my hand like it could wave her thought away. She was implying that Todd asked me to help with Mikael so he could see me. Whether it was true or not, it didn't matter. He was my boss who was now preoccupied with raising his son.

"You're trying to read more into this than there is."

"Am I? He asked us once if you were looking for a relationship."

I narrowed my eyes at her. "What? When?"

"That night you took charge of the press conference."

That was the night he was angry at me, and yet we still ended up having sex. He'd told me he wanted me. But surely, that was just sex.

"Like I said, Todd is a nice man. But we're not like you and Reed, or Ruby and Bo, or Naomi and Pierce."

Analyn shook her head. "It wasn't like lightning struck and we knew we'd found our soulmate the minute we met. Well, maybe it was like lightning, but everything you're saying, I said too. And you know Ruby and Naomi did as well." She gave me a sympathetic smile. "What do you want, Betts? How do you feel?"

I sucked in a breath and looked down, too afraid to articulate my desires or feelings.

"That bad, huh?"

"Sometimes, things just aren't meant to be," I said, hoping she'd drop it.

She studied me for a long moment and then nodded. "Okay. You know I'm here for you, whatever you need."

"I do. Thank you."

After Analyn left, I made myself some tea and took it out to the little balcony off my kitchen, needing a moment to settle.

I was going to have a baby.

My mind suddenly filled with all the things having a baby involved, such as getting a doctor and taking childbirth classes and preparing a space. Maybe I needed to look at buying a home, although I didn't have the finances for that.

I blew out a long, shuddering breath. My life, from this day forward, was drastically different. I didn't want to do it alone. To answer Analyn's question, I wanted to do it with Todd. But I couldn't allow myself to consider it.

For my baby's sake, I needed to live in reality, and the reality was that Todd didn't love me and didn't want a new family.

23

Todd

The weekend was uneventful, but that was because Dean spent most of the time in his bedroom. Since he had no interest in spending time with me, I spent time in my home office. It occurred to me that this choice of behavior was what had gotten me into this situation. Taylor and Dean had no interest in me, so I gave up trying.

On Monday morning, I'd made sure Dean got off to school and then went to work. I'd only been at my desk for ten minutes when my phone rang.

The caller ID was Dean's school's name. Fuck.

"Hello?"

"Can I speak with Mr. Marshall, please?"

"This is Mr. Marshall."

"My name is Mrs. Mickelson. I am Dean's civics teacher."

I had received a few emails from teachers expressing concern about Dean's attitude at school, but this was the first time I was receiving a phone call. "Is everything all right?"

"Last Friday was a teacher workday, so students didn't have class.

Dean was supposed to spend the day shadowing you or someone at your work and write a report about it."

Why was this the first I was hearing about it? "I see. He didn't say anything, and I didn't receive any messages from school about it."

"It went home in a letter that he should've given to you. If this were the only homework assignment he'd missed, I might—"

"What do you mean, if this were the only one?"

"He's missed quite a bit of work in the last two weeks, and I was in touch with some of his other teachers who have reported the same. Today, he's not in class. So, unless he's home sick . . .?"

Goddammit. "I'll take care of it. Would you be able to give me a list of all the homework he's missed between your class and his other classes? I'll bring him to work with me tomorrow and have him complete the assignment that he was supposed to do Friday. I'll also make sure that he catches up on all the other work he missed."

"He will be missing class tomorrow."

"Do you think missing one day will be that big a deal if he's behind, anyway?" I asked.

"I'll let his teachers know what you're planning."

WHEN I HUNG up the phone, I was livid. Energy pulsed through me. I wanted to shake sense into my son. At the same time, I continued to sit in my chair at a loss for what to do. I didn't know how to reach him. Every kind gesture was treated with disdain and disrespect. When I tried to be stern, he rolled his eyes.

Betts told me that it would take time, but I felt like I was running out of time. He wasn't an adult, but he was old enough to feel like he didn't need anybody around telling him what to do. For all I knew, he'd run away.

That thought prompted me to pull out my phone and use my app to track where he was. At the time that I installed it and connected it to his phone without his knowing, it felt a little bit like a dick move. I wanted my son to trust me, and secretly spying on him wasn't the way to do that. But trust went both ways, right? He clearly wasn't trustworthy, and therefore, as his parent, it was my duty to keep track of him.

The location the app gave me wasn't an area I was very familiar with. But I grabbed my coat and headed down to my car, determined to make an impression on the boy. At this point, I was less concerned about whether he liked me than about keeping him safe. Las Vegas had a lot of seedy elements, and I didn't need him getting involved with any of that.

My fears grew as I drove into a sketchy part of town. The tracking on my phone indicated he was at a convenience store. I drove around the store, finding him with a group of three boys who were smoking and drinking.

Jesus. A part of me thought I should send him back to his mother because he was getting worse here with me. Then again, based on what I knew about Taylor, this behavior could be normal for him. I reminded myself that I needed to be proactive.

I pulled up alongside the boys and rolled down the passenger side window. The moment Dean saw me, he tensed and rolled his eyes.

"Get in the car, Dean."

"Hey, man, that's a nice car. You didn't tell us your dad was loaded." One of the young men stepped up to the car, his gaze admiring it longingly. My first instinct was to tell the kid if he touched my car, I'd punch him in the throat.

But then I decided to go another route. "You want a ride somewhere?"

The young man stopped and looked at me, surprise in his eyes. One of the other boys made a comment about my being a pedophile. Seriously?

Dean shot the boy an angry glare. "He's not a pervert. He's just an asshole."

"Whether you want a ride or not, Dean, you're coming with me."

I gave him a look that I hoped he understood to mean that I would get out of this car and drag his ass into it if I had to. It must've worked because reluctantly, he came over and got into the front seat.

The young man who had been admiring my car came up to the passenger side window. "How did you get a ride like this?"

I looked him in the eyes. "I worked hard. I built something."

"Built something? Like a house?"

I shook my head. "I built an empire, Son. And I built it from nothing. You can do it too, but not by wasting your time smoking and drinking behind the convenience store."

There was a moment when I thought I saw a glimmer of possibility in the young man's eyes. Like he believed he could build something too. But in the next instant, it was gone.

He made a noise and stepped back from the car. "Whatever, man."

I shrugged. "I'm living proof." I put the car in gear and pulled away from the group. I didn't say anything until I was back on the main road again.

"What I saw back there breaks my fucking heart."

"Whatever." Dean kept his gaze out the passenger side window.

"You're a spoiled brat. Do you know that?"

His head jerked and he glared at me. I knew he had disdain for me, but that was the first time I saw loathing.

I flexed my hands and then re-gripped the steering wheel. "Those young men back there have a very difficult life. They see me in this car, and they can't imagine any scenario in which they could have what I have."

"Whatever."

"If I were you, I probably wouldn't go back and hang out with them."

He looked at me again with an expression that suggested that I was an old man who didn't know shit. There were a lot of things I didn't know about the younger generation, but I knew people.

"Now that they know you're my son, they'll look at you differently. They'll wonder why someone who has the resources and opportunity like you do is squandering it. At least that one who was admiring my car will. The other numb nuts are probably right now thinking about how to be your best friend so that they can get access to money."

"You don't know anything about me or my life."

The words were like little knives in my heart because they were true. "So, tell me. Why aren't you doing your homework and why are you skipping school? Because while I'm rich, you're not."

"Why do you care? Mom never did."

His words were like an epiphany. When Taylor decided to leave Las Vegas, I should've fought for custody. I knew what she was like. And yet I let Dean go live with her, thinking that because I worked so hard, I wouldn't have time to be an attentive parent. Another thing to add to my list of fuck-ups at being Dean's dad.

"Well, you're not with Mom. And I do care. So when we get home, you're going to start on all the homework you haven't done. Tomorrow, you're coming to work with me, and you're going to do your civics assignment shadowing someone at their job."

He made a pffftttt sound and pulled out his phone. I whipped the car to the side of the road, braking hard to stop. I reached over and grabbed the phone from his hand.

"Give it to me." He reached for the phone.

I exchanged the phone into my other hand and then used my free hand to push him back into the seat.

"The phone is mine until your homework is done. The same with your computer."

I thought I'd seen hatred before in his eyes, but this was pure hate. "I can't do my homework without my computer."

He had a point. "Fine, you'll have your computer, but it won't have access to games or the Internet. The world stops right here, right now, Dean, until your homework is done and you get your shit straight."

Rage radiated off him, but he must've realized I meant business. He jerked away from me, turning his head to look out the window. I pocketed his phone and pulled out into traffic again.

When we arrived home, I made good on my promise, making sure that he no longer had access to the Internet. I put his phone in the safe and just for good measure, changed the combination.

Dean had already gone to his room, slamming the door. I doubted he was doing his homework, but I was at a loss for how much more I could do to force him to get it done. At some point, I figured he'd get bored and figure out that the only way for his world to open up again would be for him to do what I said.

I gave him the night to stew in his room, but early the next day, I rousted him and reminded him of what was going on. I wondered what I was going to do if he refused to get in the car to go to work with me. Luckily, I didn't have to find out as he got in the car murmuring obscenities at me.

The disrespect tore me apart. It also pissed me off. It took every ounce of will to not lash out and punish him. But I hadn't asked him to do my bidding with a good attitude. I'd asked him simply to do it. And since he was, I'd ignore the attitude for now.

As I drove us to the office, I knew that his shadowing me wasn't going to work. He needed a legitimate work experience for his homework, not having his father looking over his shoulder every minute. I thought back to the night at the haunted house and how well Betts had connected with him. So when we arrived at the office, it was a no-brainer to take Dean up to Betts. It wasn't until I was approaching her area and she wasn't there that I wondered if she was working down in Henderson today instead. Well, I'd drive him there, if I had to.

"Hey. What are you two doing here?"

I whipped around to see Betts approaching us. Her skin was pale and there was an expression on her face I couldn't quite read. Like apprehension or something.

"Hey, I hate to spring this on you, but Dean needs to shadow someone on their job as part of a school assignment. I was thinking he could shadow you."

She looked at me and then at Dean. Finally, she returned her attention to me. "Can I talk to you for a minute?"

I nodded. We stepped aside out of Dean's hearing.

"Why doesn't he shadow you?" she said in a low voice.

"One, because he and I are both pretty pissed off at each other right now. Two, and maybe more importantly, is that you connected with him. Maybe with you, he will take this assignment seriously and won't see it as some sort of punishment."

She arched a brow. "Is it punishment?"

I shook my head. "No, this is a legitimate assignment that he skipped. The punishment is I've taken his phone and all his electronics until this assignment and the rest of his homework is done."

She studied me like she was looking for something, but I was at a loss for what it was. Maybe it was how much I asked her to do that was beyond her job. I wanted to pay her for it, but since we slept together, I worried how she might view it.

"I know I've been asking a lot from you lately, especially this. But I could really use your help right now."

She let out a sigh. "Okay. I'll do it. But Todd, things aren't going to get better with your son until you and he work things out."

"I'm trying, Betts. You were the one who told me it was going to take time."

She nodded, conceding my point.

"It's just for today. I'll come down at lunch, and we can all go eat together."

She didn't look completely convinced, but she turned. "Dean? Do you know anything about web design?"

24

Betts

When I first saw Todd by my desk, I panicked. I'd just been returning from a bout of morning sickness in the ladies' room. I knew I needed to tell him about the baby, but in the middle of the marketing department's work area wasn't the place. Then I saw he had Dean with him.

I was trying to decide whether Todd was being honest with me. Was he tapping me for this task because of our past encounters? Was he taking advantage of the fact that we'd slept together? Or was it true that he thought of me because Dean and I had gotten along okay at the haunted house?

I finally decided that maybe both were true. If I wasn't here today, he likely would have found someone else. But our relationship at times had crossed over into personal, which probably made it easier for him to come to me than to someone else.

I grabbed my laptop and took Dean to the large work table just outside my desk area. I opened the mockup of the hockey team's website redesign that we were working on.

"We are using a fairly straightforward drag and drop program, so no coding is required. This is the fundraising page. All the content is there, just needs some cleaning up and maybe a little redesign for finesse. Do you think you could do that?"

"Does this computer go on the Internet?"

I remembered Todd telling me he'd taken away all of Dean's electronics. I imagined Dean was salivating at the idea that he could go online and connect with his friends or play games. "It has limited access. There are sites that we use for things like graphics, but anything else will get the laptop shut down. So, no TikTok."

He let out a breath, and his shoulders hunched.

"If you'd rather, I could have you sift through data that we use to see what marketing campaigns are working and why."

"No, this is fine."

I left him to it, returning to my desk to review data on our current marketing campaigns. An hour and half later, I decided it would be a good time to check on Dean. I rose from my computer and stretched.

I approached him. "How's it going?"

"Looks alright to me." The smirk on his face told me something was up. I looked over his shoulder at the screen, finding it filled with gifs and memes that paid homage to potty humor.

I sat on the edge of the table so I could look at him. "How old are you?"

The smirk dropped. Clearly, he was not expecting that question. "Sixteen."

I looked at the screen and then him again. "And this is still funny to you?"

He tensed, his defenses rising.

"Did you think at all about what I asked you to do?"

"I don't really care."

Well, that was obvious. "You should care. This is your father's company."

Dean's jaw tightened. "That makes me care even less. I hate him."

I tilted my head, studying him, wondering what the right course of action was. I was a marketing director charged with showing this young man how marketing worked, not a social worker or therapist.

But I couldn't think of anything to say that would put him on the right path for both our tasks today, so I said, "Because he took your phone?"

He made a pfft sound. "No."

I arched a brow, telling him I didn't believe him.

"I'm pissed that he took my phone. But I've hated him for a long time. Not that he cares. He doesn't give a shit about me."

All his words were loaded with emotion, and I had the urge to let him continue talking. Didn't talking things out help people feel better?

"Why do you think he doesn't care about you?"

"Because he doesn't," he barked. We both looked around the area, noting a few stares from others working at their desks.

"What has he done or not done that makes you think that?" I said, bringing Dean's attention back to me.

"All he cares about is his business. You can ask my mom. When Mom and I moved to California, he stopped coming to visit except for my birthday and Christmas."

"Have you told your dad that you feel like he's abandoned you?"

Dean scoffed. "He wouldn't care." He looked down, his hard shell starting to crack, showing me vulnerability. "Truth is, neither of them cares. Neither of them wants me."

My heart broke to hear him say those words. I thought of the child I was carrying in my belly and wondered what kind of future it had with Todd as a father. It was clear that he had made a lot of mistakes, but I had a hard time believing that he didn't care about his son. I could definitely see why Dean thought that, but that didn't make it true.

"I think your dad made some mistakes, but I also believe that he loves you."

Dean looked up at me like I was nuts.

"Why do you think you're here today?" I asked.

"To do my homework."

I nodded. "Your father took your phone and dragged you down

here to do a school assignment. Why would he do that if he didn't care about you?"

He smirked. "Because it makes him look bad if I suck at school. Or maybe he wants my mom to think he's better than her."

I studied him. "Do you really believe that?"

He shrugged, his fingers playing on the mousepad of the computer. "I could run away and disappear, and they would both be relieved."

"I don't know whether that's true or not, but holding your feelings isn't helping anyone. What if you're wrong? You can't assume your dad knows you feel the way you do. If you talk to him, you give him the opportunity to understand you and change."

"He's not going to change. Neither of them will."

I wanted to reach out and hug him, to tell him that wasn't true. Aside from the fact that it would probably be inappropriate was the fact that I didn't think he'd accept it.

He shifted, straightening in his seat as he looked at the website page. "I'll work on this again." His words had a tone that told me the conversation was over.

"Okay, then. I'll check back in a little bit." As I stood, I put my hand on his shoulder, giving it a small squeeze, unable to stop myself from letting him know that he wasn't alone.

An hour later, he called me over, and I looked at the computer screen. On it was a webpage that was sleek and clean, yet vibrant.

He pointed to the screen. "These are all the pictures that you had of fundraising and charity events already on the site. These videos here, though, are stock videos. I couldn't find real videos, and since I can't go to social media sites, I couldn't find any there. But if you had some, you could put them there."

Based on what he had done before, I didn't have high hopes. As I looked over his work, I'd clearly underestimated him. The page was exactly what we needed. Fundraising and charity events were all about making money, but that was not why people join in. They join in for fun and community and service, and Dean had created a page that showed all of that.

"This is fantastic, Dean."

He flinched and stared up at me like he was wondering if I was patronizing him. I looked him in the eyes. "Really. This is very good."

He turned to look at the screen, and the tension in him noticeably lessened, and a small smile hinted on his lips. The boy was starving for praise and attention because for too long, he didn't have it. Definitely not from Todd, and it sounded like maybe not from his mother, either.

I rubbed my hand over my belly, wondering about the child growing inside me. Todd was married when Dean was born. They had set out to have a child, and even with all that, they had failed. Not only was I not married to Todd, but I also wasn't sure what our relationship was except for boss and employee. If he'd found it difficult to be there for the son he had planned to have, how was he going to be with a child who was unexpected? Would he fulfill his obligation by helping financially but withhold the attention and affection, like he'd done to Dean? Was my child destined to grow up thinking the way Dean did, that his father didn't care for him?

It will be different, I vowed. Maybe my baby wouldn't have an attentive father, but I was going to be the best mom possible. My child wouldn't be sixteen years old, bitter and angry, telling a near stranger that their parents didn't care about them or that they could run away and the parents would be relieved. No, my child would know that they were the center of my world.

I know I still needed to tell Todd, but I would also let him know that the baby didn't need him financially or emotionally. I could provide everything my child needed.

25

Todd

I felt guilty leaving Dean with Betts like I did, but clearly not guilty enough to go back and deal with him myself. I would need to find a way to make this up to her.

I took care of some business and at lunchtime, I returned down to Betts's work area where I found her and Dean sitting at a table talking. Dean was looking at her, his expression showing interest in what she was saying. Maybe leaving him with her was a dick thing to do, but it appeared that it was going well.

I smiled affably as I approached them. "Hey, guys, how about some lunch?"

The minute Dean saw me, his expression morphed back into his usual scowl.

"I'm hungry. How about you, Dean?" Betts said.

He shrugged.

"Why don't you show your dad what you did?"

He reached out and turned the laptop toward me. I reached down and tapped the space key to wake the screen. On it, I saw a webpage related to the hockey team's fundraising and charity work. It was sleek yet fun-filled with videos and pictures.

I turned my gaze to him. "You did this?"

He shrugged again.

"This is great. Damn near perfect."

He looked away as if he wasn't comfortable with my praising him.

"Let's go to lunch and you can tell me everything that you've learned so far today." I expected him to refuse, but he stood and prepared to go.

We left the office and went to a bistro just down the street from the office building.

Once we ordered, I looked across the table at Dean as he sat next to Betts. "So, how was it today?"

"It was fine."

"Did you learn anything?"

"Betts told me some things about marketing."

I looked at Betts, hoping that helplessness didn't show on my face. Why couldn't I get my kid to talk to me?

"Tell your dad about the idea that you came up with," she suggested.

I turned my attention back to Dean. "An idea? I'd love to hear it."

Dean looked down, toying with his spoon. "Betts says sometimes the hockey team does things for the community. I was thinking that maybe you could have a Junior League night where high school hockey players could sub in for the regular team after they shadowed them."

That idea wasn't half bad. In fact, it was pretty good.

"High school kids could play the first half and then the adult players could play the second, and all proceeds could go to support high school sports or whatever."

Hockey had three periods, but it was still something we could work with, and it would be fantastic publicity.

"We were thinking that maybe the Buckaroos would want to join in," Betts said.

"This is a really good idea, Dean. Maybe we could work on this idea together."

He looked at me a little bit like he didn't believe me, but he nodded, and relief spread through me.

During lunch, Dean wasn't sullen as he usually was, which wasn't to say that he had completely forgiven me and let me in. But he joined in on the conversation, particularly if he was responding to Betts. Through the conversation I realized that my kid was fucking smart. He definitely had a mind for business, and for the first time in a long time, I wondered if he'd be interested in taking over when it was time for me to retire.

I felt so much pride for him, but whenever I told him that, he would look away as if he didn't believe me. It was a reminder of how much work I had ahead of me to fix what I had broken between us.

After lunch, I walked with them back to the marketing department where Dean was going to write up his report for school.

Once he was settled at the table, I said, "I'd like to see you in my office if I could, Betts. Maybe you could walk back with me."

She looked at me, arching a brow, but nodded. "I won't be gone too long," she said to Dean.

"Okay." Dean's attention was on the laptop computer screen.

"Is he really working or is he watching social media?" I asked as Betts and I walked to the elevator.

"He's really working." She looked at me, and I could see disapproval in her eyes.

"What?" I asked.

"After everything he shared at lunch, you thought he wasn't working? Besides, with the way the Internet is set up here, he can't play around."

Guilt lanced at my gut again. "You're right. I need to have more faith in him."

We stepped into the elevator.

"I'll admit that he probably would have been on social media had he had the opportunity," she said. "The first iteration of the webpage was full of immature memes and gifs. But when he finally settled in, he did really good work. He's really smart."

I grinned with pride even though I really had no right to feel it. Dean might have been my son, but I hadn't done very much to help him become the person he was meant to be.

When we arrived at my office, I invited her in, shutting the door behind her. I watched as she walked to the middle of the room and then turned to look at me with a question in her expression.

We were at work, and I needed to behave, but she was so fucking beautiful, and I was so appreciative for all that she'd been doing for Dean. The tether on my restraint began to fray. I wanted to hold her, kiss her, and keep her near me. I wanted more time with her and Dean, enjoying a meal or doing something fun, but I also wanted time alone with her. When she was around me, it was like she was a missing piece that I hadn't even realized was gone. When she was near me, I was complete.

"I want to thank you for taking Dean under your wing. I know I was asking too much of you, but what you're able to do with him . . . I'm in awe of it."

She smiled, and the warmth of it filled my chest. I took some steps toward her, but I put my hands in my pockets, doing my best to abide by the rules of no touching while at work set at the hotel.

"What is your secret to connecting with teenage boys?" I asked.

She tilted her head to the side. "Mostly, I listen."

I stopped short, wondering what her words meant. "I'd listen to him if he talked to me."

Her expression filled with sympathy. "He's hurt and angry."

"At me?" After I asked the question, I realized how stupid it was. Of course, he was hurt and angry at me. "How do I fix it?"

She sighed. "I don't know for sure, but maybe start with an apology."

I was asking for her feedback, but all of a sudden, I felt strangely defensive. She was judging me. A judgment I probably deserved, but I still didn't like it. I was trying hard now, dammit.

"Well, I know you have to get to work. Thank you again." Dismissing her, I started making my way to my desk, telling myself what a fool I was for wanting her and wishing that she didn't see me as a horrible father.

26

Betts

When Todd invited me down to his office, I will admit, a part of me was looking forward to a moment alone with him. But we were at work, so when I entered his office, I was determined to be professional. When he shut the door and looked at me and I swore I saw longing in his eyes, I wanted to rush over and throw myself at him. When was this crazy attraction going to wane?

I was glad that he appreciated the time I spent with Dean, but I also knew that Dean's issues wouldn't be resolved until Todd took an active role in working with him. At first, he seemed receptive to what I was telling him. Then, all of a sudden, he closed up. He essentially dismissed me and was making his way to his desk. Talk over. Go away.

Maybe I should have returned to my own job, but a part of me felt that Todd needed someone to listen to him too.

I reached my hand out as he passed me and took his arm. "Todd."

He stopped, inhaling a breath as he looked down at my hand on his arm.

"You asked me my opinion and I shared it."

He gave a single curt nod but didn't respond.

I moved until I was standing in front of him. "Why are you all of a sudden upset?"

His jaw tightened. "I fucked up. I don't need to be reminded of it."

He wasn't wrong, and yet I still felt bad for him. "So, what are you going to do about it?"

He ran fingers through his hair. "I don't really know. I'm doing the best I can."

"Are you?"

His jaw tightened, and I could see him closing up again. "Yes, I am, Betts. Dean didn't come with a manual. I'm doing the best I can." He started toward his desk again.

"He thinks you don't love him."

Todd stopped, looking at me intently. "He said that?"

Maybe I shouldn't be sharing with Todd what Dean had said, but I couldn't help but feel like if Todd knew the extent of Dean's pain, maybe he'd have a better sense of what he needed to do.

I nodded. "He indicated that you didn't visit him very often, except for birthdays and holidays, like it was an obligation."

Todd's eyes closed, and I could see shame and guilt on his face.

"He doesn't seem to think his mother cares for them very much, either. He knows she brought him here because she didn't want him around anymore."

"Mother fucker."

"The point is, he doesn't feel wanted. If Taylor hadn't brought him to you, he wouldn't be here."

Todd looked at me, and I'd never seen him so vulnerable. "He is wanted. But he hasn't wanted to see me in years."

"Who left who first?"

Todd flinched. "Taylor moved him to Los Angeles. I have a business to run."

I nodded. "But is that really more important than him? You say that he didn't want to see you, but who left first?"

For a moment, I thought Todd was going to toss me out of his office. He clearly didn't like being called on his mistakes.

Instead, he turned away, walking over to the window. He was quiet for a long time, long enough that I began to think I should leave him alone with his thoughts. I was about to excuse myself when he turned to look at me.

"I've made a lot of mistakes. And I'm probably still making them, but I don't want to. I love my son, Betts. Now that he's here, I want to make it up to him. But it doesn't seem that he wants that. He might be angry and hurt, but he doesn't want to give me a chance to make it right. If only I were able to connect with him the way you do."

My heart went out to Todd because I could see that he was sincere. The guilt of his own actions and his inability to make it right weighed on him.

"Maybe it's just a matter of spending more time with him."

He shook his head. "He doesn't want to spend time with me. He'd rather be in his room." He let out a long sigh. "The only time he's willing to be around me is if you're there as well." His brow furrowed as if he'd been struck by an idea. "Maybe you need to spend more time with us."

"What do you mean?" I had this strange flutter in my belly. Like I wanted him to want me in his and Dean's life.

"Maybe I can shadow you and pick up some tricks on how to connect with Dean."

I smiled. "I think you're underestimating the both of you. You just need to try harder."

He walked toward me, and in his expression, I saw determination. "I know that I'm breaking the rules here, but your spending more time around us isn't just to help me connect with my son." He reached out, and his hands settled on my arms, rubbing gently as they inched me closer to him.

We were at work. He was my boss. This was the moment I needed to extricate myself and leave. I stared up at him.

"I've missed spending time with you." His hands moved up, cupping my cheeks. He leaned in closer, and while my mind was telling me to pull away, everything else about me went soft and pliant as I lifted my head toward his kiss. He was so good with his lips. And just like him, I missed spending time together.

The minute our lips touched, I moaned. Or he moaned. Or maybe we both did. It was a release. All the hesitation, all the restraint broke. I wrapped my arms around him like his taste, his touch, was the only thing in the world.

"You haunt my dreams." His words were said half in frustration and half in need. "Every night." He maneuvered me over to his desk as his lips trailed along my neck and his hands undid the buttons of my blouse.

I might have responded, but words vacated my brain when his lips wrapped around my lace covered nipple. Need rushed to my core, pooled in my pussy.

My fingers fumbled with his belt and pants, desperate to free him and feel him inside me. The warning bells tried to sound, but I cursed them, shut them up. My body craved this man. His touch. His taste. The way he could make me feel like the center of the universe.

I pushed his pants down, wrapping my hand around his cock and stroking.

"Oh . . . fuck . . ." He groaned into my neck. "I'm so fucking hard." He pulled my hand away and then yanked my panties down. He pulled my skirt up to my hips and set me on his desk. "You're like a wet dream come true, Betts." He plunged in, filling me hard and deep.

I gasped, clasping my hand over my mouth to keep from crying out and telling the entire building what we were doing.

This was craziness.

But oh, God, was it so, so good.

27

Todd

Had there ever been such a perfect pussy? Not that my dick had ever encountered. Betts was wet and tight, and her pussy massaged my cock until I couldn't see straight. I wanted to draw this moment out, but it was impossible. Not because we were in my office and could be interrupted at any moment. Not because I was Betts's boss. Not because my son was a few floors up waiting for her to return. No, I couldn't draw this out because the pleasure was beyond my control. Electricity shot out from my dick, lighting up every neuron in my body.

Betts pressed her face into my shoulder and let out a mewling sound as her pussy clamped down on my dick like it would never let go.

I did my best to hold back the yell of release as stars burst behind my eyes and I drove in, letting go, filling her with my essence. Hell, I was probably handing over my soul.

I never considered myself a weak man, but when it came to Betts, I clearly was. I was helpless to resist her. I had no illusions that I would be able to keep her in my life. What I had told Levi was true.

She was at a different place in her life, and becoming a step-mother to a teenage boy wasn't in her future plans. But I would take whatever she could give me. And I would ask her for more, as much as I could until she sent me packing.

We were half naked in my office, and who knew when someone could come knocking on my door. But I wasn't in a hurry to have this moment end. With my dick still seeped inside her, I cradled her face in my hands and kissed her as if through the kiss I could infuse myself in her, make her feel the things that I was feeling.

When I finished, I rested my forehead against hers. "Please come over for dinner tonight."

She pulled back and looked at me with a question in her eyes. "I don't know."

"I'll cook you a great dinner."

"You can cook?"

Admittedly, my cooking skills were limited. I could make many types of eggs, pancakes, and waffles. Dinners were usually something easy, like boiling noodles and dumping a jar of tomato sauce on them. But for Betts, I would try to cook a proper meal.

"I promise to make a great dinner."

She looked at me as if she knew my secret.

"Please." Jesus, I was about to drop to my knees.

"You drive a hard bargain."

I grinned, feeling ridiculously happy. "Good."

We got our clothes back together, and as much as I didn't want her to return to her office, I also knew that leaving Dean alone for too long probably wasn't a good idea. I didn't want to think badly of him, but the kid had skipped school, and so I had to consider that he could skip the office.

When she left, the first thing I did was pull out my phone and begin to look at easy to make gourmet meals. I made a list and then headed out to the grocery shop. In the same shopping center as the grocery, there was a toy store. I knew that Dean was too old for toys, but maybe they'd have a game or something.

When I was growing up, my parents always had a game night.

Maybe that was something that Dean and Betts and I could start together. I told myself that I shouldn't be thinking of Betts as being a part of my unit with Dean, but just like Betts herself, I found it difficult not to.

Once I had everything I needed, I returned to the office and retrieved Dean, who had written his report and had even emailed it to his teacher.

As we drove home, I asked him, "What do you know about cooking?"

He looked at me with suspicion in his eyes. "That you do it in an oven or stove."

I nodded. "I need you to be my sous chef tonight. Betts is coming over for dinner, and I told her I would cook something great."

Dean let out a laugh. While I didn't like the idea that he was laughing at me, at the same time, it took me off guard. The kid was so closed off around me. So, to see him let loose like that made me happy.

"Maybe you should order out," he quipped.

I gave him a look. "We can do this."

He rolled his eyes, but they didn't hold the disdain they had in the past.

Once we were home, Dean went off to his room, telling me he was going to finish up his homework. *Right*, I reminded myself. His schoolwork came first.

I put away the groceries and then pulled out the recipe I found on the Internet and read it through once again. The recipe was chicken piccata, which was basically chicken with capers and a lemon butter sauce. It didn't sound hard. As it turned out, it was hard. At least for me.

"What are you burning?"

I turned to see Dean entering the kitchen.

"You need to come help me or we'll end up serving a ruined dinner to Betts."

Dean rolled his eyes. "Okay, but only because of Betts."

Dean found the recipe and started going through the steps.

"Did you dredge the chicken through the flour mixture?"

I turned to look at him. "Mixture? I put flour on it."

"It says here you're supposed to combine the flour, salt, and black pepper. I think coat means you're supposed to put the chicken in the flour and get it all covered. Not dump the flour on the chicken."

I frowned as I stood next to him reading the recipe. "This is a disaster."

Dean went over to a cupboard and pulled out a bowl. "Maybe we should try again."

I watched as he followed the directions, putting the flour and the salt and pepper as the directions had said. Thankfully, I hadn't messed up all the chicken, so he took the few pieces that were left, patted them dry with a paper towel, and then buried them, one at a time, in the flour mixture until they were coated.

"How did you learn how to do that?"

He shrugged as he muscled me out of the way and put the chicken into the pan. "I learned to cook."

"Like a hobby?"

He didn't look at me as he dealt with the remaining pieces of chicken, coating each and putting them in the pan. "Mom has a busy life too."

His words stabbed me straight in the heart. The kid learned to cook because he had to.

I opened my mouth to apologize, but he interrupted me. "Do you have the wine? These are done. We're supposed to take them out and put the wine in to start the sauce."

I grabbed the wine from where I'd set it on the counter and pulled out a corkscrew to open it up.

I tried to apologize again, but once again, he spoke before I could. "Are you making something else with this? Pasta or rice or something?"

Holy hell, was I supposed to serve something else too? "What would you suggest?"

"I like pasta more than rice."

I opened the bottle of wine and then went to my cupboard, rummaging through it. "I've got spaghetti."

"Do you have egg noodles?"

What the fuck were egg noodles?

"It's a wide, wavy noodle. Oh, never mind. If spaghetti is all you have, we can use that."

"Good."

"What about a vegetable?"

We had to serve a vegetable too? I went to my fridge and opened it. "I have a bag of salad."

"I guess that will do."

It was a little uncomfortable and weird to hear such disappointment in my son's voice at my lack of cooking knowledge. I also didn't much like that the reason he knew how to cook was so he could eat. Taylor and I had really failed him.

At the same time, I enjoyed watching him excel as he turned the chicken over in the pan.

By the time Betts arrived, Dean had created the meal that I had envisioned in my mind but clearly was incapable of making.

"Wow, something smells good." She looked at me like she was impressed. "You really did make dinner?"

"Not without my help," Dean called from the kitchen.

I gave Betts a sheepish look. "Actually, I was more of a hindrance than a help. Dean is the mastermind behind our meal tonight."

Dean looked at me in surprise, as if he didn't think I would give him credit.

"Well, whatever you made, Dean, it smells delicious."

Dean turned back into the kitchen, but not before I saw a smile on his face.

I escorted Betts to the dining area and then went to help Dean serve up the plates. When we sat at the table, Betts inhaled her food as she put her napkin in her lap. "I haven't tasted this yet, but I know that if you ever want to come cook over at my place, you're more than welcome."

"Have you ever eaten anything my dad has made?" Dean asked her as he sat at the table with us.

Betts shook her head.

"I figured you hadn't because if you had, you wouldn't have agreed to come over for dinner."

"Hey." I jokingly reached out and lightly punched his arm. "I'm not that bad."

Dean grinned over at Betts. "Yeah, he is. He's pretty bad."

We all laughed, and a feeling of rightness filled my chest. This was the life that I wanted. With my money, I could do almost anything. But I realized that in my quest to have a successful business, I'd ended up alone. I'd lost my wife and alienated my son. As I enjoyed the delicious meal my son made, I felt at peace. This was what I wanted, an intimate dinner with two people I cared about . . . with family.

28

Betts

I'd been apprehensive about going to dinner at Todd's place. I told myself it was because Todd needed to learn to connect with Dean without me around. But if I was completely honest with myself, it was because I was still nervous about telling him about the baby. I considered telling him in his office except it didn't seem like the right place or time. Or at least, that was what I told myself.

I talked myself into going to dinner tonight because I figured it would be a good opportunity to watch Todd and Dean interact so I could know what to expect when I did tell him about the baby. Odds were that I was making excuses. I didn't fully understand my apprehension about Todd and the baby. I only knew that I felt it.

I was surprised to see Dean helping Todd with the dinner. The boy had been so hurt and angry only hours before. It made me wonder if he and Todd had found an opportunity to talk.

The dinner was surprisingly good considering an angry sixteen-year-old boy had made it. The kid had culinary talent.

After dinner, Todd suggested that we play a board game. He left the dining room for a minute and then came back, unwrapping plastic off the box.

"Did you buy that today?" Dean asked.

Todd set the box on the table. "Yeah. I thought it might be fun. Have you played this before?"

Dean looked at the game. "Heard of it but never played it."

Todd smiled. "Same here. We can learn it together." He turned to me. "How about you?"

I gave them both my evil grin. "I'm the Catan Queen. Analyn and I used to play this game with our friends a lot."

Todd turned his attention to Dean. "Uh-oh, Son. I think I might've doomed us."

At first, Dean acted indifferent, but as he sat down to learn the game, I got the impression that he was enjoying the attention his father was giving him.

I didn't play the game as cutthroat as I might normally have, which is not to say I didn't play to win. Several times, Todd and Dean tried to team up to thwart me, but there was no beating me in the Settlers of Catan.

When we finished, Dean stood and stretched. "I'm heading to bed."

Todd rose from his chair and patted him on the shoulder. "We'll get her next time."

My stomach fluttered at the idea that there would be a next time. I didn't understand what our relationship was, yet it was clear that I wanted it to be something. At least something beyond my being the mother of his child. Maybe that was why I was hesitating in telling him. Maybe I wanted him to want me first. Not because of a baby, but because of me. Of course, if that was going to happen, I'd need to let go of my concern that he was my boss and what that would mean for me at work.

Todd reached into his pocket and pulled out a phone. "I'm giving this back to you because I'm more comfortable knowing that you have a way to reach me if you need me and I can reach you. You still need to finish all the homework you haven't finished yet, but I'm going to trust you to do that."

Dean shrugged like it was no big deal, but I got the feeling it was an attempt to hide how pleased he was. "I'll get it done." Dean looked over at me. "Good night."

I smiled at him. "Good night, Dean."

He headed off to his room, and it was only when I realized I was alone with Todd that my nerves kicked up. The last time we were alone, we had sex on his desk.

He smiled at me. "Progress."

I nodded. "Yes. I'm happy for you both." This was it. This was the moment I needed to tell him about the baby. But once again, I found myself nervous. This evening was so nice. And the truth was, I liked being around Todd, even not knowing how he felt about me. Once he learned about the baby, that would all change.

I rose from my chair feeling like a coward with my intention to leave.

"Can you stay a little longer? Maybe have a glass of wine?"

No, I couldn't have a glass of wine. I couldn't have it because I was pregnant. The pregnancy I still hadn't told him about.

"I'm stuffed. Your son is a very good cook." God, I was a horrible person.

Todd grinned with pride. "Tonight was amazing with him. It wouldn't have happened without you." He stepped closer to me, and while my instinct told me I needed to leave, I stayed right where I was.

"I think you two will connect eventually. Maybe I helped hasten that a little bit. "

"You hastened it a lot." His hand cupped my cheek, and I couldn't stop myself from leaning my head into it. What was it about this man that enraptured me? I was unable to resist him, and at the same time, I was too afraid to trust him. Or maybe I wanted to experience this thing between us for as long as I could, knowing that when he learned about the baby, it could all go away.

"I can't seem to get enough of you."

My heart picked up the pace. "You just had me earlier today."

He smiled. "And here I am wanting you again."

"I'm not sure that's a good idea with Dean in the other room."

He grinned. "But it was okay with everyone who was working right outside my door?"

I laughed. "I wasn't thinking. You have that effect on me."

His expression suggested he was really pleased by that comment. He bent closer, his lips a whisper away from mine. "Let me fog your brain again. And then I'll take you to my room, which is at the opposite end of the house from Dean's." His lips touched mine, and all my concerns vanished.

He scooped me up, eliciting a surprised cry. "This time, I'm getting you naked."

I looped my arms around his neck. "You've had me naked before."

"It's been a long time. I need to reacquaint myself with your body." He carried me into his room, setting me by the bed and undressing me. "You have a fantastic body, Elisabeth."

I nearly swooned. I loved it when he called me by my real name. My conscience tried to nudge me to tell him about the baby, but I ignored it. Right now, I'd enjoy him and let him enjoy me, then I'd tell him. Maybe.

"Yours isn't so bad either," I said, running my hands over his chest and then under his shirt to pull it over his head.

"For an old man, you mean?"

"For any man." I wondered if his age was really an issue for him. I didn't mind. I didn't even notice unless he brought it up.

He sat on the edge of the bed and pulled me to him until I was straddling his thighs. He tugged me down, and then his mouth was on my breasts, sucking, nipping, sending delicious sensations through me.

I moaned, arching into him. I rubbed my pussy over his dick.

He groaned, and a moment later, I was on my back. "What's your fantasy, Elisabeth?"

I stared up at him, unsure what he was asking me.

"What would rock your world? I want to do it to you. Whatever you want, I'll do it."

My brain went blank. "I like everything you do."

He smiled, dipping to kiss me.

Then it occurred to me that maybe he had a fantasy. I wasn't particularly inventive in bed, and maybe he wanted that. "What's your fantasy?"

"You." His lips trailed along my neck and lower.

I took his face in my hands. "No, really. What would rock your world?"

He looked at me with amusement in his eyes. "Each time I'm with you, you rock my world. Everything about you is sublime."

When he said things like that, my insides went gooey. I tried to keep from sinking into the fog of sensations. "But what would you really like?"

He looked down at me, and something crossed over his face. Something I couldn't read. "I like touching and tasting you. I like it when you touch and taste me. I like being in your mouth or your pussy. I like taking you on top, from behind, or on the bottom. I like it all, Elisabeth. Every fucking bit of it."

"You said I haunt your dreams. What do I do then?"

He laughed. "All of it."

I pushed him back. "Do I suck your dick?" Then I straddled him. "Yes."

Looking down on him, I felt powerful. "Like this, or are you standing?"

"Like this, standing, sitting, sixty-nine ... every way."

Sixty-nine? My ex-fiancé wanted sex in strange positions, but I never found them exciting. It felt awkward, not arousing. But with Todd, I found myself feeling more adventurous. I gave him a flirty smile and shifted until I straddled him facing his legs.

He groaned. "You're going to kill me, you know that?" His hands went to my hips, tugging them up his chest.

I answered him by gripping his dick and then sucking it deep.

"Holy fuck . . . God . . . Elisabeth." His hips bucked up and his fingers dug into my hips. This had to be a sign I was doing it right.

A few seconds later, his tongue teased my pussy, distracting me from his dick.

"You're making this hard."

"Come here." He maneuvered me until I was again straddling him, facing him. He pulled me up until my pussy was over his mouth. "Hold on to the headboard."

I did as he said, and thank God I did because when his mouth once again was on my pussy, I had to hold on for dear life. Sensation rolled through me, driving me as I rocked over his face.

"Oh, God . . . Todd . . . I'm going to come . . . ." And then I was there. I cried out, throwing my head back and arching as pleasure rocketed through me. The orgasm tore through me until my thighs gave out. When I sank back, though, Todd wasn't there. Without my realizing it, he'd scooted out from under me and was now behind me, his hands caressing my shoulders and arms, his lips cascading kissing along my neck.

"When you're ready, I want you like this."

I gripped the headboard again and rose to my knees. "I'm ready."

He moved closer, his hands sliding to my hips. "Ready for what, Elisabeth?"

"You."

"Me what?"

"Fuck me, Todd."

He let out a growl and then he drove in, filling me to the hilt.

29

Todd

She drove me mad with her questions. Of course, I had fantasies, but I wasn't sure how adventurous she was in bed. I didn't want to scare her off by sharing something that made her uncomfortable.

When she adjusted her body to sixty-nine, my head about exploded. She was sucking my dick while I had a stellar view of her pretty, delicious pussy. For a moment, I savored it. But I had to do my part, and so I was devouring her pussy. When she said she was distracted, I took advantage, changing her position so that her pussy was still over my mouth, but she could ride my face with the support of the headboard. Jesus, fuck, I was in heaven. Especially when she said she was coming and her juices filled my mouth. I could have come right then, but luckily, I had enough control that while she caught her breath, I was able to move behind her.

"Fuck me, Todd."

I sank into her realizing I'd been wrong before. This . . . her telling me to fuck her and then driving into her body . . . this was heaven. Her body swallowed up my cock like they were made for each other.

I withdrew, biting lightly on her shoulder. "More?"

"Yes. More. Don't stop."

Good, because I'd about hit the limit of my control. "More what?"

"Fuck me."

I thrust in, electricity sizzling through my veins. "So fucking perfect." I withdrew and plunged in again, and again, and again, until I was like a racehorse heading home at a full sprint. I neared the finish hoping Betts was with me. She let out a strangled cry and her body went taut, her pussy gripping my dick hard.

I hit the line, yelling out as pleasure consumed me. I continued to move, in and out, in and out, drawing out the pleasure until my body went boneless. I collapsed, pulling her with me until we were lying entwined on our backs.

I couldn't ever remember feeling so much contentment as I did at this moment. It was like finally, after forty-nine years, all the pieces of my life fit together perfectly. My son was sleeping in the other room, and while I had no illusions that moving forward things would be perfect, I truly felt that we had made progress.

And now in my bed, in my arms, was a woman I couldn't seem to get enough of, and I wasn't just talking sexually, although even now, she stirred my libido again. My attraction to Betts felt deeper than just lust. When she asked me what I wanted from her, the word "forever" flashed in my head.

Betts was smart, kind, and patient with me and Dean. I found myself wanting her to stay here the night . . . hell, all the nights. The only thing that kept me from asking her to stay was Dean. Now that we were finally making progress, I didn't want him to think that my attention to him would be divided. Especially since I still didn't know where I really stood with Betts. All the issues that were getting in the way between us still existed.

Still, I felt compelled to let her know how much I enjoyed being with her. I tugged her in closer, kissing her on the temple. "Thank you so much for being here for me."

She tilted her head up and smirked. "I was glad to help. It would be uncomfortable to walk around aroused like that."

I laughed. "I wasn't talking about that, but I appreciate your taking care of my dick as well. I meant for me personally, and for Dean. I know that things are still complicated between us since I'm your boss, but I'd like to continue to explore this connection."

Her brow furrowed. "Is that a good idea?"

"From where I stand, it is. I understand that it's different for you, but before Dean came to stay with me, I thought that we were going to continue to spend time together. I still want to do that."

Her gaze drifted down, and it made my heart stutter in my chest. She cared for me as a friend, clearly with benefits, but not more than that.

"I'm wondering if this is a good time to do this, though, considering you're building a relationship with Dean."

"I think I can do both. I've always been good at multitasking." Even as I said it, I knew I had to be careful that Dean didn't feel like he was being ignored. I brushed her hair from her face. "I'm not ready to let this go."

She was quiet for a moment, and then she rolled away from me and got out of bed. I watched her, a feeling of desperation growing in my chest. How could I make her understand how much I needed her?

I got out of bed and found my lounge pants, slipping them on. Then I made my way over to her and waited until she was dressed before I reached out to her. "I'm sorry if I said something wrong."

She shook her head, her gaze downward. I put the crook of my finger under her chin, lifting her head so she could look at me.

"It's just like you said, there's so many complications."

I nodded. At the same time, I wondered if there was something more. I knew I couldn't push her. She had more at risk, and I needed to give her time to decide whether I was worth it.

"Tell me you'll think about it," I said.

Her eyes were wary, but she gave a slight nod. "Okay. I'll think about it."

I wouldn't lie that her resistance hurt, but I reminded myself of all that she was risking to be with me. And it wasn't like I was such a catch. Sure, I was rich, and she seemed to enjoy our time in bed, but I was so much older and had a teenage son and an ex-wife. That, added to the fact that sleeping with the boss could hurt her reputation at work. I should have been questioning why she was here.

I walked her to the door. "Thank you again for all you've done for me and Dean."

She smiled. "Of course. I'm glad to see the two of you starting to grow together."

"I hope you'll come over and have dinner with us again sometime." I kicked myself because I was pressuring her again.

The wariness in her eyes told me she wanted me to stop pushing it, but she managed a wan smile. "I'm surprised you'd want me over again after I kicked both your butts in Catan."

I laughed. "I've had many lessons in humility lately. I suspect I needed them." I needed to let her go. What was the saying? If you love something, set it free. If it comes back, it was meant to be? "You're going to be okay getting home?"

She nodded. "Yes, I'll be fine."

I walked her to her car and watched as she drove off. A sense of wrongness filled my chest. She should be here with me and Dean. An image of us living together as a family flashed in my mind. Hell, maybe we could have more children. It was the first time in a long time that the idea of remarrying and having a family not only seemed possible, but something I wanted.

I was in love with her. That had to be it. It was the only explanation.

There was something between us, I was sure of it. Was it just that I was her boss that kept the wall between us? Was there anything I could do to convince her that we might have a future? Or maybe she didn't feel the same. Maybe it really was friends with secret benefits.

The answers weren't going to come to me standing in my driveway watching as her tail lights disappeared. As much as I wanted to call her or chase after her, I knew that despite the epiphany that I loved her, she needed time and space. Just like Dean needed time to trust me again, she'd need time to see that we could have something special.

30

Betts

I was a terrible person. And a coward. Todd had been so sweet, telling me that he wanted to spend time with me. It was the perfect opportunity to tell him I felt the same, and about the baby.

But I didn't.

I was having a hard time understanding where my cowardice was coming from. The truth was, while Todd wanted to continue this relationship, he wasn't saying he loved me or promising ever after. He hadn't asked me to stay the night, and I understood that. He likely didn't want to explain me to Dean since to him I was just his father's friend and employee. Plus, with my concerns at work, I was equally as eager to keep our relationship a secret.

But secret relationships never lasted.

I'd run off out of fear and guilt, and I was still avoiding him by working most of the time down in Henderson at the rink. After a couple of days, I wondered if he meant what he said as he hadn't been in touch with me. One minute, he was saying he wanted to pursue this thing between us, but now a few days later, I hadn't had a text or call from him. Of course, I hadn't texted or called him either. He had asked me to think about us, so maybe he was waiting for me to contact him. Why was this thing between us so confusing?

Right this moment, I had more important things I needed to concern myself with, primarily the baby that was growing in my belly.

I left work at the rink early today, returning to Las Vegas for my doctor's appointment. My appointment was in the birthing center because I was going to have an ultrasound. I was brought into the examining room, and the doctor met with me, first asking questions about how I was feeling, and she shared information on what to expect during the pregnancy. The more she spoke, the more guilty I began to feel knowing that Todd should be here with me. I needed to tell him.

Once the talking portion of the exam was done, she had me lie back on the table and expose my belly. She squeezed some gel and then pressed a wand over my little mound.

"Let's see your baby." She moved the wand over my belly and then stopped, tapping something on her keyboard. She did that a couple of times while I watched the screen, not knowing what I was seeing.

"Here's your baby." She pointed toward the screen. "Here's the head. See this fluttering? This is the heart."

Emotion overwhelmed me, tears coming to my eyes as I looked at my baby. It felt like a miracle that a life was growing inside me.

"I'll print out a picture for you. And here are a few brochures covering what we talked about. Make sure you're taking a prenatal vitamin. You can exercise, but avoid anything too strenuous. Sex is fine as long as you feel fine."

I gripped the brochures and picture, studying the image of my baby. I decided I would show the picture to Todd when I told him about the pregnancy. This experience made the situation so much more real. It wasn't nebulous. Not some theory. There was a person inside me. A person Todd helped create. I had to tell him.

I walked out of the appointment, leaving the birthing center. The medical complex was huge, with many other clinics. It was busy

today, and I ended up parking near offices used by general practi-
tioners.

I started over to my car, thinking about how I should tell Todd
about the baby.

"Hey, you're the marketing person with the Silver Nuggets. The
one who's dating Mikael Virtanen."

I tensed as I looked at the man stepping into my path. He looked
down toward my hand where I held the brochures and picture.

I opened my mouth to tell him that I wasn't dating Mikael, but
before I could speak, he held up his phone and took a picture. "Are
you and Mikael having a baby?"

What? "No. And you need to delete that photo. I'm not dating
Mikael." I reached for his phone.

He stepped back. His smile was greedy and cruel. "I'm going to get
a pretty penny for this."

"But it's not true." Panic nearly choked me.

He shrugged. "Fans will love it." He looked at the picture on his
phone, whistling as he walked away.

I followed him. "Hey. You can't just go around taking pictures and
posting lies."

He didn't acknowledge me. He trotted off through the parking lot
and to a car. Why had he been here? Was he following me? Or had he
been at a doctor's appointment and it was bad luck that he recognized me?

I let out a low growl of frustration and burst into tears.

"Betts?"

I whirled around, wondering who else was there who would
know me.

Pete stood, his expression filled with worry. "Hey. Are you okay?"

Embarrassed that I was blubbering, I worked to pull myself
together. "Pete. Hi."

"What's wrong? Do you need a doctor?" He looked toward the
medical offices.

"No. I'm fine. Really. How are you?" I remembered how poorly I had treated him at Naomi's wedding. "Listen, I'm really sorry for what happened at the wedding."

He shook his head. "It's fine." He gave me an affable smile. "You could buy me a cup of coffee to make it up to me. There's a little coffee shop across the street."

I had the feeling he was inviting me to make sure I was okay. But it would be rude to blow him off again, so I agreed.

We walked across the street, and he ordered a coffee while I got tea. When we sat at the table, he said, "It appears you're having a baby. Congratulations."

My brow furrowed, wondering how he knew that. He nodded toward the pamphlets I had set on the table when I sat down.

Oh, right. Just what I needed, another person knowing about the baby before I told Todd.

"Yes."

"How's it going? Swelling feet? Cravings? Morning sickness?"

"How do you know about all that stuff?"

He laughed. "I've got four sisters, all of whom have kids. I have been through pregnancies with all of them. I've heard it all."

I smiled. "I have had morning sickness, although that seems to be easing up. I don't really have any cravings, at least not yet."

"Well, if you have any questions about how to relieve nausea or back pain or sciatica, let me know. I've become an expert."

I felt grateful for having run into Pete. He really was a nice man, and he deserved better than the way I had treated him at the wedding. "I'll keep that in mind. Right now, I'm trying to figure out my future."

"Like work or home?"

Like telling my baby's father. "Yes."

"You have a cushy job at a big corporation, though, don't you? They usually have the best healthcare and family leave."

He really did know a lot.

"Yes, you're right. I suppose I'm most concerned about my living situation. I mean, I know babies are little and not very mobile, but I need to think about the future. I have an apartment, and I'm not sure that's very conducive to raising a child."

He perked up. "Are you looking for a new place to live?"

I shrugged. "Maybe."

I knew plans could change once I told Todd, but since I hadn't heard from him and still couldn't be sure how he would react, I needed to rely on myself to make my own plans.

"My sister and brother-in-law have a duplex. They live on one side and rent out the other. Their current tenants are getting ready to move out and they're looking to rent it to somebody. It's nothing fancy, but it does have three bedrooms and a yard. Plus, there's a school and a park in the neighborhood."

In some ways, running into Pete felt like running into a guardian angel. He'd shown up when I was in distress, he was calming, and he was potentially an answer to my living situation.

"How much is it?" Todd paid me well, but I also had to consider that I might need to leave my job, depending on how Todd reacted to the baby. I didn't think he'd fire me, but if he took it badly, I wasn't sure I wanted to work for him. It would be awkward if not hostile.

Pete smiled. "I'll help you negotiate a good deal. They've gotten a lot of free babysitting out of me."

"I suppose I wouldn't mind seeing it, then."

He checked his watch. "They're both at work, but if you wanted, I could call them and make an appointment for us to go over this evening."

That fast? Suddenly, life was moving at the speed of light. On the other hand, if it turned out to be a good deal, it would be easier to move now than later in my pregnancy.

"Yeah, okay."

"Excellent. Maybe my sister will pay me a finder's fee."

I was worried about the photograph that slimy man had taken, but I was happy to have run into Pete and have the opportunity to apologize to him and settle my nerves.

When we left the cafe, I went back to my car and pulled out my phone. I dialed Todd's number, but he didn't pick up. When his voicemail answered, I sat for a moment wondering what to say.

Hey, Todd, I'm pregnant.

Hey, Todd, I need to talk to you about something.

Unsure of what to say, I hung up, deciding I'd call him back later.

I started the car to head home when my phone pinged with a text. Looking at it, I saw it was from Todd.

Sorry, can't pick up. In a meeting. Have a dinner engagement later but will call you after.

My stomach fluttered with nerves. Tonight, I would tell Todd about the baby, and then I would know for sure whether I was going to do this alone or not.

31

Todd

When my phone rang and Betts's ID popped up on the screen, I was excited and frustrated all at once. She was finally calling, but I was on a videoconference with the head of one of my subsidiaries in Asia and couldn't take her call. I started to text her back to let her know that I saw she had called, and I would contact her after the meeting, but then I wondered about the wisdom of looking too eager. Sure, I'd been on the edge of my seat since we'd last been together waiting for her to let me know what she thought of my proposal that we give this thing between us a go. I was giving her the time she needed to think about it, but did she need to know I'd been sitting by my phone waiting for her answer?

I put myself out there time and time again, and each time, she was hesitant. I was willing to gamble in business, but there was a limit to the risks I wanted to take with my heart. After my divorce, I felt certain I would never love again. Betts was seriously testing that theory, and while a part of me wanted to jump in the deep end with her, the memories of how everything went so wrong with Taylor had me wondering if I should rein in my enthusiasm. I learned from

Taylor that my heart wasn't a very good judge of women. I needed to use my head a little bit more.

So instead of saying I'd call her right back, I let her know that I would be out for a little bit this evening and would call her later tonight. That wasn't a lie. I had arranged to have an early dinner with Levi, who was back in town and interested in meeting Dean. But after I sent the text, the only thing I could think about was why she was calling. What was she going to tell me? Was she going to agree to give in to this attraction we had, or was she going to tell me that because I was her boss, we couldn't? I was afraid of the latter, which made me concerned about talking to her. The idea that she had my emotions—hell, my life—tied up in knots was unsettling.

After my videoconference, I headed out, having my driver bring me home. I found Dean in his room doing his homework. We had seemed to have turned the corner in our relationship. Sure, he still rolled his eyes a lot, but didn't all teenagers?

In giving Betts the time that she needed, I was able to focus on Dean and make sure he knew I was here for him. Not that I hadn't been focused on him before, but now that he wasn't so adamant about staying away from me, we were spending more time together. We began working together on the charity junior league hockey game project. I reached out to Reed Hampton and Pierce Jackson, co-owners of the Buckaroos, to see if they would be open to such an event. They indicated they would enjoy hearing a proposal, so Dean and I were working on one, and I planned to have Dean be a part of the presentation to them.

I leaned against the door jamb of his room. "How was school?"

He shrugged. "Fine."

I was pretty sure that was a normal response. "We have to leave in ten minutes to make it to dinner on time."

He looked up from his laptop. "Is Betts going to be there?"

I cocked my head to the side, a little surprised by the question. "No. I think I told you that we're meeting a friend of mine from college. He's still one of my best friends. You've met him before, but you were just a little kid. You probably don't remember him." Taylor didn't much like Levi, so I didn't see him as often during our marriage.

"Are you going to be seeing Betts again?" Dean asked as he closed his laptop and stood to get his jacket.

I wasn't sure what to tell him. I hoped so, but at the same time, I hadn't talked to him about my relationship with Betts. It wasn't that I didn't want him to know about us. My hesitation was because I wasn't sure how to define my relationship with Betts. "I imagine sometime, we will."

He shrugged his coat on. "Are you two fighting?"

I shook my head. "No, why?"

He stared at me, and I got the feeling that he knew I was bullshitting him about something.

He shrugged. "No reason."

I pulled the car out of the garage and allowed Dean to drive us to the restaurant. I'd arranged to get his driver's permit, so he could drive with an adult. I still hadn't gotten him private lessons yet, but I was teaching him myself until then.

Dean followed the rules and did his best to be an attentive driver, but being his passenger still scared me to death. Thankfully, the restaurant we were going to was on the outskirts of town, and traffic wasn't too thick.

It took him two tries to park between the lines, but finally, he parked and turned off the ignition.

I patted him on the back. "You're getting it."

He didn't look at me, but I could see the smile on his face, and that was worth every gray hair I'd sprouted during the drive over.

We walked into the restaurant and in the back corner, Levi held up his hand, waving to let us know that he was already there.

"Is he going to have cool stories about you in college?" Dean asked as we wove our way through the restaurant.

"I bet he does, but if he tells them to you, I'm going to have to kill him."

Dean shook his head. "Yeah, right."

"What does that mean?"

"I bet you were a total square."

I wanted to deny it. I could deny it. But I decided it was better for him to think I was a square than to know the truth. At least for now.

When we arrived at the table, Levi stood and held out his hand to Dean. "Levi Wexford. Your dad's oldest friend."

Dean took his hand and shook. "Dean Marshall, your friend's oldest son."

Levi looked at me and laughed. "Chip off the old block."

We sat down, ordering drinks—nonalcoholic for Dean, of course—and reviewed the menu.

Once we ordered our meals, Levi asked Dean, "So, how are you enjoying life back in Las Vegas?"

Dean shrugged nonchalantly, but at least he didn't hold the bitterness that he'd had not so long ago. "It's all right."

Levi arched a brow at me.

"I think the whole situation probably sucked for him, but we've settled in and I think things are going pretty well. Dean, why don't you tell Levi about the charity event you're working on?"

Dean's cheeks flushed as if he was embarrassed by my trying to brag about him. It was something he was going to have to get used to. I was proud of my son. Not just for his charity event ideas, but for surviving me and Taylor. And for giving me a second chance.

Dean explained the idea and how far we'd gotten so far in planning it.

Levi smiled at him. "You really are a chip off the old block." He looked at me. "Why didn't you think of that? You always come up with these crazy ideas that should never, ever work, and yet somehow, they do."

I shrugged. "It is what it is."

Levi turned his attention back to Dean. "You think you're going to take over your old man's empire someday?"

Dean looked at me and blinked. Clearly, it hadn't been something he'd ever thought about. "I don't know."

All of a sudden, I was concerned that he would feel pressure to make a lifelong decision when he was still so young. "Dean still has high school to get through, and then college, and then figuring out where his passions lie. And if it's with me and the company, great, but if there's something else, I'm more than fine with that too."

Our dinners arrived, and we continued chatting and eating, and I was so pleased that Dean was engaging with Levi.

Just as I was finishing up the last of my steak, my phone vibrated in my pocket. It wasn't the first time. It had been buzzing every few minutes for the last ten minutes or so. I had news alerts for many areas of my business, but most were benign. The frequency with which these were coming in began to concern me. I had a vision of Mikael doing something crazy.

I pulled my phone from my pocket, holding it in my lap and surreptitiously looking at it to see what was going on.

The alerts all had to do with Mikael, and worried that he was creating a media nightmare, I clicked on the link to see what was going on.

SILVER NUGGET STAR MIKAEL VIRTANEN *is having his own nugget.*

WHAT THE FUCK did that mean? Reading on, it appeared that Mikael had gotten someone pregnant. I shook my head. Of course he did. He probably never had the birds and bees discussion.

I scrolled down, and my heart stopped when I saw a photo of Betts.

MIKAEL'S BABY *mama appears to be Silver Nugget marketing director, Elisabeth Adams.*

I STUDIED the photo thinking it had to be a mistake. Perhaps it was an old photo or some sort of AI deep fake. In the picture, Betts looked to be standing outside a medical clinic. The photo had circled an area that showed a brochure she was holding.

Top Ten Things to Expect When Expecting.

For a moment, I could only sit and stare at the picture. It was like there was a buffer in my brain, not allowing me to fully comprehend what it was I was reading. But finally, reality burst through, and hurt and anger exploded. She lied to me. She told me there was nothing between her and Mikael, and now, apparently, they were having a baby.

So why the hell was she sleeping with me? It didn't make any sense, and yet, once again, there was irrefutable picture evidence that she and Mikael were having an affair. Or, more likely, they were together, and the affair was with me.

"You alright over there, Todd?" Levi pulled me from my swirling thoughts.

I looked up at him and then over to Dean. Because I didn't need Dean to know about the soap opera going on in my life, I shoved the phone back in my pocket and managed a smile.

"Yeah, sure. Just stuff going on. You know how it is."

"I've got to use the bathroom," Dean said, scooting out of the booth.

Once he was far enough away, Levi said again, "No, really, what's going on? Is your empire burning down?"

No, this felt worse. "No. I'm getting alerts that Mikael, the kid I brought over to play hockey from Finland, has fathered a child."

Levi frowned. "Well, if this was the sixteenth century, that might be a problem, but today, it's not very unusual for a young man like him to sow his oats. We did it too, if I recall."

I swallowed, finding it very difficult to say the next words. "It's with Betts."

Levi's brows rose. "Your Betts? The one who's more than the flavor of the month but that you won't share your true feelings with? That Betts?"

I nodded. "How do I do that?"

"What?" Levi asked.

"I have the worst luck in picking women."

Levi cocked his head to the side. "Well, it seems to me that until you talk to her, you don't really know what's going on."

I scoffed. "There's picture proof that she's pregnant."

"Well, you slept with her. How do you know it's not yours?"

Until that moment, I hadn't considered that. The wave of emotion that slid through me shocked me. It was disappointment that the baby was Mikael's and not mine. How fucked up was that? I'd already proven to be a bad husband and father, and here I'd been thinking that maybe I could give it another go with Betts.

I shook my head. "She would've told me."

He shrugged. "If you think she's lying about all the men she's sleeping with, why do you think she would tell you about the baby? Unless of course she's a gold-digger like Taylor, in which case she absolutely would tell you about the baby."

I was having a hard time following what he was saying. It was like it could all be true and yet at the same time, it made no sense.

"You really need to go talk to her." Levi looked toward the restroom where Dean had disappeared. "If you want, I'll take your son home."

I shook my head. "No. I can't do that. I can't leave here acting like there's something out there that's more important than him. Not when he's finally coming around."

I pulled it together, and after dinner, I drove us home. Once home, Dean headed to his room, telling me he wanted to watch a livestream.

The photo of Betts was searing my brain. I had to go talk to her. "I need to run out and take care of something. Are you all right here?"

"Sure."

"If you want, I can do it another time."

"No. I'm just going to watch this livestream."

With a nod, I left Dean and headed back out to my car. As I drove over to Betts's, my mind was a whirl trying to explain away what the article said. It wasn't like the media never made mistakes. There had been a time the media reported my head coach, Naomi, was dating one of the players, which was wrong.

But in that case, the story hadn't been refuted like it had been in the case of Betts and Mikael. As I thought about it, I couldn't remember reading anything that the story of Betts and Mikael had been put straight.

When I arrived at Betts's apartment, it took forever for me to find the courage to knock on the door. I was about to get my heart broken, I knew, and yet I needed to confront her.

When she opened the door, her eyes widened in surprise.

"Expecting Mikael?" I all but snarled.

She retracted from me, looking at me with concern and confusion. "What are you talking about?"

I stepped into her apartment as I pulled out my phone and held up the story. "Didn't you know? You're having Mikael's baby."

She studied my phone and then looked up at me and blew out a breath. She knew. She knew, so this had to be true.

"Todd, it's—"

"First, you tell me you're not dating Mikael and now, are you going to tell me you're not carrying his baby? Jesus Christ, Betts, you're pregnant? You're letting me fuck you while you're pregnant with somebody else's baby?"

She looked up at me, and it was almost as if she didn't know what to say. "No. None of this is true. How could you believe that?"

"How? Because twice now, the media has pictures with you and Mikael."

She shook her head. "I wasn't with Mikael when that picture was taken."

It occurred to me that she wasn't denying being pregnant.

"Mikael isn't the baby's father."

For a moment, everything inside me went still. If Mikael wasn't the father, did that mean I was?

A knock sounded on the door, and Betts looked at me and then at the door. "Give me a minute." She left me standing in the middle of her living area to answer the door.

"Ready to go look at new places to live?" The voice wasn't Finnish, so not Mikael. But it was definitely male.

I made my way to the door to see who was going to get a new place to live with Betts. The man was familiar but I couldn't place him. He looked at me and then at Betts.

Betts sighed. "Pete, this is Todd. My boss. Todd, this is Pete."

Two things hit me at once. The first was that she introduced me as her boss, which told me how much of a fool I'd been for falling for her. The second was realizing Pete was the man she'd been with at Naomi and Pierce's wedding. The man who had to be her baby's father.

The world stands still for a moment when it's crumbling, I discovered. But finally, I was able to propel myself forward. "Congratulations," I said as I walked out the door.

I made a beeline for my car and started driving, trying to figure out what the fuck had just happened. How had I so misjudged Betts? How had my heart fallen for a woman who was cheating on the man who was her baby's father?

I was such an idiot.

32

Betts

I felt like I was hit by a freight train. Todd had come blasting in, accusing me again of sleeping with Mikael and now having his baby. Before I could really respond, Pete showed up to take me to see his sister's duplex. I couldn't be sure, but I suspected the look on Todd's face was deciding that Pete must be the baby's father. I couldn't be sure because he stormed out, leaving me standing there stunned.

My initial instinct was to go after him, but then the anger and hurt kept me in my spot. He'd essentially accused me of being a cheater. And a liar. And then he left without hearing the truth. He, of all people, should know that the media made stuff up. He'd used that to his advantage on more than one occasion.

Then there was the fact that he'd had sex with me. A lot. And it didn't occur to him that he could be the father.

It hit me that this was the point. He didn't want the truth because he didn't want to be my baby's father. Perhaps this was his way of denying it. He could clear his conscience if he believed the baby was somebody else's and I was the type of woman to cheat on a man. That was what really stopped me from going after him.

Sure, I wanted him to believe me and know the truth, but mostly because I wanted more from him. But tonight, he showed his true colors. His ability to care for people was limited. His wife had come across as a gold-digger, but maybe she just got tired of competing with Todd and his business. Todd was struggling to raise his son, and tonight it was clear he didn't want another one. So, I let him go.

"Hey, Betts. Is everything all right? Are you having problems at work?" Pete asked as he stepped into my apartment.

It took every bit of strength I had to pull myself together. "Yes. Everything's fine. You know how it is at work."

He gave me a sympathetic nod. "You would think being an elementary school teacher was easy-peasy and without bureaucracy, but you would be really wrong."

I managed to smile.

"So, shall we go see the duplex?" he asked.

I didn't really want to go, yet it was now clearer than ever that I was going to be a single parent. I needed to take control. That didn't mean I wouldn't try to tell Todd the truth, but I knew that I was on my own. He didn't want me or the baby.

So, I went with Pete to see a possible new home for me and the baby. The duplex was nice, but I wasn't ready to commit to it yet. The truth was, my mind was still whirling at what happened with Todd, and I knew I couldn't make a decision under the influence of hurt and anger.

THE NEXT DAY, I drove down to Henderson to work at the rink. The entire way, I was wondering what everyone on the team was thinking about the story and the picture posted online last night. The first thing I planned to do was put the kibosh on it with the media and everyone at work. After that, I would drive back to Las Vegas to the corporate headquarters and deal with the marketing team up there and their response to the story. And then I'd deal with Todd.

As I made my way through the hallways of the rink, a few people were looking at me in a way that I felt like they had read the story and were talking.

When I arrived at my office, Mikael was standing outside. Just what I needed. I glanced around, wondering who could be there to see him waiting for me. It would be bad enough to have staff around, but if there happened to be a sports writer or photographer, it would be even worse.

"I made the news people go away," he said.

God, I wanted to hug him. "Thank you."

Then he dropped to one knee.

"What are you doing?"

"I know I'm not your baby's father, but I will marry you and raise the child as my own."

I reached down, grabbing his arms and pulling him up to his feet. "The last thing we need is to end up in the media again with the news that we're engaged."

"But that is my intent."

I took a deep breath so I wouldn't take all my anger and frustration out on him. "You're a good friend, Mikael, but we can't do that. I appreciate your offer, but it wouldn't be fair to you or the baby." It wouldn't be fair to Todd, too, probably, although at the moment, it felt like he deserved it.

Mikael shrugged. "I just wanted to help you because you have helped me."

I nodded. "And I appreciate it. The best thing that you can do now is to tell the truth. Tell it to everybody. Tell it to the team and anyone else who asks. I'm going to do the same. But we really have got to stop the story."

He smiled and gave me a salute. "I will do it."

He exited my office, but right after him, Naomi walked in. She had an expression on her face that was a mixture of hurt and anger.

"I hope you're going to tell me that the news about your having Mikael's baby is not true. I know I've been preoccupied with the triplets, but we're still friends, aren't we?"

I motioned her into my office. She came in and shut the door.

"Mikael is not the father of my baby."

She arched a brow. "But there is a baby?"

I sighed as I sank down in the chair behind my desk. I was so tired. And it wasn't just being pregnant. Emotionally, I was exhausted. "Yes, there is a baby, but I'm not ready to talk about it right now." I looked up at her, hoping she could read in my expression that I really needed her to respect my desire not to talk about Todd right now.

She studied me. "Okay. Does Analyn know?"

I didn't want to lie to Naomi and tell her no. But I worried that by telling her yes, I would make her feel bad. Analyn and I had been friends since childhood, so we were close. But Naomi and I worked together.

"I hope she does. I hope you're talking to somebody. I know for a fact that secrets and lovers and babies can make a toxic combination if you don't have someone to support you."

Relief filled me. "Things are difficult right now, but I am dealing with them."

"Well, if you need anything, you let me know, okay?"

I nodded.

"The other thing I want to talk to you about is this charity event Todd has contacted Pierce and Reed about. It sounds like he and his son are organizing it, but knowing Todd, it's going to be some crazy marketing ploy. I figured I'd check with you to make sure you knew what was going on."

I had forgotten the discussion of the charity event, and for a moment my heart filled with warmth that Todd was following through and working on the event with his son. But then I remembered that he'd called me a cheater and walked out.

"I am aware of the event, but I don't know the details. I'll make sure somebody looks at them in marketing. I imagine since Pierce and Reed are going to be involved, they'll have some input as well."

Naomi nodded. "You're right. Well, I've got to get back to the team. I have to say you worked miracles on Mikael, so I can see why people are speculating."

"Mikael's a nice kid, but he's not my type. I am glad to hear that things are going well between him and the team."

When Naomi left, I set out executing my plan of putting out the proper press releases that had a hint of a threat of legal action, although I wasn't sure I had any legal leg to stand on.

Once I had taken care of everything at the rink, I left and returned to the corporate office in Las Vegas. I headed to the marketing executive's office and explained to him everything that was going on and the information that I had put out on behalf of the team.

He was a long-time marketing person, so he knew how stories could be skewed. I was grateful that he understood. He called an impromptu meeting with all the marketing staff, and I was able to share the information with them as well.

With that out of the way, I made my way up to Todd's office. I didn't bother checking in with his secretary. I just opened the door and walked in, not caring what he was doing.

He looked up from his desk and scowled. "I'm not interested in talking."

"Good, because I'm not interested in what you have to say. You're just going to sit there and listen."

He sucked in a breath.

"The baby is yours."

For a moment, I thought I saw emotion swim through his eyes. But very quickly, it dissipated and was replaced with a sneer. "Why should I believe you when you've been cheating with Pete this whole time?"

Well, that told me I was correct in thinking he believed Pete was the father. "Pete is not my boyfriend. I went to the wedding with Pete, and I didn't see him again until yesterday. He found me crying after that stupid man took a picture of me and asked if Mikael was the father. Pete was a friend when I needed one." I wondered why I couldn't like a man like Pete. "And since you clearly don't ever want to have a family and can barely be a father to the son you have, it occurred to me that I would be raising this baby all by myself. Pete told me his sister had a place to rent that was a little bigger and had a yard, and he agreed to show it to me. You're the only man I have been with, and you are the father of this baby."

He studied me for a moment, but it was clear he still wasn't believing me. "Is that true? I mean Pete seems like a nice guy, but life with him would be a financial struggle, right? Me? I've got a lot of money. You wouldn't be the first woman to deceive me or take advantage."

I could only gape. He looked like Todd, but this wasn't the man I knew. Or at least, not the man I thought I knew.

"Is that what this is all about? You found out you were pregnant, and when you figured out that I was attracted to you, you saw the answer to all your problems? I'm older and richer."

I couldn't decide whether I was more hurt or angry by his words. Both emotions threatened to knock me to my knees.

When I was finally able to suck in a breath, I found the strength to say, "I accepted a long time ago that you are not a family man. I hope that things go well between you and Dean, but you don't have to worry about me or this baby. I don't want anything from you, ever. Except maybe for you to sign away your rights."

On shaky legs, I turned and rushed out of his office. I was able to make it to the elevator, and once the doors closed, I sank down and wept.

33

Todd

The minute my office door closed, I stood up and hurled my laptop against the wall. Anger and frustration and something worse, fear that I was wrong, swirled in a toxic mix. Twice she suggested that I couldn't be a family man, I couldn't be a father, and it gutted me. But the words that sent a chill down my spine were when she suggested that I sign my rights away. Did she say that just to fuck with me? Was the child really mine?

If it was mine, why hadn't she told me? Once again, her harsh words about my not being a family man came back. Maybe she hadn't planned to tell me. For reasons I couldn't explain, that hurt worse than the idea of her trying to pawn off a child that wasn't mine. It told me she really didn't care for me. She didn't think I was capable of being a husband and a father. Any way that I looked at the situation, it was clear that Betts didn't think much of me.

The intercom on my phone buzzed. I pressed the button.

"Mr. Marshall, is everything okay? It sounded like there was a crash in there."

"Everything's fine," I assured my secretary. It wasn't fine, of course.

But I was the owner and CEO of a billion-dollar company. I couldn't look like I was losing my grip.

I walked over and picked up the shattered pieces of my laptop, deciding they were a metaphor for my life. I set them on my desk and walked over to the window. I stared out over the desert as if it would have answers.

My phone rang, and at first, I thought I would ignore it, then I worried it might be Dean. I pulled my phone from my pocket. Looking at the caller ID, I saw it was Levi.

"Hey," I said.

"I'm heading out in a bit, but I want to check in and see how your talk with Betts went."

"It's all gone to hell." I pinched the bridge of my nose with my thumb and index finger.

"Want to meet?"

"I don't know what I want to do."

"Come meet me for a drink, then."

Levi told me where to meet him, and while I didn't really want to go, neither did I want to stand here in my office looking out the window, wondering how much I'd fucked up my life.

I walked into the casino bar, finding Levi already had a table. It wasn't even noon yet, but I ordered a double shot of whiskey and explained to him what happened last night when I'd gone to Betts's and Pete had showed up. I told him how she'd come to my office today telling me that the child was mine.

"You know, there are DNA tests to determine paternity," Levi said.

"She said she wrote me off as someone who could have a family. Twice. She even sounded skeptical about my ability to fix things with Dean."

He winced, and I was glad he recognized how much her words had hurt me.

"I've fallen for a woman who thinks I am incapable of being a husband and father. She told me she wanted me to sign my rights away."

He frowned. "It's a shitty thing to ask. With that said, it sounds like she's not lying about your being the father."

"I don't think she was going to tell me. She was outed by that story. But now that I know, she doesn't want me to be a part of its life." God, it ripped my heart apart knowing she felt like that about me.

"Too bad for her because I know otherwise."

I looked down into the amber liquid in my glass. "Maybe she's right. I fucked up pretty badly with Taylor and Dean. Maybe it isn't in me to be a good husband and father."

"Give me a break, Todd. First of all, you and Taylor were no great love story. For her, you were rich. For you, she was pretty and willing to act the part of a trophy wife. But don't pretend like she was the love of your life."

I took a sip of my drink, glaring at him over the rim, mostly because he was right. I'd cared for Taylor, and I think she did for me too, but it wasn't love. At least not the depth of love required as a foundation for marriage.

"And as for Dean, you're a great dad. Maybe you had a few missteps, but what parent doesn't? And you're doing everything you can to fix them. You're a good person, Todd. One of the best people I know. Betts is wrong if she thinks you're incapable of loving. Personally, I think you should be with her, proving what I'm saying is true."

I shook my head. "It's clear the feelings are one-sided." I lifted my head and looked him in the eyes. "She doesn't love me, but I am going to be a father to that baby. There was a time when I thought going away would be better for everyone involved, and all I ended up doing was fucking my son up. I'm not doing that again."

He patted me on the back. "Good. I can stay longer if you'd like. I can be your wingman, so to speak, when you talk to Betts again."

I shook my head. "No. I need to do this on my own."

WHEN I LEFT THE CASINO, I didn't head back to the office to talk to Betts. Instead, I drove out into the desert, parking at one of the hiking trails and taking a walk. I had to get my shit straight. I had to figure out how I had gotten here and what I was going to do moving forward.

It appeared that Betts had come to the decision that I wasn't worthy of her or the baby. She was wrong. Not that I was perfect, but I was capable of love. I'd wanted to give it to her. I wanted to give it to the baby.

What I had to figure out was how we'd move forward. She didn't love me, and after today, I was pretty sure she didn't respect me. The best I would be able to hope for would be a civil coparenting relationship. I knew I could do that as most of the time, Taylor and I got along all right.

Thinking of Taylor brought me to Dean. I wasn't sure what I did or said that had us turning the corner, but things were definitely in a better place now than they had been when he arrived. He'd spoken to Taylor a couple of times since he'd been with me, and so far, she hadn't made any statements to indicate she was ready for him to go back to Los Angeles. But I knew I couldn't rely on her indifference. I needed to take steps to make sure that Dean at least stayed with me until he was eighteen.

By the time I headed back to my car, it was time for me to head home as Dean would be arriving home from school shortly. One of the things I came up with as I sat in the desert was that I should have been clearer with Betts about how I was feeling. I didn't know that it would have made a difference, especially since it appeared she wasn't the type of woman I thought she was. But it made me realize that not sharing what was going on led to a breakdown, so I needed to be more open with Dean. So I didn't have to think about dinner, I ordered a pizza on my phone and picked it up on the way home.

When I arrived home, I made my way to his room, finding him at his laptop. "How was school?" I did my best to sound normal.

As usual, he shrugged. "Fine."

"I picked up pizza for dinner. You ready to eat?"

He nodded, closing his laptop and standing. "Extra cheese and pepperoni?"

I nodded, smiling and feeling grateful that he was here with me. "Of course. Is there any other kind of pizza?"

We headed out to the kitchen, and I got plates for the pizza while Dean filled our glasses with water to drink.

Once we sat down to eat, I asked, "How are you feeling about being here with me?"

He stopped mid-bite of pizza and looked up at me.

"I know it was tough at first, but things are going well, right?"

He nodded. "It's okay."

My heart sank a little bit because I was hoping being here with me was more than okay. "Are you wanting to return to Los Angeles with your mom?"

He stilled, his eyes widening as he looked at me. "You're giving me up again?"

Holy shit. "No. Not at all. What I'm trying to say, very poorly, apparently, is that I want you to stay. I want to make it legal. I want to have full custody."

I watched Dean as he sat back in his chair and studied me. "For how long?"

"Until you're eighteen. I know I wasn't a good dad for a long time, and I've been trying to change that. I like being your dad. I want you here."

Emotion swept over his face. He looked down and shrugged. "Yeah, okay."

I smiled, knowing that his nonchalance was covering up happiness. "There's something else I want to talk to you about."

"Is it Betts?" he asked.

My brow furrowed. "How did you know?"

He rolled his eyes. "I'm not an idiot. I know you guys like each other. Are you getting married?"

I studied him for a moment, wondering what he'd seen between me and Betts that I hadn't. "No." I tilted my head to the side. "How would you feel about it if I did?"

He plucked a pepperoni off his pizza and popped it into his mouth. "It would be okay. She's cool."

A wave of sadness washed through me that marriage wasn't an option for me and Betts. "I'm glad that you like her. But we're not getting married."

"Are you guys fighting? Did you break up?"

I let out a sigh. "I'll be honest with you, Dean. I don't know how to qualify the relationship I had with Betts. It was complicated because I'm her boss."

He frowned. "Is she suing you or something?"

I shook my head. "No, nothing like that. There's just a lot of things that went unsaid, a lot of misunderstandings. She questions my ability to be a family man. And she doesn't seem to be the woman I thought she was."

"Why not?"

"Because she hasn't been honest with me."

"Are you talking about that thing with the hockey player? Because today, it's all over my feed that it's not true."

I hadn't even checked the newsfeed to find out what, if any, additional news had come out about Mikael and Betts.

"Is that why you're mad? Because people think your baby was his?" Dean asked.

I'm glad I hadn't taken a bite of pizza because I might've choked on it. "You know about that?"

He rolled his eyes and smirked. "She's having a baby, and I know you and her like each other, so I just put two and two together." He leaned forward toward me. "But maybe sometime, I should give you the talk about the birds and the bees."

I barked out a laugh. The situation wasn't funny, and yet my son had just brought levity, breaking the tension that had been coiling to the breaking point in my chest.

"I might take you up on that," I said.

We started to eat again when Dean said, "Betts says that you should share your feelings with people. That you just can't assume that people know how you're feeling."

"She said that?"

"Yeah. So maybe you should tell her how you feel."

The words she'd said to me earlier that day about how she knew I couldn't be a family man made it very clear how she felt about me. "She told me how she felt, and it was clear that my feelings for her wouldn't change that. But I do plan to be involved in the baby's life. How do you feel about that?"

Dean seemed to think about it. "I guess that would be all right. I don't want to change diapers, though."

I smiled. "You got it."

I knew I needed to talk to Betts again. I needed to let her know that in no uncertain terms, I wasn't going to sign away my rights to my child. Whether she believed I was capable of loving or not, I was going to be in my child's life.

We'd just finished eating and were cleaning up when I got an email notification. Checking my phone, I saw it was an email from Betts with the subject line—*Resignation.*

34

Betts

After my cry in the elevator, I returned to my desk. For a moment, I sat in my chair feeling numb and uncertain as to what to do. I couldn't reconcile the man I had come to love with the one in his office accusing me of trying to trap him with a baby that wasn't his. Just a few nights ago, he had asked me to consider having a relationship with him, and now he'd called me a gold-digger.

The pain was still acute, but the anger was finally giving it a run for its money. The man had accused me of sleeping around and trying to trick him. I couldn't work for somebody who believed I was that sort of person.

I got to work getting all my projects organized and ready to pass on to someone else. By the end of the day, I had everything in place except for one final item. I opened up a blank document and wrote out my resignation letter.

I read it over and for a moment wondered if this was a wise action to take. I was a pregnant woman who couldn't afford to be out of a job. But in the end, I knew I couldn't continue to come to work and see Todd knowing the things he thought about me. So I copied the letter into an email and sent it off to Todd. I sat back in my chair, wishing I could feel relief, but I'd only just made my life harder. Now I needed to find another job.

I left the office and headed home, feeling lost and alone. Once home, I called Analyn knowing I needed to talk to someone. And being the true friend that she was, she was in my living room within twenty minutes, holding me as I cried on her shoulder and told her everything that happened today.

"I should've known better. I'm not the type to hook up with somebody, especially my boss. I should've stayed with Pete at Naomi's wedding."

"That's just your sadness and anger talking," Analyn said, handing me another tissue.

I looked at her through bleak eyes. "But it's true. If I hadn't been in such a foul mood and stayed with Pete, I wouldn't be in this situation." I wasn't sure when I got pregnant, but I knew that if I hadn't lit the inferno with Todd at the wedding, I wouldn't have slept with him.

"That might be true, except the attraction was there. Whether you saw him at the wedding or another place, you probably would have hooked up."

I shook my head. "Before the wedding, he hardly knew I existed."

"All right, let's say what you're saying is true. Do you really wish that you never had the experiences you've had with him? What about the baby?"

My hand went to my belly. She was right. If I hadn't hooked up with Todd, I wouldn't have this life growing inside me. I'd wanted to be a mom, and now that was going to happen.

And I couldn't deny that Todd and I had some good times together. Not just the sex, but times when we talked and laughed.

"The truth is that love can make you do foolish things. And because it's scary as hell, it can make you think or overthink things that aren't true," Analyn finished.

I scoffed. "Do you think it's love that has Todd thinking that I cheated on him or that I got pregnant and decided I would tell him it was his so I could get money?"

Analyn took my hand in hers. "It's possible."

I arched a brow at her. "How is that possible?"

"Well, consider the fact that he discovered you were pregnant from a news item that said Mikael was the father. It wasn't that long ago there was another news item that said you and Mikael were dating. A man in love might be jealous to find out that the woman he loves is with another man and having his baby."

"But it's not true. Todd should know it's not true."

"Why should he know it's not true?"

I tensed and pulled my hand away. "Are you questioning me too?"

"No, honey. But I've known you most of my life. Todd hasn't."

I nodded. "He should know that I'm not that type of person."

She cocked her head to the side. "Are you sure he should know that? I know that after everything that happened after your engagement broke off, you shut down a little bit. How much have you opened up to Todd? Does he know that you're in love with him?"

I looked down. "I've been spending time with him and his son. I've been sleeping with him. I've worked with him."

"But have you told him how you feel? Has he told you how he feels?"

I shifted, feeling uncomfortable. Between the two of us, Todd had been the most open to saying what he wanted. He never said he loved me, but he said he wanted to continue to see me. "It's just been so complicated. He's my boss."

Analyn took my hand again and gave it a squeeze. "I get it. You know I do. I ended up marrying my boss. Remember how I said that sometimes love is so scary that you end up thinking things that aren't true? Maybe that's why he's kept his feelings close to the vest."

"His life is about building his business. I was there when his ex-wife would call, and he was always brushing her off. For years, he was estranged from his son."

She gave me a hard look, and I felt the shame she wanted me to feel at blaming Todd and making him be the bad guy. He said some terrible things to me, but hadn't I said them as well? I had said to his face what I had just told Analyn. And I knew the words hurt him because I saw it on his face.

"Let me play devil's advocate," Analyn said.

"What have you been up to until now?"

"Picture yourself in Todd's shoes. He cares for a woman who works for him. But she is concerned about what could happen if it's learned she's sleeping with her boss. He sees two news articles connecting her with a younger, stronger hockey player. And instead of learning from her that she's pregnant, he sees it on a social media newsfeed. And then she tells him the reason she didn't tell him about the baby was because he's not family material."

Guilt burned deep in my gut, and I was angry at Analyn for making me feel that way because I knew she was right. But it didn't matter. We'd said too many hurtful things to each other.

"We're beyond the point of no return."

"That may be. But there's a baby to think about. No matter what, the two of you need to work something out," she said.

I wasn't sure how we were going to manage it, but I knew she was right.

"I don't know Todd well, but he strikes me as a decent man. He will provide for you and the baby, I'm sure of it."

I sighed as I scraped my hands over my face. "I know. But I don't want to rely on him. Which means tomorrow, I have to start looking for a new job."

"Did he fire you?" She looked at me indignantly. "If he fired you, that changes—"

"No. I quit. I just couldn't work for a man who believed I would lie and cheat."

Analyn put her arm around me and tugged me close. "It sounds to me like you and Todd still have a lot more talking to do. And even if things don't work out between you two, you need to find a way to get along for the sake of the baby. I can understand not wanting to continue to work for him and wanting to be self-suffi-cient, but don't dismiss his support. Not just financially, but as a parent as well. It's not easy being a parent. I can't imagine doing it alone."

I nodded. "Thank you for being here."

"Of course. It's the least I can do for all the times you've been here for me."

We sat quietly for a few minutes. I was so grateful for Analyn, for the strength and support that she gave me. Even when I made mistakes, she was always there for me.

A knock on the door made us both startle.

"Did you invite Ruby and Naomi over as well?" Analyn asked.

I shook my head as I stood. "No. I haven't told them anything. Well, Naomi knows I'm pregnant, but she doesn't know all this with Todd." I walked over to the door, looking through the peephole.

My heart rate sped up as Todd stood on the other side of the door. I craned my head around toward Analyn. "It's Todd."

She stood. "Good. You two have a lot of things to talk about." She nodded toward the door. "Maybe you should let him in."

I sucked in a deep breath and opened the door. Todd looked as emotionally worn out as I felt.

Analyn stepped up next to me, giving me a hug. "You got this, babe." She stepped through the door as Todd moved aside so she could exit. She looked up at him. "Love can make you say and do and think stupid things. Remember that."

He looked from her to me as if he didn't understand. I simply shrugged. He looked back at Analyn. "I'll remember that."

Analyn walked off, and I was left alone with Todd. The last time we talked, we both said very hurtful things. I wondered if this time, it would be more of the same. But Analyn was right. No matter what, Todd's and my life were connected through this baby, so I needed to find a way to get along with him.

35

Todd

"Love can make you say and do and think stupid things. Remember that." Analyn's words echoed in my brain as I stepped into Betts's apartment. Why did she say them? She couldn't know how I felt about Betts. Was she implying that Betts loved me?

The kernel of hope bloomed in my heart even as I told it not to. Her words earlier in the day and her resignation this evening told me all I needed to know. What she needed to know was that I would not sign over the rights to the baby. She was stuck with me for the long haul, even if she felt I was incapable of loving my child.

I followed her to her living area, both of us silent. Finally, when we were both standing and staring at each other, I said, "I guess Analyn knows."

She nodded. "She's a good friend to me."

"I suppose she was the first one to know." I tried to keep my voice calm, even though deep down, the idea that Betts hadn't told me first about the baby was like a stake through the heart.

She looked down. "Yes." When she looked up at me, I saw regret in her eyes. "I'm sorry about that. And I'm sorry for the things I said to you earlier."

I nodded, my own guilt and regret replacing the pain of her betrayal. "I'm sorry too." This time, I was the one looking down in shame. Finally, I lifted my gaze to hers. "Dean told me that you said we needed to talk about our feelings. I know you think I don't have them or that I'm incapable of love or being a good parent—"

She shook her head vehemently. "Todd—"

I held my hand up to stop her. "I can understand why you might think that based on my failed marriage and relationship with Dean. So now I'm going to do what you told him to do and tell you how I feel."

She swallowed and waited.

"I love you."

Her eyes widened, and she gasped in shock.

"I have for some time, although I only just recently realized it. But I was too cowardly to say anything. I tried to inch toward it by asking you to be with me, but your resistance made me afraid to tell you the truth. I know that this may be too little, too late, or maybe you just don't feel the same for me, and I accept that. But I'm going to be a part of this child's life. You can't keep me from that."

She shook her head, and I felt it like a vise around my heart. The very thing I was trying to avoid was happening. She was rejecting me.

She stepped forward. "I don't want to keep the baby from you." She wasn't saying she loved me back, but at least she was accepting that I was going to be in the baby's life.

"Why didn't you tell me?"

"I was going to, but like you, I was afraid. I don't think you are incapable of loving or being a parent. I just thought that it wasn't something you wanted. I believed that when I told you, everything would change, and I didn't want it to change."

I cocked my head to the side, not understanding what she was trying to tell me. "What would change?"

"I was afraid that when I told you, you wouldn't want me or the baby."

My jaw tightened. "Because you didn't think I could love you or the baby?" Was I really such an emotional wasteland?

"Not that you couldn't, but that you wouldn't want to. You've been single and alone for so long. I thought that was on purpose."

She wasn't wrong, but it was only because I hadn't met anyone to make me change my mind until her.

She blew out a breath. "That's only part of it, really. The truth is, Todd, I knew that when you learned about the baby, however you felt about it, you would do the right thing. You would provide for me and the baby."

"And that's a bad thing?"

She shook her head. "Not at all. But . . ." She looked down. "I wanted you to want me for me."

I stared at her, not sure I heard her words correctly. "I did tell you I wanted you."

"Yes, but I thought it was just the sex. Or for help with Dean."

It made sense why she wouldn't be confident about my feelings, but it didn't make sense that she wanted me to feel them considering the boundaries she'd put around us. "You said that because I'm your boss—"

She waved her hand. "I know. I told you that we had to be a secret, and I was resistant, so I know I was being unfair to you."

"I guess Analyn is right in that love makes people say and do and think the wrong things."

She let out a small laugh. "Boy, does it ever." I waited for her to elaborate, but she didn't. She didn't love me, and my having said the words to her hadn't changed her mind. But I knew that before I came over.

I shoved my hands in my pockets and sucked in a breath. It was time to move on. "Are you still planning to resign?"

She looked at me and blinked.

"I understand why you would want to. But if you want to stay, we can work things out where you wouldn't be uncomfortable."

She frowned. "Uncomfortable?"

"We can avoid each other altogether. We need to work together for the baby, but I can make sure to stay away at work."

She looked at me like I'd grown a horn. "Stay away?"

Her obtuseness hurt. Was she going to make me spell it out?

"You said you loved me. But now you want to avoid me?" she asked.

"I said I loved you, but you didn't say it back. And I understand. It's not your fault if you don't—"

She slapped her palm against her head and then looked at me. "Of course, I love you, Todd." She shook her head. "I'm sorry I didn't say it sooner. I thought I had."

I wanted to grab her words like a lifeline, but I was too afraid to do it. So I remained where I stood. "You said you wanted me to want you, but you didn't say you loved me."

She stepped closer to me, reaching out toward me. My hands instinctively came out of my pockets and took her hands in mine. Touching made the longing in my heart painful.

"I've made such a mess of things. I'm sorry. What I meant was that I wanted you to love me for me, not just because I was carrying your child. I didn't want you to feel obligated."

The noose around my heart loosened, and I reached my hand up to cup her cheek. "My desire to be with you is not out of obligation or duty." I let out a small laugh. "The reason I brought Mikael over and wanted you to work with him was so I could be around you. Nearly everything I've been doing is to be around you because I can't seem to be away from you."

Her smile was like the sun coming out after a storm. "And I want to be with you not because you are rich or handsome or—"

I flashed a grin. "You think I'm handsome?"

She rolled her eyes. "More handsome than anyone has a right to be."

Unable to hold back, I tugged her in close, wrapping her in my arms and vowing I'd never let her go. "I'm sorry I've been such an asshole. I'm sorry that I hurt you and said awful things to you. I think you know jealousy makes me crazy."

She looked up at me. "You don't have to be jealous, Todd. You're the only one I want."

I stared down into her beautiful green eyes, feeling myself tumbling into them. "What about the fact that I'm your boss?"

She smiled. "Well, technically, you're not my boss anymore."

I took that to mean that she didn't plan on coming back to work. I didn't want her to go, but I also wanted her to be happy.

She walked her fingers up my chest and gave me a flirty smile. "Now, tomorrow, maybe you'll accidentally delete that resignation letter, but right now . . ."

I grinned. And then I plastered my lips over hers, kissing her until I couldn't breathe. I pulled back. "Just tell me you're mine."

"I'm yours."

I dipped to kiss her again, but she stopped me. "Tell me you're mine."

"Don't you know, Elisabeth? I've been yours ever since you seduced me in the library at Naomi's wedding. I haven't stopped wanting you, thinking of you, needing you since."

Her eyes filled with tears. "Me neither. I'm sorry I made this so hard."

I wiped a tear from her cheek. "We both made it hard. From now on, let's be honest. Let's follow your recommendation to share our feelings."

"Deal."

"Can I tell you how I'm feeling now?"

Her smile turned flirty. "Does it involve getting naked?"

"It does." I scooped her up into my arms and carried her to her bedroom.

We stripped at a world-record pace, but once we were on the bed, I slowed things down. I was going to take my time so she knew without a doubt that I loved her, that I wanted her for her and not out of obligation or duty. There was so much I wanted to say to her like how I wanted her to move in with me and spend the rest of her life with me. But for now, I stuck with words of love.

"I love you, Elisabeth." I whispered it with each kiss I cascaded along her jaw, down her neck, and lower to her belly, where I kissed the place where our baby grew.

"Todd." Her arms held me tightly, and I couldn't ever remember feeling as loved as I felt from her. "I love you."

I spread my body over hers. Lacing my fingers with hers, I pulled her hands over her head. "Look at me, Elisabeth."

Her beautiful green eyes shone up at me. With our gazes holding, I slid inside her body. Finally, after so much uncertainty and pain, my world righted itself.

36

Betts

Was I dreaming? I hoped not. When Todd arrived, I didn't in a million years think we'd end up here, making love. To think I almost ruined it by not telling him I loved him when he'd said the words to me. I was so shocked to hear them. And then, all I could think about was making him understand my thought process for the decisions I'd made.

I had no illusions that everything would be smooth sailing. He was still my boss . . . well . . . if he deleted the resignation letter. There was much to talk about and work through. But we knew we loved each other and wanted this thing between us to work. That was a start.

"What are you thinking?" he asked as he slowly withdrew and slipped back in, like he had all the time in the world.

"That I might be dreaming."

"Are your dreams usually this good?" He moved again, making it hard for me to think.

"No. This is better."

He smiled and then kissed me. "All the pieces of my life have finally come together. Do you feel it too?"

I nodded, marveling that he'd perfectly articulated what I was feeling. "I feel it too."

"It feels good." He moved again, this time a little bit faster, harder, deeper.

I gasped and arched. "It feels beyond good."

After that, there weren't any words, just sighs and moans as our bodies rocked in perfect sync, driving together toward the ultimate pleasure. We hit the pinnacle at the same time, and together, we flew, soared into bliss.

For long moments, we held each other as our breaths and heartbeats returned to normal. Finally, Todd rolled to his back, tugging me into his side. I rested my head on his chest, feeling the beat of his heart, a heart I knew beat for me.

"You know, I could stay here forever," he said.

I lifted my head to look at him. His smile was so sweet and serene.

His brow furrowed. "Actually, I really could."

"You could what? Stay here forever?" It wasn't a bad idea, but there was Dean and this baby we needed to attend to.

"Well, maybe not right here forever, but I could resign from work too. I could focus on you and Dean and the baby." His hand pressed over my stomach.

It sounded lovely, except . . . "You're the owner and CEO. I don't think you can resign."

"I can resign from being CEO. I could sell or have someone else run things."

"But you love business."

His eyes filled with such love, it made my chest swell with emotion. "I love you more. And Dean and this baby too. The only thing you all are asking of me is to love you, and so that's what I'm going to do."

"What about you and what you want?"

"I want to be a good husband and father."

My heart beat wildly, wondering if he meant that he wanted to be my husband.

"I want to love you, and I want you to love me back."

"I do." This was no wedding ceremony, and at the same time, I felt like I was committing my life to his.

I lifted my lips to his and kissed him. He rolled us until I was underneath him. His fingers pushed back my hair from my face. "Just so we're clear, what I'm saying is I want to make a life with you, Elisabeth. I know I come with a lot of baggage, and I'm going to be a senior citizen way before you—"

I pressed my fingers over his lips to stop him. "Do you know what I want?"

"Tell me. Whatever it is, I'm going to give it to you."

I smiled as I traced his lips with my fingers. "I want to be a good wife and mother."

It took a second, but then realization showed in his eyes. "You're okay with the fact that I come with a teenage son? A teenage son who, by the way, thinks you're cool. Oh, and who knew we were an item before we did."

I laughed. "I'm glad that Dean is here. I want us to be a family."

He closed his eyes as if he were savoring my words. "That's what I want too, baby. You and me and Dean and this little guy."

"That little guy might be a girl."

"Boy, girl, either way, I'm happy."

Then he kissed me, and I kissed him back, for the first time, really understanding what it meant to love. And what it felt like to be loved.

ONE OF THE advantages of living in Las Vegas was how quickly a marriage can take place. Not that we rushed from bed down to the nearest chapel of love, but we did plan and execute a wedding within two weeks.

I walked down the aisle toward Todd. The love shining in his eyes made me feel like the center of the universe. Next to him stood Dean as his best man, and my heart was filled to capacity to think we were about to be a family.

All our friends were here, Analyn, Ruby, and Naomi along with their husbands, and Todd's best friend, Levi. I really enjoyed Levi. He came off a bit like a playboy, but I could tell that he cared for Todd a great deal. He was to Todd like Analyn was to me.

After the ceremony, we had a small reception, and then Todd whisked me away to a beach in Mexico, leaving Dean behind with Levi. Todd worried a little bit about what Levi might expose Dean to while we were gone, but I assured him that Dean was a smart kid. He'd keep Levi in line.

The second morning of our honeymoon, I felt the baby move for the first time. I reached across the bed for Todd's hand, placing it on my stomach.

He looked up at me with awe in his eyes. "It feels like you've got an athlete in there."

I nodded.

"Maybe he'll play for the family hockey team."

I smirked. "It could be a girl."

He grinned. "Don't you know, baby? I'm all for women in hockey. I'm the one who hired a woman to coach a men's hockey team. I have no problem with putting a woman on the team."

I laughed and pulled him to me for a kiss. "Anything for publicity, right?"

He rolled over me, settling his hips between my thighs. "Here's a press release for you." He thrust inside me, and all words were gone for the next hour.

When we returned from our honeymoon, ship with the boss, I didn't care. Besides, Todd wasn't going to be my boss much longer. His first priority when we returned was planning the charity hockey game with Dean. It was determined that the event would take place at the end of the season and after the playoffs.

The second order of business was to prepare for his retirement. The baby was due in five months, so March was his goal to find a new CEO and fully transition out and retire.

When we weren't at work, we were at home. Our life might've seemed quite ordinary to the outside world, but to me, it was perfection. In the morning, I woke up next to the man I loved and the child we made kicking inside me. We had breakfast as a family. After school and work, we were home together. Dean sometimes taught Todd how to cook. Other times, Todd was taking Dean out to drive. Dean had just started private driving lessons with the goal to have his license by Thanksgiving.

Sometimes, we played games, although not Catan. I think they both got tired of losing all the time. On the weekends, Dean was out with friends or with his new girlfriend. I mentioned to Todd that perhaps he needed to have a talk with Dean about the birds and the bees. Todd laughed and told me how when he had explained to Dean that I was pregnant, Dean was the one who said that perhaps Todd needed the lesson.

By late February, we were nearly ready to enter the next phase of our lives. I was large and sometimes wondered if maybe there was more than one baby inside me. My doctor was adamant that there was only one. Todd and I decided that we would wait until the birth to know whether it was a boy or girl, so the nursery was made up in neutral colors.

It was a regular Saturday. Todd had gone into the office to do some work. Since the beginning of the year, he had spent more weekends at the office, but I knew it was only so that we could meet our deadline for his retirement when the baby came. Today, he was down in Henderson, dealing with hockey business while Dean and I remained at home.

Dean was watching a livestream in his room while I was sitting and relaxing, having a cup of tea. But I was having a difficult time getting comfortable.

I rose from the couch and went into the kitchen to re-warm my tea when I felt a sudden wetness between my legs. For a moment, I stood in the middle of the kitchen looking down. Had I just wet my pants? And then I realized . . . *No. My water broke.*

I put my cup in the sink, and as I turned away, the lower part of my belly tightened hard, making me catch my breath.

"Dean?" I gripped the edge of the counter.

"Yeah?" he bellowed from his room.

"Can you come here, please?"

"I'm kind of in the middle of something."

"Dean. I think I'm in labor."

Two seconds later, he came flying into the kitchen, his eyes wide and crazed. "What?"

"My water broke. I'm going to call my doctor, but I need to go to the hospital. Can you drive me?" I was thanking God that he had succeeded in getting his driver's license.

"What about Dad?"

"We'll call him too. He's down in Henderson."

Dean looked nervous, like he was afraid the baby was going to drop right there. "I think Dad put your bag in the car already, right?"

I nodded. "You just need to get the keys and your wallet. I'll grab my purse, and we'll go."

A few moments later, we were in the car. I called my doctor, who told me she'd meet us at the hospital.

My next call was to Todd. His voice came through the Bluetooth speaker of the car. "Hey, beautiful. I think I'm going to be done here—"

"My water broke and I'm in labor. Dean is driving me to the hospital."

"Oh, my God. Okay, I'm on my way. Dean? Are you all right?"

Dean's fingers gripped the steering wheel at ten and two, his eyes darting around as if he was terrified that at any moment something would go wrong. "You should be here, Dad."

"I'm on my way. I love you both."

For all our planning, we hadn't anticipated this. But I knew that Todd was on his way. As long as this baby didn't do something crazy and come faster than all the baby books indicated a labor took, we should be fine.

37

Todd

If I didn't get a ticket, it would be a fucking miracle. I sped along the highway, weaving around traffic. I was glad that I had made the decision to drive myself today instead of having a driver because there was no way he'd drive like a bat out of hell to get to the hospital in record time.

I replayed Betts's call in my mind. She sounded strained, but I suppose labor could do that to a person. Dean sounded nervous. Why the hell hadn't I been there?

Dean is a good driver, I reminded myself. And women had babies every day. But even telling myself that didn't alleviate the quantum stress I was feeling. The truth was that my stress wasn't so much related to worry about Dean or Betts, although that was there.

No, my concern was missing the birth of my child because I was at work. Even when Dean was born, I'd taken time off work to be there.

I'd been feeling guilty about working so much over the last couple of weeks, and even with Betts's assurances that she understood that I was working so much now so that I didn't have to work at all once the baby was here, I still felt guilty. This was the behavior that had led to the breakup of my marriage and the estrangement from my son. I couldn't miss this child's birth, their first day here on earth because I was at work.

Granted, the baby was two weeks early, but I couldn't use that as an excuse. I'd promised Betts and Dean and myself that I would be present. The family would be first in everything. I made that vow to Betts as soon as I could after she agreed to be my wife. I'd made it to Dean on the day we submitted custody papers to court.

Taylor hadn't fought me on it, which was a mixed blessing. I was glad not to have to go to battle with her, but I didn't like the message it gave Dean. So, I doubled down, making sure that no matter what, he knew how important he was.

But I was on the verge of fucking it up on the first day of my new child's life. I couldn't have that. I sped into the hospital parking lot and screeched to a halt by the front doors, rushing in, not caring if my car got towed.

I hurried to the nurse's station, giving her my name and asking her about Betts. I scanned the waiting area for Dean but didn't see him.

The nurse told me where I could find Betts. I decided I would check on her first and then look for Dean. I hurried down the corridor to the labor room. When I walked in, she was doing her breathing learned in childbirth class, and Dean was standing by the bed, counting.

Relief like I'd never known filled me, followed by an intense love. Here was my family.

I rushed into the room, and when Dean saw me, he stepped away, relief filling his expression. I took Betts's hand and set my other hand on Dean's shoulder. "How are you?"

Betts let out a breath. "I'm ready for the baby to be here."

I lifted her hand to my lips and kissed it. Then I turned to Dean. "Thank you so much for getting her here, Son." I squeezed his shoulder to accentuate my appreciation.

He nodded. "You're welcome."

"Are you going to stay here or are you going to head home?"

Dean looked over at Betts, his face going pale. "Maybe I could just wait in the waiting room?"

I realized he was nervous about seeing the birth of a baby.

"It could be a while. It's okay if you go home," Betts said to him.

"No, I'll wait."

I handed him my keys. "Would you mind parking my car, assuming it hasn't been towed yet? It's right out front. Oh, and would you mind calling Analyn, Ruby, and Naomi? I'm sure they'd like to know that Betts is having a baby today."

He nodded and seemed glad to have a task he could do outside the labor room.

When he left, I turned back to Betts, leaning over the bed and kissing her temple. "I'm so sorry I wasn't here."

She managed a sweet smile. "You're here now. That's what matters."

SIX HOURS LATER, I watched as the head of our baby emerged from Betts's body. I remembered back to when Dean was born and the sense of awe that I had felt. It was a fucking miracle that two people having sex could create something as miraculous as a person.

With a final push, the baby was born. Betts collapsed back in the bed, and I leaned over, whispering in her ear, "You're fucking awesome. I love you so much."

She squeezed my hand in response as her breathing was still labored.

"It's a girl."

Tears welled in my eyes as the nurse set the baby into Betts's arms. What the hell did I do to deserve this? A second chance at life. A second chance to do it right.

Betts looked up at me. "Are you okay that it wasn't a boy?"

"Are you kidding me? You and I made this beautiful being. It could've been born purple with twelve toes and I still couldn't be happier."

Across the room, the nurse made an "aww" sound.

"I'm glad it's a girl. Not that I'd be unhappy if she was a boy, but I don't want Dean to feel displaced."

Just when I didn't think I could love Betts any more, she'd say something like that. Something that showed how much she didn't just love me and our child, but Dean is well.

"I think Dean would be fine either way." I looked down on our brand-new daughter. "What are we going to name her?" We had gone through a zillion boys' and girls' names but could never quite settle on one that we both loved.

She looked up at me with a smirk. "I was sort of thinking of Mikaela."

I liked that name. "It's nice. What made you think of it?"

"For Mikael."

My smile faltered. "You want to name our daughter after Mikael."

She shrugged. "You once told me that the whole reason you brought him here was so that you could spend time with me. And if you think about it, a lot of the significant points of our relationship related to Mikael. We don't have to tell him, of course."

"I guess it's a way to pay homage to what worked to get you to fall in love with me," I said.

Betts reached up her free hand, putting it around my neck and pulling it toward her. "Or what made you fall in love with me."

I smiled and then kissed her, pouring every ounce of love I had for her into the kiss.

When she pulled back, she held the baby up toward me. "Would you like to hold your new daughter, Mikaela Deanna Marshall?"

"Deanna?"

"That pays homage to Dean, who drove like an old lady to get me here, but he got me here safe and sound."

I laughed and then took Mikaela Deanna Marshall into my arms.

My eyes welled with tears as I looked at the beautiful being in my arms. I glanced at Betts. "Thank you."

"You're welcome. For what?"

"For giving me the chance to be a better man. To have love. To have a family."

This time, her eyes welled with tears. "Thank you for giving all that to me as well."

We had to be quite a sight. The two of us crying over a brand-new baby. I suppose the nurses had seen it before, but I doubted anybody had ever felt such an overwhelming intensity of love as I felt at this moment. And the best thing was, I had the rest of my life to love this woman, and Dean and Mikaela and any other children we might have. I was the luckiest man in the world.

EPILOGUE

Todd

Sun, surf, sand, and family. Was there anything better?

I sat in my lounge chair, watching as the waves came in. Dean dropped his skim board onto the sand and water, hopping on and gliding across the beach. It looked like fun, but I discovered that looks were deceiving. When I made an attempt to skim board, I was reminded that I was a fifty-year-old man. I landed hard in the sand and still had abrasions from it.

I turned to the right where Betts was reclining on a lounge chair. She was slathered in sunscreen and wore a hat while she sat under the umbrella. I didn't blame her. With all her gorgeous red hair and fair skin, she was sensitive to the sun. Her eyes were closed, and so I took a moment to admire her beauty.

To look at her, no one would guess that four months ago, she'd given birth. Her tits were still a bit larger from nursing, but her stomach was flat and her hips were round. I loved playing on the beach, but I eagerly awaited bedtime when I could run my hands over her sublime body.

I settled into my chair, also underneath the umbrella, and kissed the top of baby Mikaela's head which lay against my chest. She was sleeping soundly, cuddled up against me. Sometimes, it was still amazing to me how I had gotten so lucky to have all these beautiful people in my life.

Life was a bit of a whirlwind after Mikaela's birth. When she was two weeks old, I was finally able to relinquish control of the company to a new CEO. I continued to work with Dean and the Buckaroos on the Junior League hockey event. First, we had to get through the season and the playoffs. For the second year in the row, the Silver Nuggets won their division, and I used the money from the bet with Levi to purchase this small island in the Caribbean.

The charity event was a big hit. Our junior hockey team kicked the opposing team's butt, but the Buckaroos, for the first time in over a year, beat the Silver Nuggets. Since it was all for charity, I didn't mind losing.

Once the event was over, I packed us up and brought us to the island with the intention of staying here until school started. Betts wondered if that was a good idea, since Dean would be away from his friends. Dean didn't complain, but we made arrangements to have his friends come visit a few times during the summer.

The sound of a boat took my attention away from my family. In the distance, a boat approached the main dock.

"Is that them?" Betts asked next to me.

"I imagine it is." I rose from the chair, adjusting Mikaela and then reaching down to help Betts up.

"Dean," I called out.

Dean picked up his skim board and trotted back toward us.

"Our guests are here."

He looked over toward the dock and then tossed his skim board on his towel.

As a family, we walked to the dock where we greeted Reed and Analyn, Pierce and Naomi, and Bo and Ruby with all their children in tow. They had also brought with them Dean's friend, David. The two of them high-fived and then ran back to the house so David could change and they could skim board.

"Welcome," I greeted our guests.

"This is lovely," Analyn said, hugging Betts and then taking a peek at Mikaela.

"It's not bad," Betts agreed.

We led them back to the main house and then showed them to their private bungalows that had been a part of the purchase of the island.

Once they were all settled in, they joined us at the main house out on the large lanai where we had arranged to have lunch. Dean and David joined us, eager to eat and get back to the beach.

"This is fantastic," Bo said. "Do you have an extra skim board? I'd love to give that a try."

"You might want to wear knee and elbow guards," I quipped.

Dean rolled his eyes, but everyone else laughed.

"You know, I could afford an island," Reed said to his wife, Analyn.

"Maybe you should buy one," she answered.

Lunch was filled with chatter and laughter, and I was again reminded of what a lucky son of a bitch I was.

The sound of a helicopter beat overhead, causing all of us to stop talking and look up.

Betts smirked at me. "He always has to make an entrance, doesn't he?"

I nodded as I rose from my seat. "Excuse me. We have one more guest to welcome."

I made my way down the beach and then through the pathway toward the landing pad the previous owner had built. I waited as the helicopter landed and Levi emerged.

He came over, giving me a hug. "So this is what you did with that money you won from me?"

"Yes. Come and say hello to everyone."

We walked together back toward the house. "You know, I thought you were pressing your luck by taking on that last bet with me. I can't believe after everything, the Silver Nuggets won again. That has to be the biggest payoff from a gamble you've ever received."

I shook my head. "No, my biggest payoff on a gamble was in giving my heart to Betts and living this dream."

He looked at me like I had said something schmaltzy, which I had. But it was the truth.

He laughed. "That reminds me. I have something else for you."

He reached into his pack and pulled out a six-inch tall trophy with a man and a woman holding hands. I read the plaque.

Best Family Man

I laughed. "This was well-earned."

We arrived back at the house, and I showed Betts the trophy.

Betts laughed. "What a great prize."

I shook my head and took her into my arms. "You are the best prize." I bent her over and kissed her, hearing all my friends say "aww" except, of course, for Dean, who made gagging sounds.

Levi was probably right. I was pressing my luck to take his second bet. There was no reason to think the team would have a successful season, much less win the championship the second year in a row. But whether I'd won the bet or not, it had brought me close to Betts. The moment she told me she was mine and I was hers, I'd achieved all the excitement, adventure, and success I could ask for.

THANK you for reading Betts and Todd's story. I hope you enjoyed it. **You can binge read the entire series here.**

Bet On It: Analyn and Reed

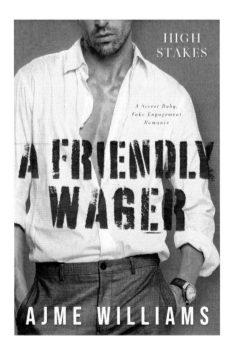

A Friendly Wager: Ruby and Bo

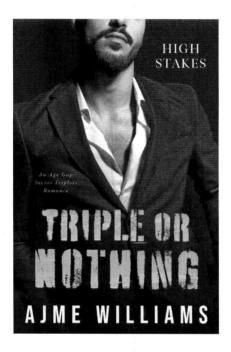

Triple or Nothing: Naomi and Pierce

BET ON IT (SNEAK PEEK)

DESCRIPTION

Being a billionaire had become boring until a stranger showed up to a conference and spiced things up...

Curvy, sassy, and dangerously younger than me...

Analyn was everything that a former hockey player needed to stay away from.
I was used to women falling all over me.
But Analyn's pretty mouth that never shut up was still tempting.
Especially when I made a bet that she couldn't resist.

Analyn had no idea she was setting herself up for failure.
Little Miss Sassy came back to me, this time looking for a job.
And I knew it was my turn again to suggest a wager.

Our one-night stand had to be forgotten.
But I couldn't *not* notice that cute pencil skirt she'd wear to the office.

All eyes were on me... on *us.*

And my eyes were on the only woman I could *bet* would never trust me.
Or would she?

PROLOGUE

Analyn

Men are scum. Especially Chase Tolliver, the man I was sure was going to propose to me. I was right. Oh, did he ever propose to me. Except it wasn't marriage. It was an open relationship.

As it turned out, we'd been in an open relationship practically since we started dating. I just hadn't known it.

When he'd suggested the new arrangement, we were at a fancy restaurant in Chicago, my heart beating a million miles a minute, at first in joy and then in shock. Did he really mean that he wanted an open relationship? Did it go both ways?

I pointed toward a handsome man sitting at another table and asked, "So if I wanted to sleep with him, you'd be all right with that?"

He gave me an affable smile. "Sure. That's the point, isn't it?"

I wasn't sure what hurt more—that he didn't feel sex should be monogamous or that there was no sign of jealousy at the idea of my sleeping with another man. Both were bad. Both indicated that I wasn't in the type of relationship I wanted.

"And what if I didn't want that?" I'd asked him.

He didn't say anything at first, but that pause told me everything I needed to know. He hadn't been faithful while we dated. He wouldn't be faithful in a marriage. A marriage he hadn't even proposed. Chase wasn't the man for me, after all.

I put my napkin on the table. "Let me save you the trouble. You're welcome to screw around with all the women you want, but when you need a plus-one or a girlfriend, don't call me."

I stood and walked away from the table to leave the restaurant. When he didn't call after me, I began to wonder if my reaction was exactly what he wanted. He'd set me up to break up with him so he wouldn't have to break up with me. Coward.

Men are scum and cowards.

The best way to get over a breakup is to spend time with your best friend. Unfortunately for me, my best friend lived in Las Vegas while I was in Chicago. No worries. I simply packed a bag and hopped a plane and was now spending a week with my best friend, Betts. In the few days I'd been there, we had done all the things required to get over a man, which involved copious amounts of ice cream and wine. We were having such a great time, she invited me to be her roommate if I wanted to move to Las Vegas. I was seriously considering that idea.

Unfortunately, tonight Betts was on a date with her boyfriend, Paul. They had an on-again-off-again relationship that had been off when I arrived, but then he called earlier tonight, and it appeared that they were on again.

She felt bad leaving me at her place alone while she made up with Paul, but I assured her that it was okay. I wanted her to be happy, and if Paul was the guy who was going to make her happy, then she needed to see him.

After she got all dressed up and headed out to meet Paul, I putzed around her condo for a little bit, but I didn't like being alone. I started to think about Chase, and instead of thinking what an asshole he was, I got down on myself.

What was wrong with me that I wasn't enough? I determined the best way to combat self-pity was to go out and live it up. I was in Las Vegas, Sin City, after all.

There had to be a reason the motto of Las Vegas was, "What happens in Vegas stays in Vegas." Surely, that meant I could let go of my inhibitions in an effort to forget Chase and not worry about any ramifications. That sure sounded better than hanging around Betts's condo feeling sorry for myself.

I did a quick Google search looking for the best places to go that weren't about gambling, or at least only about gambling. In Las Vegas, I swear there were slot machines in the bathrooms. But I didn't have any money to lose, so I just wanted a nice club where I could drink and let my hair down.

I decided on the Golden Oasis. According to Yelp, it was the coolest club because it included tech features like holograms with famous celebrities of Hollywood's golden era. I dressed for a night at a club, which included a red dress that clung to my ample curves, styling my long, dark hair into thick waves, and putting on enough makeup to suggest I was interested without being trampy.

I studied the result in the full-length mirror in the guest room of Betts's condo. "Eat your heart out, Chase."

I ordered a rideshare that dropped me off in front of the club. I walked in and was pleased to see that it was as cool as the Yelp reviewers and images had made it seem. On one wall, a hologram of Marilyn Monroe in her iconic stand over a vent moved until air blew her dress out. A few drunk men joked around like they were trying to look up her dress. Women took selfies of themselves modeling the same stance as Marilyn.

The drunk men notwithstanding, the place had a young, hip, yet sophisticated vibe. I patted myself on the shoulder for making a good choice.

I made my way to the bar, taking a seat on the stool. I should have ordered something exotic, but I couldn't think of anything offhand so I started with a plain white wine.

As I drank, I watched the activities in the club. A crowd filled the dance floor, where new arrangements of old standards played. More holograms of Hollywood's shining stars shimmered among the dancers.

I finished my wine and ordered a cocktail that included cranberry juice and vodka and continued to watch the crowd. I could tell the people who were single, looking for a good time, apart from those who were couples.

Couples just had a vibe about them. It was like I could see the bond between their hearts. The more I thought about it, Chase and I didn't have that bond. I thought we had true love, but clearly, we didn't. It was time I stopped grieving over losing something I didn't have.

What better way to forget one man than by spending time with another one?

I didn't know where that thought came from, but after a glass of wine and a cocktail, it made perfect sense. A titillating thrill shimmered through me at the idea of meeting a stranger in a bar. Betts would probably be worried, because neither she nor I was the type to go clubbing and hook up with men.

Did I want to hook up? No, I told myself. But I wouldn't mind having a man notice me. Or pay attention to me. I could enjoy the company of a man without it ending up as a hookup, right?

I scanned the bar looking for someone with the potential of enjoying an evening of drinking and maybe dancing. There were many men to choose from, but some I dismissed off the bat, like the ones trying to look up Marilyn's dress. Sure, I'd like to spend my evening with someone handsome and sexy, but it would be nice if they had a little substance as well.

My gaze settled on a man sitting at the end of the bar looking bored and maybe disgruntled. Like his life hadn't turned out the way he thought it would. *Welcome to the club, buddy.*

He appeared older than me, maybe in his mid-forties, but he was definitely handsome. He was the epitome of distinguished, with short brown hair with a little pepper of gray, lines along his eyes that hinted at wisdom or experience, and a strong, chiseled jaw. He wore a T-shirt that showed muscle definition a man half his age would envy. I decided he was the perfect one for me to make friends with tonight.

I made a beeline toward him, taking a seat in the stool next to him. "Can I buy you a drink? And before you say no, or yes, I just want you to know the only reason I'm over here talking to you is because you look like you're alone, and so am I, and I'm looking for someone to have a good time with tonight."

His head turned, showing pale blue eyes that made me think of a meadow stream. His arched brow suggested he thought I was a lunatic.

Only then did I realize how he could take my words.

I gave my head a quick shake. "I mean a good time as in having drinks and talking and dancing. You look like you could benefit from having your mind taken off whatever it is you're ruminating over. And I'm here to forget a man, whose name will never cross my lips again."

I half expected him to get off the stool and walk away without a word. Instead, he tilted his head to the side. "What makes you think I was going to say no?"

His question took me off guard, mostly because I expected him to respond to my bad attempt to buy him a drink.

I shrugged. "I don't know. I've never actually gone to a bar and talked to a stranger. You might think I'm crazy. I'm not, unless approaching a stranger in a bar is crazy."

His lips twitched upward. "Sometimes, crazy is a good thing. Makes life interesting."

I nodded.

"I could use something interesting in my life right about now." He held up his hand toward the bartender. "Josh."

Yay. It was working.

The bartender headed over to us. "What can I get you?"

My new friend looked at me. "What would you like?"

"I'm buying, remember? What do you want?"

He flashed a grin, revealing a dimple, and holy cow, he really was handsome. He turned to Josh. "I'll have a bourbon and water."

"And I'll have another one of those cranberry vodka things."

Josh went to fix our drinks.

"You must come here a lot if you know the bartender's name," I said.

"I come here enough. It's not really my ambiance, but the owners run a good club. I know one of them and have been bugging him to open one like this but with a sports theme."

I frowned. "Aren't there a lot of sports bars?"

"Yes, but I mean like this with the holograms. Imagine being able to sit with a hologram of Babe Ruth or Wayne Gretzky."

"Wayne who?"

He closed his eyes and shook his head.

I felt a little dumb not knowing who this Wayne guy was.

Finally, he opened his eyes, his baby blues showing humor. "Wayne Gretzky, probably the single best hockey player ever."

"I'm sorry, I don't know hockey."

He sighed, like he'd heard that more than once. "The point is a place where fans can come and be with their all-time favorite sports giants." Movement caught his eye, and he raised his hand again. "As a matter of fact . . ."

A couple approached him at the bar. "Hey, Max, Amelia." He turned to me. "This is . . .?" He laughed sheepishly. "I'm sorry, I haven't gotten your name."

"Analyn."

"This is Analyn. She might be crazy, but in a good way."

The heat of a blush came to my cheeks, but I extended my hand to the man and woman.

"This is Max Clarke and his wife, Amelia. They own this place."

"Nice to meet you." I'd never met the owner of anything. In movies, it always seemed like knowing the owner, or the owner knowing you, meant you were a big deal. I wondered who my new friend was.

Max laughed. "We were having dinner when we realized that the kids were over with Amelia's brother and his wife and decided that we would have a night on the town. In fact, we're talking about maybe getting a suite at a local casino."

"Not just any suite," Amelia said, waggling her brows at her husband. "The suite that started it all."

I watched them with envy, wondering why I hadn't been able to have that sort of relationship with Chase. I didn't know Max and Amelia, or about the suite that started it all, but in the few seconds I'd been with them, I knew that they had something special.

"Well, don't let me keep you from your night on the town," my drinking buddy said.

"You have a good evening. Both of you. It's nice to meet you, Analyn." Max turned his attention to my new friend. "And the next time my brother Sam is in town, we'll get together and talk about that sports bar idea of yours."

"Sounds great."

As Max and Amelia walked off, Josh, the bartender, served our drinks.

I held up my drink to click with his, but first . . . "I think you should tell me your name, and then we can cheers."

He held up his bourbon and water. "I'm Reed."

"Here's to crazy, new, interesting friends."

"Cheers to that."

We clicked our glasses and sipped, and then we started talking about anything and everything. Well, maybe not everything. We didn't talk about work, or even much about our personal lives short of telling him about my ex and his desire for an open relationship.

Reed showed the right amount of disgust at the idea. "I don't think I'll ever understand that. If you find somebody you want to be with, it seems to me you need to hold on tight and not let anything get in the way."

I studied him. "Have you ever had that?" I wondered if he was divorced or widowed. He couldn't be married and believe in monogamy unless he was playing me and his reaction was all an act. I sipped my drink and pushed that thought away. It didn't matter. We were in Vegas, and once I went home to Chicago, it wouldn't matter.

He shook his head. "I haven't had much luck in that department."

I must have gaped because he laughed. "Why does that surprise you?"

"Because of all this." I made a motion toward his face and the hard planes of his chest etched in the fabric of his T-shirt.

He shrugged. "I suppose I'm looking for somebody who wants a little bit more than this."

I nodded. "I hear you. Well, actually, I don't because I don't have this . . ." I made a motion to my own body. Don't get me wrong, I don't think I'm unattractive, but I'm no super model.

He frowned. "What do you mean, you don't have this?" He motioned to me. "If you weren't here sitting with me, any one of the single men—hell, maybe even some of the married men—would be coming over here to make your acquaintance."

I shook my head as I sipped my drink. "That's nice of you to say, but I doubt it."

"I bet you that if I left, there would be a man, several probably, who'd show up. Whereas I've come here plenty and never had a woman hit on me."

"I did . . . hit on you . . . I mean . . . well . . ." God. Why did everything I say suggest I wanted to have sex with him? I let out a sigh.

"Perhaps we'll have to agree to disagree because I don't really want to take that bet."

I went all warm inside as I took his words to mean he was enjoying my company, awkward as it was. "I guess it just goes to show that there's much more that goes into a relationship than just attraction."

He held up his bourbon. "I'll cheers to that, too."

We continued talking and drinking. I wasn't drunk, but the inhibitions were down, the music was pumping, and I could feel it vibrating in my blood. "Do you happen to dance, Reed?"

He shook his head. "Not very well."

"Me neither."

"I don't believe it."

"I bet you're better than me," I said, playing off the "bet" he'd made earlier.

He grinned, and for a minute, I was blindsided. "I'll take that bet." He stood, and I was able to note that he was tall. Tall and broad, like a football player. He held his hand out to me. I placed my hand in his, and it was large like the rest of him. I had a moment to remember the adage about a man's hands being reflective of the size of his package. I let out a giggle and immediately tried to take it back. How mortifying.

"What's so funny?"

I shook my head. "Nothing. I was just noting the size of your hands."

His eyes narrowed, and I swore there was a wicked feral quality to it. "It's true, you know, about hand size."

All my girly bits flared to life. "No, I wouldn't know."

The music was a fast rhythmic beat, but he put his hand on my hip to keep me close to him as we danced on the crowded dance floor. I might have thought he'd respond to my comment and was a little disappointed he hadn't. I reminded myself that I didn't want this to be more than a night of drinks, dancing, and scintillating conversation.

He was right. He wasn't a great dancer, but neither was I. Neither of us cared as we allowed our bodies to move to the beat. I felt free and uninhibited. I wasn't worried about what others thought. I just let go and lived in the moment. It was the most fun I'd had in a long, long time. In fact, I'm not sure I ever had so much fun with Chase.

The song ended and the DJ came on. "Time for the true Mr. Blue Eyes himself." A hologram of Frank Sinatra appeared near the stage. The music swelled, and the hologram sang *Strangers in the Night*.

My chest filled with a strange sensation as the words of the song mixed with Reed pulling me close. "Shall we keep dancing?"

"Yes, please." I didn't want the night to end. I felt like Cinderella, afraid of the clock hitting midnight and this wondrous night coming to an end.

"I suppose we haven't resolved the bet. I'm pretty sure I've lost."

I shook my head. "I think it's a tie."

He laughed as he pulled me to him for the slower dance. As we moved, our bodies drew closer until I was flush against him. My hand settled on the hard, warm plane of his chest. Lower, I felt something else hard. Something that proved the point about large hands. I looked up at him.

He gave me a sheepish smile. "You'll have to excuse my friend."

Arousal rushed through my body. I wanted to strip this man down and drag my tongue over every inch of him. It was unsettling and exciting, and I laughed, feeling a little bit giddy about it all.

He leaned his head closer, his lips just along my ear. "If you had any interest in seeing the proof about hand size, I'd be happy to show you."

I'm pretty sure I groaned. Not a groan of dismay, but a groan like I was about to orgasm right there on the dance floor.

I wasn't a prude, but neither was I a woman who normally went home with strange men for a hookup. But the bartender, Josh, knew him. And the owner, Max Clarke, and his wife knew him. That had to mean he was an okay guy, right?

Plus Josh, Max, and his wife knew he was talking to me. If I turned up dead, they'd be able to tell the police I was with him. God, I watched too much true crime TV.

I pushed that away and reminded myself that I was here tonight to live life out loud and not worry about ramifications, of which there would be none because this was Vegas, baby.

"Your hands are impressive," I said with a sexual bravado I'd never felt before.

His hand slid down to my ass, tugging me a little bit closer, letting me feel the steely length behind the zipper of his jeans. "How about we find a place more private to dance?"

The next moments were a blur as we left the club and entered one of the nearby casino hotels where Reed had a room. Then we were in the elevator, where he pressed me against the wall, his hard length teasing me and his lips giving me a searing kiss that almost had me orgasming right then and there.

Our hands were all over each other's body as the doors of the elevator opened, and we managed to make our way into the hall and toward the room that he'd rented.

By the time we entered the room, he had lifted my dress so that when the door closed behind us, he'd slipped his fingers into my panties and yanked them down. Thank God I went with the lacy red thong.

Then he dropped to his knees, lifting my leg over his shoulder. His hands ran along my thighs as he looked up at me. "I hope you don't mind my putting off showing you the proof of my size. If I don't go down on you now, I'm going to go fucking mad."

"Okay," I squeaked as the intensity of his eyes and the hoarseness of his voice stole my breath. He was like a fantasy come true.

The minute his tongue slid through my folds, my world tilted on its axis. His tongue was hot and wet and oh, so very talented.

I gripped the door handle to keep me from tumbling over. My hips gyrated, and the one leg I was standing on trembled.

His tongue licked, flicked, and sucked and at one point, dipped inside me.

"Oh, my God."

His lips moved away, sucking on the inside of my thigh.

I whimpered, wanting him back on my clit. "Don't stop."

He looked up at me again. "I'm not stopping. You taste so fucking good, I don't want it to end too fast."

Yeah, no. I couldn't wait. Maybe his other women could hold off, but I'd never needed to come so badly in my life. "I'm sorry. I need to come."

He gave me a sweet smile. "Don't be sorry. If you need to come, then I'll make you come."

Then his mouth was on me again, and holy smokes, I felt like I was on a runaway freight train about to fly off a cliff, but in a good way. He inserted a finger inside me, and his lips wrapped around my clit. The two of them working together shot me off to the stratosphere. My entire body went rigid and then shuddered as wave after wave of pleasure rolled through me.

He made an "mmm" sound, as if he were having a sweet dessert. Then he slowly stood, his immense body blocking me in. He brought one hand in front of me, holding it in front of my face, splaying his fingers wide. "Are you ready to experience the proof about hand size?"

I nodded because I still was unable to form words. He took my hand, bringing it up to his lips and kissing it and then pulling it down, pressing it over his hard shaft.

I looked into his eyes, finding my voice. "I'm going to need more proof than that." I found my strength next, pushing him away from the door and toward the bed, knocking him back until he was lying on the mattress.

I did a striptease, feeling wanton and sexy and at the same time safe. His eyes flashed with wild passion as my dress dropped to the floor along with my bra.

"So fucking sexy."

I crawled over him, straddling his thighs as I unbuckled his belt and then undid the button and zipper of his jeans. I tugged and tugged at his jeans and boxers until his dick sprang free. The rumor about hand and dick size was true, and then some.

1

***

Reed—one month later.

I really shouldn't complain. How many men in the world could make money hand over fist in business while spending the morning in their office drinking coffee and watching the hockey highlights from last night's game?

I bet there were many who couldn't, yet here I was, sitting at my desk while I watched the home team star player, Bo Tyler, score two goals on the big-screen TV in my office. I justified having the TV because as CEO of a billion-dollar daily fantasy sports site, I needed to know what was going on in sports. It was a fucking fantastic excuse to watch TV.

At the end of the game highlights, the commentators switched to showing Bo's after-game antics in which he was caught celebrating his success by getting drunk and sneaking onto a golf course to play drunken golf with glow-in-the-dark golf balls.

I shook my head as I watched him get escorted off the course by the golf club's security. I smiled wryly, wondering how my best friend,

Pierce Jackson, coach of Bo's hockey team, was faring this morning. He had to be happy about winning the game, but he wasn't going to be thrilled about Bo's nocturnal golfing habit.

I clicked off the TV, tossing the remote on my desk. As I looked at all the paperwork scattered on it, I had to remind myself again how lucky I was. As the owner of the number-one daily fantasy sports company, I made more money than I could ever spend in my lifetime.

My kids—hell, my grandkids—probably wouldn't be able to spend it all. Not that I had kids or grandkids because I didn't and it was unlikely I ever would.

My dating life was shit.

I was a forty-five-year-old ex-hockey-star turned billionaire who couldn't find a woman who would stick. And it wasn't from a lack of trying.

During my hockey days, I didn't date. I hooked up. But once my business hit a million dollars in net worth not long after I started when I was forced to retire from hockey, I decided I'd find someone to share my newfound wealth. But every woman I dated dropped off the radar after a few dates. It was annoying, although today, I couldn't remember much about any of them, except for one.

Analyn.

Ever since that night a month ago, she had become my fantasy sex sport, starring in my dreams and my daytime jerk-offs. I couldn't quite pinpoint what it was about her that stuck with me, compared to the other women I had dated.

Yes, she was beautiful and sexy, but so were the other women. There was something sweet and vivacious about Analyn. There was an authenticity about her that was refreshing. She said what she thought and didn't act with any guile or pretense.

When she'd first come to sit next to me at the bar, I wasn't sure what to think. To be honest, I wasn't in the mood to be picked up by a woman. I went to the bar to lament, as had become my habit, on how boring my life had become. I wasn't sure I had ever gotten over the fact that my hockey career came to an end earlier than I would've liked due to an injury. Now I was a billionaire with the world at my feet, but I was alone and bored out of my gourd by life.

Sometimes, I thought I should have gone into coaching, like Pierce had. But at the time, I didn't think I could handle watching all the players on the ice and not be able to skate with them. Hockey had been my dream, and then my life, and then it had all come to an end.

Of course, I understood what a whiner complaining about my charmed life made me. When I quit playing hockey and started my business, my dissatisfaction only continued to grow. I thought maybe if I were to find a good woman and have a family, that would be the answer. As it turned out, finding a good woman wasn't so easy.

Now, over ten years since my forced retirement from hockey, I was still unmarried and childless. There must be something wrong with me that after a few dates, the women would disappear. It took Analyn one night. I woke up the day after having the most amazing sex I'd had in a long time, maybe ever, ready to fuck like rabbits again, only to find the bed empty. The disappointment was acute.

But it wasn't just that there wasn't going to be any more sex with her that bothered me. I really enjoyed her company. I would've liked to have seen her again. I was aware that she was from Chicago, but maybe I could have flown out to visit her or flown her here to visit me. On the one hand, it seemed like a lot of work to date a woman long-distance, but since she was the first woman in a long, long time to get me out of my funk, it would've been worth it. Imagine the phone sex!

But it wasn't to be. Not only had she left while I was sleeping, but there was no note. I wondered what happened when she woke up next to me. Had she regretted it? Had I done something to offend her? Maybe in the early morning light, without the haze of alcohol, she realized how much older I was than her. I had to be at least twenty years her senior, practically old enough to be her father. I shook my head free of that thought because it was disturbing.

The intercom on my desk buzzed, pulling me out from my ruminations. I poked the button. "Yes, Catherine?"

"I just want to remind you that you're interviewing for the new social media marketing manager today. The first candidate is in twenty minutes. Would you like me to bring in the file for the applicant now?"

I scraped my hand over my face. Sometimes, I really hated my job. "No. I'll look at it when it's time."

"Very well."

The line clicked off, and it occurred to me that Catherine often spoke to me in a tone that made me feel like she was disappointed in me. Considering I was a billionaire who spent his day whining, I couldn't blame her.

A few moments later, there was a knock at my door, and Catherine poked her head in. "I brought you some coffee. It sounded like you could use it."

That was the other thing about Catherine. She was fucking efficient. She was so good, it was probably why I found my work boring. She could anticipate anything, so I very rarely had to deal with any sort of crisis. Everything at work ran smoothly, almost like I didn't even need to be here. There was a thought.

"Thank you. I appreciate that."

She walked around my desk to stand next to me as she set the mug on the blotter. She rested her hip on the desk and smiled down at me. She was a professional, and at the same time, we'd been working together long enough that there was a familiarity between us. I wouldn't say we were friends, but we definitely had a connection that made us work together well.

"I suppose you caught the news footage of Bo last night," she said.

I picked up the mug, taking a sip of the hot, dark brew. Another thing that Catherine excelled at was coffee. "I did. I imagine Pierce is having a conniption fit."

She laughed. "No doubt." She tilted her head to the side. "Were you like Bo when you were playing?"

"No." Not even a little bit. I had dreamt of playing professional hockey my entire life, so when I finally made it, I was focused on staying there. That wasn't to say I didn't sow my oats and party. I just didn't do it to the level that Bo Tyler was able to do it. Bo got away with it because he was so fucking good on the ice. It was possible he'd surpass Gretzky as the greatest of all time.

Catherine gave my shoulder a light push with her perfectly manicured hand. "Oh, come on. You can tell me."

I shook my head. "Nope. I was living the dream back then. I wasn't going to fuck it up, no way, no how." I supposed it wasn't good to use the F-word in front of my administrative assistant, but she didn't seem to care. In fact, I think a part of her appreciated that while we had a professional relationship, around her, I could be myself.

She laughed and then straightened from my desk. "Well, I'll give you a few minutes. I'll let you know when your appointment is here."

"Thank you, Catherine."

I watched as she left, reminding myself how lucky I was. I had an extremely successful company, in part because my administrative assistant was the epitome of efficiency. She was smart and clever, and when she needed to be, she was the best damn gatekeeper any CEO could have. I had friends that asked whether I'd ever fucked her on my desk because she was also attractive. The answer was no, I never had, and in fact, I had never thought about it.

Catherine had a lot of things going for her, but I didn't feel sexually or emotionally attracted to her. The truth was, while I occasionally might have been sexually attracted to a woman, I had never been emotionally attracted or felt a pull beyond my dick for any woman except Analyn. And goddammit! Now I was thinking about her again. Maybe I needed to go out and get laid to get her out of my mind. With my luck, I'd fantasize about her, maybe even say her name while I came, ruining it with the woman I was with.

I forced myself to focus on work, pulling up recent data files to see how well the company was doing. There was a time when looking at my numbers gave me a thrill. Today it was more of the same.

A few moments later, Catherine knocked at my door again.

"Your appointment is here. I've put her down in the conference room."

I nodded and stood, putting on my coat and straightening the tie I'd loosened when I'd arrived. I felt like a dead man walking as I exited my office, which again made me feel pathetic considering how fortunate I was in my life.

I walked with Catherine down the hall to the conference room. Catherine entered first, and I followed behind.

I stopped short when I saw the curvaceous dark-haired woman standing next to the conference table. Holy fuck, it was Analyn.

Her eyes rounded as recognition came. Well, at least she remembered me. The way she had left, I wondered if she would. I had spent that night getting to know every inch of that woman and knew that I would never, ever forget her.

"Analyn Watts, this is Mr. Hampton, the CEO of Dream Team." Catherine handed me the folder with Analyn's application. "Mr. Hampton, this is Analyn Watts."

Watts. We hadn't shared our last names a month ago. I'd cursed that since I couldn't find her, but then I realized that had been the point. She hadn't wanted to be found.

"Would you like me to get you another cup of coffee? Ms. Watts has already declined one."

My gaze stayed on Analyn as dueling emotions ran through me. On the one hand, I felt hope. Here was the woman I couldn't get out of my mind. Maybe I'd be able to see her again.

But another part of me had a growing anger at the way she had left after that spectacular night we'd had. It was stupid of me to be pissed off. It'd been a hookup. There had been nothing about that night to suggest that it was any more than that. But by the time I was drifting to sleep that night, I knew I wanted more than a hookup, but she had taken off without a word, taking away that opportunity.

"No, thank you, Catherine. That'll be all for now."

Catherine left the room, shutting the door, leaving me alone with Analyn. I had so many questions that I wanted to ask her and none had to do with the job. I reminded myself that she was expecting a job interview, which had me wondering why she was here. Had she lied to me about being from Chicago?

I motioned to the chair in front of her. "Have a seat, Ms. Watts." I had to be professional, and if she thought maybe I didn't remember her, that would be okay too. Petty, I know.

She stared at me, and for a moment I thought she was going to leave. I arched a brow, in my mind, challenging her, asking her if she was going to bolt again. She let out a sigh, as if she was resigned to the moment. For some reason, that angered me more.

She pulled out the chair and sat down.

I sat in my chair, opening the file. "Let's start by having you tell me, have you ever walked out on anyone?"

End of preview. **Get the complete story here.**

ABOUT THE AUTHOR

Ajme Williams writes emotional, angsty contemporary romance. All her books can be enjoyed as full length, standalone romances and are FREE to read in Kindle Unlimited .

Books do not have to be read in order.

High Stakes (this series)
Bet On It | A Friendly Wager | Triple or Nothing | Press Your Luck

Heart of Hope Series
Our Last Chance | An Irish Affair | So Wrong | Imperfect Love | Eight Long Years | Friends to Lovers | The One and Only | Best Friend's Brother | Maybe It's Fate | Gone Too Far | Christmas with Brother's Best Friend | Fighting for US | Against All Odds | Hoping to Score | Thankful for Us | The Vegas Bluff | 365 Days

Billionaire Secrets
Twin Secrets | Just A Sham | Let's Start Over | The Baby Contract | Too Complicated

The Why Choose Haremland (Reverse Harem Series)
Protecting Their Princess | Protecting Her Secret | Unwrapping their Christmas Present | Cupid Strikes... 3 Times | Their Easter Bunny

Dominant Bosses
His Rules | His Desires | His Needs | His Punishments | His Secret

Strong Brothers
Say Yes to Love | Giving In to Love | Wrong to Love You | Hate to Love You

Fake Marriage Series
Accidental Love | Accidental Baby | Accidental Affair | Accidental Meeting

Irresistible Billionaires
Admit You Miss Me | Admit You Love Me | Admit You Want Me | Admit You Need Me

Check out Ajme's full Amazon catalogue here.

Join her VIP NL here.

WANT MORE AJME WILLIAMS?

Join my no spam mailing list here.

You'll only be sent emails about my new releases, extended epilogues, deleted scenes and occasional FREE books.

Made in United States
North Haven, CT
23 June 2023

38139142R00146